THE CONFESSION

"Sit here," Don Ettore instructed Olivia, indicating an old couch with a fading needlepoint of a Moorish garden. It was customary for Don Ettore, when hearing children's confessions, to seat them in his lap so that they could whisper their secrets into his ear. But with Olivia, he had qualms about this.

He sat beside her on the couch. "There now," he said reassuringly. "Would you like a lemonade?"

She smiled at him. "No, *grazie*, padre." Her fair, lovely face, the large eyes, reminded him of a Botticelli cherub he'd once seen in the Palazzo Pitti.

Then—even as he was thinking this—Olivia did a strange thing, which for a moment startled him. She took his large hand into her own tiny one, and pulled it to her lap. At first he was shocked, annoyed by her boldness. But those eyes were smiling into his own, and all the bad thoughts seemed to evaporate.

Then it began. . . .

A TERRIFYING OCCULT TRILOGY
by William W. Johnstone

THE DEVIL'S KISS (1498, $3.50)
As night falls on the small prairie town of Whitfield, red-rimmed eyes look out from tightly shut windows. An occasional snarl rips from once-human throats. Shadows play on dimly lit streets, bringing with the darkness an almost tangible aura of fear. For the time is now right in Whitfield. The beasts are hungry, and the Undead are awake . . .

THE DEVIL'S HEART (1526, $3.50)
It was the summer of 1958 that the horror surfaced in the town of Whitfield. Those who survived the terror remember it as the summer of The Digging—the time when Satan's creatures rose from the bowels of the earth and the hot wind began to blow. The town is peaceful, and the few who had fought against the Prince of Darkness before believed it could never happen again.

THE DEVIL'S TOUCH (1491, $3.50)
The evil that triumphed during the long-ago summer in Whitfield still festers in the unsuspecting town of Logandale. Only Sam and Nydia Balon, lone survivors of the ancient horror, know the signs—the putrid stench rising from the bowels of the earth, the unspeakable atrocities that mark the foul presence of the Prince of Darkness. Hollow-eyed, hungry corpses will rise from unearthly tombs to engorge themselves on living flesh and spawn a new generation of restless Undead . . . and only Sam and Nydia know what must be done.

Available wherever paperbacks are sold, or order direct from the Publisher. Send cover price plus 50¢ per copy for mailing and handling to Zebra Books, 475 Park Avenue South, New York, N.Y. 10016. DO NOT SEND CASH.

THE TRIDENT

BY JOEL HAMMIL

ZEBRA BOOKS
KENSINGTON PUBLISHING CORP.

ZEBRA BOOKS

are published by

KENSINGTON PUBLISHING CORP.
475 Park Avenue South
New York, N.Y. 10016

Copyright © 1981 by Joel Hammil
Reprinted by arrangement with Arbor House.

All rights reserved. No part of this book may be reproduced in any form or by any means without the prior written consent of the Publisher, excepting brief quotes used in reviews.

2nd Zebra Books printing: February 1985

Printed in the United States of America

To Ursula

And with special acknowledgement, affection and gratitude to Albert and Mary Salvatori

PART ONE

CHAPTER ONE

He watched the stranger from behind the mausoleum, the gray granite of the stone and the shadows of the cypresses almost perfect camouflage. The sun was at its noonday height, almost directly overhead, and Don Ettore, the priest of San Eustacchio, was anxious not to be seen—not yet. His courage hadn't yet peaked for that confrontation he had dreamed of for years.

A stranger—a chic, unusually beautiful woman at that—was a rare event for La Rocca, an Italian village which could be seen from the new expressway crossing il piano del Abruzzi between L'Aquila and Chieti, just south of il Gran Sasso. Unless one had a friend or a relative in the medieval, walled village with its high church spire and its tile-roofed houses outgrowing the ancient wall sprouting in clusters called *frazioni*, visitors were rare except on festa days.

Olivia Amontaldi di Donati had left her beige Ferrari sportster at the old iron gate of the cemetery and made her way through the perimeter of cypresses so indispensably Italian. Making her way along the weed-strewn walks, she spied a caretaker laboriously raising a stone grave marker toppled by one of the area's frequent earth tremors. "Where can I find the grave of Giovanni Gracchi?" she called to him in local dialect.

Startled, the wizened old man whose face seemed grown from the earth let the heavy stone down gently, then straightened as best he could. Approaching slowly, his olive-pit eyes narrowed with peasant cunning. Just before her, he cocked his head quizzically to study the stranger.

Pretending to be unaware of this intense interest, she asked the question again. "Please tell me where Giovanni Gracchi rests."

"Giovanni Gracchi," he said, repeating the name as his slow mind groped for a connection.

"Yes."

It was more than the usual distrust of strangers which prompted the curiosity of Augustino Smarella, who had been around La Rocca long enough to know everyone's story. Appropriately enough, considering his trade, he was also the village's unofficial historian and genealogist. The fact he was a simpleton didn't seem to matter. The caretaker certainly recalled the peasant Giovanni Gracchi, as well as his present, permanent location. But he also recollected the man's daughter, and this is what presently interested him, since the child had earned a fearful reputation. Her very name evoked terror throughout the area. What had happened to her was a mystery, but few cared to inquire. Just that she was gone one day was good enough.

The old man took off his battered hat which had known many seasons and many weathers, and from its sweatband produced a half-smoked Toscano, an evil-looking cheroot of twisted tobacco. After lighting it, his face twisted with a gap-toothed leer. "Ciu-ciu. He was called Ciu-ciu." The leathery face screwed into even more wrinkles as he cackled triumphantly, startling a flock of crows into flight. La Rocca's idiot savant welcomed every opportunity to prove his singular skill.

"Ciu-ciu?" the young woman replied softly, disingenuously.

"You didn't know, eh?" he grinned.

The visitor shook her head, even though she of course knew. It was her own father they were discussing. It would put the idiot off, she thought. Why give him any ideas to carry down into the village? Ideas she was back. The *iettatrice* had returned. The word, she knew, would spread like a brushfire. She therefore listened to the story she knew all too well.

Ciu-ciu Gracchi had come by his name in an unusual way, but the days following the world war had been unusual times. Things had been so very bad—so disorganized—that there was no work of any sort to be found. People went hungry. Giovanni Gracchi, the peasant, living in his tufo hut with neither goat nor chickens—merely had a wife and seven children. But he had found a simple solution to quell the hunger in at least the children, and this had brought him a certain fame and a nickname which clung to him. Every evening he would line up the children, all seven of them, one behind the other, each holding on to the one in front. It was a simulated train in which he played the locomotive. He would then race through the house, out the front and back into the rear, again and again, all the while bellowing, "Ciu-ciu! Ciu-ciu!" The children would eventually drop out exhausted, one after the other, and fall asleep forgetting their hunger.

"Very sad," the young woman said, shaking her head. The movement in the sunlight drew fire from her penny-copper hair.

The caretaker's hands made an eloquent gesture which could be interpreted as: those days everything—everyone—was sad. "He's back there," he said aloud, pointing. "Next to the De Lutis stone. You'll see the fresh earth."

Don Ettore stealthily drew closer to the woman standing motionless beside the new grave. She wouldn't be praying, he thought. Oh, not her. So why did she return, he asked himself. Could it be she was vulnerable to that indomitable family loyalty in the Italian blood? Had this brought her back? Had she at least this humanity about her? He felt a surge of hope.

Olivia stood erect, motionless as still another stone madonna that was everywhere about. The thought came to Don Ettore that she was seeing into the grave herself, seeing past the plastic-wrapped wreath of already withering field flowers. She was seeing what she wanted to see. Obstacles—the laws of nature—didn't apply to her. Her gaze was penetrating the earth, the lid of the plain pine box, and finally was peering at the man's for-once-untroubled face still unspoiled by the corruption.

How was it possible, he thought, that that swarthy, taciturn ox of a man, little brighter than the *asino* that carried the firewood down from the mountains on its delicate legs—how could such a dolt have produced that flame-headed enchantress? What aberrant seed could he have shot into the passive, worn body of the woman who was his wife as their children listened with curiosity from the next bed? The red hair and translucent complexion emerging in a black-haired, swarthy family was not unique or unusual in the region. After all, it had been the battleground—the invasion route—of history's countless armies including Vikings, Celts, and more recently the hated blond Germans, who had sowed their genes among them.

The day was warm. Windless. Insects whispered. It was September and the foliage was already poised for its final gasp of color. He became alert. Was she shaking her head? What thoughts could she be having? Was she perhaps denying any connection with the man in the ground? He was her father. Or was he indeed? And if not . . . Involuntarily, he crossed himself.

She moved, turning. Now! he thought. Now, or the moment would be gone. The moment he had awaited—schemed for. As quickly as his thick, aging body permitted, he stepped around the stones to confront her.

For several moments it was still. He perceived the recognition in her eyes and this pleased him. Here he was, years—eighteen years—older, to be exact, an ordinary village priest in a dusty, black suit, and she remembered.

Olivia did indeed recollect the florid face with its large nose twitching rabbitlike when he was nervous or upset. The hair, grayer now, was still cut short in a Teutonic bristle. The rimless glasses seemed thicker, giving his dark eyes an owlish look.

"Don Ettore—" she murmured, smiling. "La Rocca's prickly morality in person." Her voice, he noted, had changed. The local accent gone. It was cultured, sure of itself. The sarcasm of her words—the mockery in the tone—were inescapable. He wasn't accustomed to this, but showed no offense.

There were too many things to say. Eighteen years . . . he felt like a shy, tongue-tied schoolboy. He hadn't wanted their greeting to be this way. He had visualized it so differently. Not give her the slightest advantage. Use his pompous style of slight condescension fitting to his office. But the years of anxiety and longing spoiled his plans. The words he meant to say delivered in that mellifluous voice betrayed him. The sleepless nights composing them were wasted. He observed how beautiful she was, and thought sadly evil has no right to such beauty; but of course—it's the devil's trap. So I know this, he thought unhappily. What good has it done me?

"You mock an old man," he said.

"Padre! You, old!" she said, mocking. "With those thoughts I see dancing in your eyes?" Her voice lowered, taking on the vulgar, leering intimacy of a prostitute, as she added, "Hey, how about another visit to your study, eh?"

He felt he had been struck a blow. Obscenity! How unkind! And yet in his confusion, he realized he could expect no kindness from the likes of her. He mustn't be surprised at anything she says or does.

Her face saddened, took on a look of compassion. "To think," she said, "all those years—even after your own true nature and fantasies were shown you—to think you did nothing about it. Or am I mistaken? Did you?"

With utmost gravity, or so he thought, he said, "I've waited for you."

"Ah!"

"Eighteen years—"

"Yes."

"So long—"

"Yes," he agreed.

"I mean not to see—not to hold in your white hands some young man's cock."

He shut his eyes. Hers were as cold as an iceberg's shadow. When he again opened them, she was walking off. He now became aware he had been clutching his silver crucifix.

She had said the truth, he knew. Eighteen years—even long before that—he had lived the lie. His cloth—the faith—the rituals, lies too, covering his cowardice. His heart ached with misery. How he had tried to put down the demons in him, and oddly enough the worst times were not the night but certain hours of the day. The devil's hours, he had thought of them. Even while he was giving strength to others. Relieving them of their guilts. Whom did he have to confess to—even if he would?

She had been called an *iettatrice*—a witch. Yet he knew he would have sold his soul just to have led her into one of the musty mausoleums, and there amidst the shelved bones and solemn orderliness let her cast that spell over him as she once had done. As a child, she had been called *iettatrice;* now she had come of age into her full powers.

God help him. God help all of them.

CHAPTER TWO

Imperceptibly she sighed, even though the lovely, mature face showed nothing but the enigmatic, serene smile of the well-bred hostess. The fine-boned face with black hair drawn back severely into a bun might have been a ballerina's slightly past her prime. The beauty was still there, of another sort, as well as the authority and above all—the cachet. At the moment, the Principessa Beatrice Amontaldi di Donati was bored with her luncheon guests, each day the same except when family or friends came to the village; each day the same local petty politics and bickering. She glanced down the long table to her husband, the prince, flanked on either side by the so-called important and respected ones of the village. These were the secretary of the *comune*, the mayor, the doctor and the inevitable Don Ettore, with his gift of unction. He was her priest and confessor while the family was in residence. For him she had more than bored indifference. She held a cold hatred of the man for the misfortune he had imposed on the family eighteen years before. However, her devout religious nature tempered this at times. He became less man than God's instrument. But she could never forget it was he who had brought that cursed child into their lives. Nevertheless, Don Ettore remained their priest, conducting mass in their private chapel, listening to her confession, if not her husband's.

What a splendid actor he is, she mused, looking toward her husband, the prince. Listening to their stupid chatter, pretending interest, and all the while dreaming himself *banco* at some casino or other. He had the gift, she thought. His eyes take no part in what he thinks.

She wasn't involved in the table's conversation. Princess or not, it was men's talk. The new women's liberation was battering at but hadn't yet breached La Rocca's rotted walls. Instead she amused herself speculating what the homelife of these pompous asses was like, especially in the bedroom. Wicked thoughts, she realized. At least six Hail Marys' worth, yet worth it. She suffered these luncheons, knowing their necessity, as well as that of their September visits. It was noblesse oblige—to show the prince's interest in his people and the land no longer his. It was the tradition.

Before the Great War, the villa had been the base—the bastion—of the Amontaldi di Donatis. It was the heart of their principality extending hundreds of hectares in every direction. The abandoned ruin of the castle higher on the mountain had been the medieval fortress from which the prince's forebears and their horsemen had swooped down upon the merchants and travelers traversing the single main road below, demanding tolls, fighting off competitive dukes and bandits, on occasion joining together against some invading army. The abdication of the monarchy in the forties and the establishment of the republic had changed the class structure of the nation. The power of the great families was gone, and the taxation system expropriated the great land holdings of the nobility in a gradual process, leaving a dubious collection of high-sounding titles, remnants of former giants left with diminished estates, some foreign holdings and an elitist society clutching at their memories and good manners.

Of the main principality, once a veritable state, the Prince Amontaldi di Donati had remaining to him his villa, a few hundred hectares of olive and almond trees, some vineyards and a few tenant farmers increasingly resentful of Don Giulio, the prince's factotum and general manager in La Rocca. Nevertheless, some of the old ways persisted. In some odd way, the village still considered him their prince. Honoring an age-old tradition, they felt a certain fealty toward him, even as he accepted a responsibility toward them. Therefore, each September the prince and principessa would come from Rome or Monte Carlo for a few weeks at the villa to be brought up-to-date with the village's problems. He listened patiently—aware, even as they were, that there wasn't very much he could do about them except offer a word of advice, perhaps arbitrate one of the continuous quarrels between this faction or that.

Except for Don Ettore, the town dignitaries represented, as was usually the case, opposing political factions with violent differences of opinion regarding the smallest problem. Any concession reflected a sign of weakness, and loss of respect—that magical word. The prince listened patiently to their heated debates, trying to be even-handed and Solomon-like in his comments; careful not to be misconstrued, since a mere nod of approval could be exaggerated that evening in the men's social clubs, the *circoli recreativi*, the political dendrites of the nation. Only Don Ettore, behind his thick-lensed glasses, remained outside these heated disputes. Many felt him an opportunist, waiting for the whole structure to collapse so that the old order could return.

Mayor Aristide de Santis, Christian Democrat, as well as the village barber, was describing to the prince how a coalition of the socialists and communists was holding up an appropriation which would connect the village to the new expressway. "The truck drivers must go almost to L'Aquila to connect up! And tourists! What tourists? La Rocca gets no tourists! Sali and Populi, they get the tourists and their money! You can't park a car on their piazza for the damned German buses. La Rocca meanwhile sleeps in the sun, except for the few days each year for some festa."

Alessandro Sieppi, the secretary of the *comune*,

was a Communist, as everyone knew. As a youth, he had fire-bombed a German S.S. lorry of soldiers, after which he had hidden in the mountains. After the war, he had become something of a local hero. It was he who had scrawled graffiti on the village walls: hammer and sickles—*"morte ai fascisti e ai monarchisti."* And yet Alessandro had a sickness. In dealing with the prince—whenever he was in his presence—something within him collapsed. He became the most hat-in-hand, bowing and scraping, Your-Excellency-this-Your-Grace-that, sycophant imaginable. It was the joke of the entire village, his own people not excepted. "How far that day did Alessandro get his nose up the prince's purple ass?" And the pity of it was, he knew it. He knew it, and could do nothing about it. Despite all his extremist, inflammatory rhetoric against the upper classes, in the prince's presence this all melted, as if they had come under a hot sun. The only thing certain was that his self-hatred would take expression in violence toward his wife, Elvira. As it was said, "September not only the olives and almonds blossomed in La Rocca, but also the bruises on Elvira Sieppi's body."

The youngest of the guests, Dottore Martin de Cecco, was the only one with a beard. This was to make him look older. More professorial. But it was a failure—a ridiculous, scraggly affair. While the mayor and the secretary were flinging hot words at each other, he peered down at the locally made porcelain plate before him. Beneath peach pits and grape pits, he perceived the proud crest of the Amontaldi di Donatis topped with the *"Corona chiusa"*—the closed crown which signified that the family title had been awarded no less than a thousand years ago by a Holy Roman Emperor. Only five families in all Italy could boast such a heraldic privilege as the *corona chiusa*. It also made the family *"nobiltà' bianca,"* white nobility, as compared to titles awarded by some pope or other. But despite this, there was the anomaly that the Amontaldi di Donatis could boast of no less than three popes throughout the dynasty.

As gestures and hot words, restrained somewhat by the presence of the principessa, were flung back and forth across the table, the young doctor ruminated about a certain evening a year ago. He had been summoned to the villa, where he had found the prince in his enormous four-poster bed agonizing from a gallbladder attack. He recalled looking down at the gaunt body of the sixty-two-year-old man, marveling what Brioni tailoring could do to camouflage a man's appearance. Aside from a variety of other ailments as a result of a lifetime of good if not spendthrift living, there was the pelvis smashed as a result of having been shot down over Tobruk, ending a spectacular career as a fighter pilot. The surgeon in the British hospital had done a botch job, as a result of which the prince lived in almost constant pain, relieved when it became unbearable by his *"medicina."*

Looking down at the ruin of the man, he had at the time mused, Sic transit gloria mundi—fit to be declared an unrestorable public monument. And as he had slipped the needle of morphine into the body fragile and worn as one of the old Fragonards below, he had noted the ravages of an indulgent, profligate life.

That had been a year ago. Now, sitting silently at the table, he glanced at the principessa, so vital, aloof—and beautiful—and wondered what it was like for her, life with this fading and fragile museum piece.

The Principessa Beatrice Amontaldi di Donati sat absorbed in peeling a fig. Cutting the top and bottom of the fruit, her delicate fingers wielded the knife like a surgeon as she stripped away the green outer skin, leaving bare the white rind. A sickening memory came to her. Once, as a teenage girl, in her own family's country villa outside Firenze, she had happened on an unforgettable scene. A pig was being butchered. The blood—the almost human cries and squeals. Finally it had been done and the skin stripped away. The bloody horror had been replaced by a startling pure whiteness beneath. She recalled her fascination and awe; also the shock at discovering that her underthings had become unaccountably very wet.

Eighteen years ago, perhaps almost to the day, she had come to Don Ettore. It had been less than a year after the sumptuous wedding in the Rome palazzo, a magnificent international event covered even by America's *Life* magazine people. It was a wedding of two great families, one *nobiltà' bianca*—white nobility, loyal to the royal court. Her family, the Marquis Grisoldi, were *nobiltà' nera*, black nobility, titled by a seventeenth-century pope, and their allegiance was therefore to the Church.

Months later, Beatrice, concerned there were no signs of pregnancy despite the prince's ardent attentions, had gone to a Firenze specialist. The news was grim. The prince was at fault, not her. Some deficiency in him. But how was he to be told? He was Italian, an Italian prince, and a man of enormous pride. It was an impossible situation.

Being in La Rocca at the time, and devout in the best *noblità' nera* tradition, there was the compulsion to tell her priest the truth. After listening in silence, Don Ettore had removed his glasses and, with appropriate solemnity, had instructed her to lie to the prince. Say her barrenness was God's will.

Damnable lie! Damnable priest! she now thought and not for the first time. But why! Why! she wondered. Where had she been remiss? Deserving of this punishment?

The advice had proven a catastrophe. The prince almost immediately had lost interest in her. She was bewildered. She couldn't at first understand what was happening. Was she somehow imperfect? Less a woman? This loving, passionate man who night and day—at all hours—had demanded her kisses. Her body. His vows of eternal love. Then all at once it had gone. It was finished, even though his good manners and gentleness to her had remained. Some part of her hadn't then—and even now—blamed him. She had been raised in a society where progeny were all-important. Titles were to be passed on. It was a responsibility.

The belief her husband was having other relationships at first came as the faintest ripple on the placid waters of her life. It was the beginning. Words were never said by friends or acquaintances. Nothing was seen. It was all very discreet, but she knew. The cut-off conversations at her appearance, the averted eyes—even the subtle offerings of sympathy—these were all unnecessary. Before her marriage she had heard whisperings of his reputation as a prodigious lover. He had even been compared to the notorious Victor Emmanuel whose courtiers had been procurers for his bizarre taste for peasant types. His minister, the clever Cavour, spent more time covering up scandals than at his intrigues.

Don Ettore had been quick with his reassurances that everything would turn out well. That she hadn't sinned by her lie, since it was done out of consideration for her husband.

"The lie isn't my concern!" she had cried to him. "I'm losing my husband! His love!"

"God will provide a solution," came the pious pronouncement.

Now, sitting at the table, peeling the fig, she recalled the damnable solution. She vividly recalled the moment it had been proposed. It had been in the garden. Dusk. The wisteria and jasmine had perfumed the place, the night-blooming flowers starting to open. The marble statues lining the walk always seemed more lifelike at this hour, she had always thought. Those Roman reproductions of the classic Greek masters. The same gods and goddesses—Roman, Greek, but with different names. Many of the statues had been unearthed in the area, buried not only under the debris of time and natural cataclysms, but deliberately concealed to protect them from pagan-hating, Christian zealots of one kind or another.

She recalled Don Ettore walking beside her, the crunching of gravel and the final evening cry of some bird. Then, all at once, everything had hushed.

"I've found a solution," the priest had said.

She had stopped walking. She turned to him filled with hope. Expectation. The Holy Grail—salvation was being held out to her.

The memory made her feel ill. She rose to leave the table. Conversation stopped and chairs scraped the marble floor as the men stood in unison. The prince limped about to her.

"Beatrice?" he said, solicitously, "are you all right?"

"A little headache, Antonio. I'll go to my room." She smiled wanly toward the table. "Gentlemen—"

Don Ettore, watching her leave, was troubled. He knew the havoc he had done to her life, and he suspected what her feelings toward him might be. The return of Olivia, her daughter, could only exacerbate old wounds. The incident in the cemetery with Olivia just a few days ago had unsettled him as well. He could only speculate what was happening in the household. How careful he had been through the years. It seemed to him now his whole life had been spent on some bleak wasteland, dissembling, hiding from the truth of himself. The principessa had never expressed her feelings toward him, and yet he knew that a word from her to his bishop in Chieti and he would be shipped off to some hell in Sardinia or Sicily. It didn't matter that the bishop had approved of his plan to help the principessa, and the child Olivia as well—even perhaps saving the latter's life. But then he hadn't told the bishop everything. Everything! he thought. Sweet Jesus! If he only suspected the truth . . .

CHAPTER THREE

Evil, it is said, has its opposing counterpart.

In another part of the world, far from an Italian woman many years ago called an *iettatrice* by the local, superstitious peasants, there was a man who, unlikely as it might seem, was to become antagonist to the Gothic horror represented by a flame-haired Italian beauty. The elements of an epic confrontation were shifting into place. White knight moved into position, threatening the dark queen.

The town of Pojoaque, New Mexico, closer to Los Alamos than Santa Fe, was little more than a wide spot on U.S. 285; and other than being a gas and water oasis, it had two other reasons for existence. There was a small borax plant on the outskirts of town, and a little further out was the Bandelier National Monument, an archaeological phenomenon known as the Puye cliff dwellings.

High on the side of the red sandstone cliffs, a thirteenth-century tribe of Pueblo Indians had once lived there as a community. Wooden ladders had interconnected the cavelike dwellings, also giving them access to the desert floor below.

For no reason other than the stubbornness of Walt Heffernan, its owner and publisher, Pojoaque had a newspaper, the *Pojoaque Double-Dealer*, with a circulation of 483, with regular advertisers consisting of Hal's Texaco Service Station, Minnie's Truck Stop and Gus Hollander's Trading Post. The most exciting feature was a column called Sheriff's Calls carrying such items as: a bridle reported missing had been found off the main highway; a reservation Indian had been picked up carrying a stolen electric clock and a three-inch sterling silver statue of King Kong.

It was a surprise, therefore, when one afternoon publisher Walt Heffernan received a call from New York City with an offer to purchase his paper. "You don't want it, young man," he said after hearing the proposal. "Your local high school's probably a better paper. Besides, the new relay brings in 'Laverne and Shirley' and Harry Reasoner. With them, who bothers with a newspaper?"

"You advertised," was the reply. "I saw it in the *New York Times*."

"My wife did that. She's got no conscience, not to speak of being anxious to get away from sand and saguaros."

Dave Turrell, sitting in his Madison Avenue office, nevertheless persisted, even mentioning a price which convinced Walt Heffernan he was dealing with a certifiable lunatic.

"What do you know about running a paper?" Heffernan asked.

"Not a thing. I'd expect you to show me what you can."

Walt Heffernan, a decent man with a conscience, tried again to discourage his caller, whom he now considered one of those Easterners with romantic visions of the Old West. Dave Turrell upped his offer by five hundred dollars, at which point the publisher shrugged and, in the spirit of caveat emptor, said, "I warned you, young feller, remember that. I'm telling you now you'll find this a sorry place. The press is an old Webendorfer jes' dyin' to be set out to rust. You won't find parts for it, either. You'll mostly set type yourself since Leo's gettin' old and prefers his Old Overholt. You can't depend upon a kid to drop off the papers. You'll even do that yourself, and as for stories to print, outside stuff'll be what you can lift from the Albuquerque or Santa Fe press."

"What about local news?" Dave said, in an effort to sound professional.

"Local news? Let's see. Last year's big story was of course the borax mill strike. We have the Santa Clara reservation close by. There's always trouble when the plant lays some Indians off for not showin' up for work when they're havin' one of their celebrations. You said your name was—"

"Turrell. Dave Turrell."

"Well, Mr. Turrell, have I changed your mind?"

"There'll be a check in the mail, Mr. Heffernan,

and I'll be out in about three weeks."

"Your funeral, sir," were the publisher's last words.

Dave Turrell was a victim of his own success. As creative director for a major ad agency, he had had a major role in snaring a Japanese auto account which everyone on the street had been after. The executive placement people were already wooing him. The word was out on Dave: a vice-presidency was in the offing. His life—all was coming to a head. He was at a crossroads. Here he was—a thirty-five-year-old, single, attractive enough to be in one of his own TV commercials—and the pit known as success was yawning before him. Gilding the lily perhaps, the trap was baited with a chic, long-legged beauty. Janet Blucher, despite a promising career in merchandising young fashions at Bloomie's, had nevertheless decided she preferred a home, husband and babies.

One Sunday morning while Janet was in the kitchen doing one of her incomparable omelets, Dave lay back in his loft bed recollecting that earlier that morning he had taken a very large, if not dangerous step. He had said he loved her; what was worse, he believed it was true. Speculating upon his life ten years down the line brought him into an acute anxiety. Careful! Careful, it said. Bells rang, lights flashed. Other men in his agency came to mind with the frightening paradigm. This could be your life, Dave Turrell. The lovely house in the suburbs, the too many martinis, dropping Valium, the country club talk, the big deal when a golf handicap was lowered a point, or who got whom in a Calcutta, the great blow-job available from this or that secretary, the stunning cost of orthodonture, and that ulcer guessing what some asshole client or his bigger asshole wife should think of this or that campaign, double-ply toilet tissue for instance.

For the first time, Janet's omelet tasted lousy, the coffee was bitter. When she said they were to visit some friends in Westport, panic set in. All her friends they visited weekends just so happened to live an idyllic existence. Dave thought of his Nam days: when the jungle seemed most innocent and peaceful—bang!

He dropped the bomb at dinner several evenings later in a Third Avenue seafood house. The shrimp-stuffed bass was excellent, the house Chablis awful. Janet, no fool with Dave or any other man, knew something was in the wind, and called it.

"What is it, Dave?" she said, poking at her salad.

"I bought a little newspaper. It's out west, near Santa Fe. The *Double-Dealer* it's called." He laughed nervously. "Imagine. *Double-Dealer*." Even as she stared at him, he went on extolling the virtues of clean air, the peace and serenity of the West. He heard himself using expressions such as rat race, knowing he was speaking quickly. Too quickly. Selling, yet not convincingly. "And the view of the mountains! I was in the area once. A tobacco commercial. You want to reach out and touch them, and they're fifty—a hundred miles off."

"The mountains," she said dully.

"The mountains."

"I don't like mountains, Dave. They make me nervous."

"Oh." He looked at her hopefully. "Give it a try, Janet."

"Why do you want this, Dave?"

He knew he was speaking in clichés, which he professionally despised. He spoke of urban blight, of subways and fifty-minute sessions on psychiatrists' couches.

"Dave," she said slowly, "when was the last time you were in a subway, or on a psychiatrist's couch for that matter?"

"I feel—"

"What?"

"Pushed."

"By what?"

"Time. Commitments," he said, shrugging. Even as he said these things, which he knew sounded contrived, unconvincing and trivial, for the very first time he had the old perception there was more—something much more over which he had no control and which was, in some fashion, making these decisions for him, decisions that were putting his life into turmoil, leading him in weird directions that he found hard to explain or convincingly justify.

"No, Dave," Janet said, her voice even, her gaze holding his, "it's not awful. It's just that you're so full of shit." She then delicately wiped her lips, stood—and walked away.

Dave squashed with his shoe the fifty-eighth

scorpion in the room he'd rented by the week in the Mountainview Motel, distinguished by beds which vibrated for five minutes for a quarter, but which actually stole quarters and didn't vibrate; but then very little worked as it should in Pojoaque. Many times he'd thought of Walt Heffernan's warning: your funeral, young man. It was damn fast becoming that.

"I've something to show you, Dave." The speaker was a young, full-blooded Indian, sitting on the Naugahyde chair drinking a Coors from the can. Dan Crespi was a member of the Santa Clara tribe who also happened to be an anthropologist with a Ph.D. from Santa Fe College, where he presently taught.

"I got to rouse Slim Buchwalter to fix my air conditioner, else there'll be no edition this week," Dave said, slipping on the shoe after scraping scorpion remains into the metal wastebasket.

"This is more interesting," Dan said. "I've got the jeep out front."

Dave and Dan Crespi had become truly good friends in the four months since Dave had arrived entertaining the wild speculation that perhaps fate had said, Let's see if Dave Turrell can make a Pulitzer winner of this mess. A Pulitzer by now had become as ephemeral as the magnificent lake which could be seen shimmering in the distance on any hot day on the nearby desert. Both fata morganas. Dan had come to him to aid him in his stories of the Santa Clara Indians. Washington would run hot and cold with each new administration. Help the poor Indian, became the cry.

This help, however, was usually confused. First it would be: keep the Indian culture pure, don't let's assimilate them into the American mainstream. Then, down would come the edict: bring industry to the Indians. The trouble was: the Indians, with no preparation for American industry, often failed at it. Dave had found Dan Crespi an invaluable aid in his editorials, which displeased the local whites.

The jeep ride to the Puye cliff dwellings was short. Dave had been there before, but just at a viewing point at the bottom. He had wondered the obvious: how could anyone survive up there? What could life have been like climbing ladders and vine ropes, clambering from one place to another? How was food grown? Gathered? Hunted? It must have been a siege mentality that had chosen such a precarious life.

Dan had the permission of the rangers, and now they were in the dwellings themselves, reaching them after a hazardous climb down from the plateau on top.

Erosion had softened the lines of the sandstone ruins in a relentless dissolution. The two stood silently in the midst of what once had been a living quarter. The crumbled outer wall opened to the desert beyond, and the mountains in the distance were already purpling. People once had lived and loved here, Dave reflected, somehow moved. He couldn't dispel the notion he was in some hallowed place. A small dust devil swirled up red earth in a hot wind.

The Indian read his friend's thoughts. "It's why I chose anthropology rather than archaeology," he said.

Dave nodded. He understood. Old places shouldn't be disturbed. Searching out old roots was one thing; desecrating them, another.

"This isn't what I want to show you, Dave."

The two made their difficult way through passages open to the sky. Above, on the plateau, they came to an unusual structure. It was an old, crumbling abode built into a large domelike structure strengthened by timbers. Dave estimated it as thirty yards across.

"What is it, Dan?" he asked.

"It's called a kiva house. It's where the shamans—the medicine men—performed their rites."

"I don't see any entrance."

"There's a hole in the roof at the very top. Follow me."

Clambering up an obviously new ladder. Dan led the way to an opening in the roof about a yard in diameter. Inside was another ladder, and the two descended to the earthen floor. The walls once had been covered with colorful wall paintings, but these had been ravaged by centuries of vandals. Dan explained that the various wall apertures were places where the shamans flitted in and out in order to dazzle with their magic, even using life-sized Kochina dolls. Along the wall were rocks of various shapes and sizes that might have been seats and benches. The most arresting feature of the dome-shaped theater was a large stone of a material alien to the region. It rested precisely in the center, and was obviously the focus of whatever ceremonies took place there.

Dan, approaching the stone, said, "What do you make of it?"

Dave recalled seeing something like it in a museum somewhere. He ran his hand over the pitted surface. "A meteorite?" he said.

"Imagine the fiery ball coming down from the sky, making a great noise."

"The Indians would worship it."

"So they would," the anthropologist said. "A fetish object. The African primitives would call it a juju. And yet why *this* meteorite, Dave? Meteorites aren't that rare in the desert. This one perhaps had something special about it. Look at it closer."

Examining it from every angle, something at the very top caught his attention. On the rough surface there appeared to be a deep carving. It resembled a sign. A symbol. He leaned closer.

"Interesting, eh?" Dan said.

"A trident. It appears to be a trident."

"Yes."

It did indeed resemble a trident with the shaft broken off quite close to the head. Dave's attention was caught by tiny glints framing the symbol, giving it a bizarre emphasis.

"Diamonds?" Dave said.

Dan nodded. "Crude bits of diamond, suggesting the heat and pressure of a tremendous impact with another body. Was it another asteroid?" He hesitated a moment. "Or was it something else?"

"Then it wasn't your shamans who carved this."

"I honestly believe it was a message."

"A message—?"

"Yes. A heavenly message, if you'll allow that."

"Dan—"

"I'm a scientist, Dave. But I respect what's beyond the books. The computers. My Indian heritage? I don't know."

"But from whom? A message from whom?"

"Good question." Dan then went on to explain that the Indians of the time had no written language. Wars, great events, anything of interest in fact, certainly unnatural phenomena—these were all passed along by song. "The Sioux Indians—they're plains Indians who use sweat lodges in which purification is done before sacred rites are performed. I once heard a song in one of them. It had to do with a fiery stone that fell from the sky. It warned of the day the earth would darken for the Indians of all tribes. People would die. The tribes would die."

The yellow light that came into the chamber from the hole above created an eerieness. Crespi's companion fell into the introspective mood as he felt himself infected some with his friend's natural mysticism.

Dan abruptly laughed, saying, "Nonsense, of course, eh? A rock, a song. Any conclusions from them couldn't be called scientific. Empirical, right? Okay, let's go back to the jeep."

Dave, entirely puzzled, watched as his friend poked about the rear of the jeep to come up with a manila packet of photos that he spread out on the hood of the car.

"Have a look at these, Dave."

Dave Turrell saw the same object in a series of perspectives. It appeared to be a huge, carved stone of granite or basalt. The designs were of an intricate pattern, not altogether unfamiliar to him.

"Mexican," he said. "Pre-Columbian."

Dan Crespi nodded. He went on to explain they were photos of a Mayan stele, a stone monument that, not unlike Egyptian obelisks, was used to record noteworthy events of the time.

"This was found at Uxmal on the Yucatan peninsula. Look closely, Dave. Tell me if you see anything familiar." He waited for several moments as Dave examined one photo, then the next. He noticed his friend arrested by a detail. "You see it, eh?"

"The trident."

"Exactly!" Dan said. "These hieroglyphs have been translated by Professor Clark of Yale University who found the stele, and it tells the story of a young woman taken captive during a raid. Beautiful enough to be sacrificed to the gods Tepeu and Gucumatz, believed to be the ancient forefathers. But as she was being prepared by the priests, this sign—the trident—was discovered on her body. The priests fell down before her, bowing. The woman was not only spared but was given the status of a goddess. Hundreds—maybe thousands—were subsequently sacrificed to her."

"Why?" Dave asked.

Dan shook his head. "It doesn't say. Perhaps to fend off some catastrophe. To propitiate her. We do know what happened to the Mayans."

"The same as what happened to the Puye cliff dwellers."

The Indian didn't reply. He was staring off into the distance, across to the mountains sliding into blue shadows. It was becoming late in the day, and the moonscape desert floor seemed empty and desolate, except for the thin, straight line of the highway going off into a Daliesque infinity. Far off, an aluminum trailer rig caught the last of a sun's ray and glistened in the remnants of the golden sun. As the rig approached the road cutoff to the viewing point, it sounded its horn, a lonely, eerie sound trailing off in some Doppler effect, which, unaccountably, reminded Dave of a moan of despair.

CHAPTER FOUR

"Ciu-ciu" Gracchi had known almost from the birth of the child that she was different from the others. It hadn't been just her red hair—the difference in complexion. Among other things, it was her strange stillness, never crying or complaining, not even when the lack of food was at its worst. Deprivation seemed to have no effect upon her, or was she susceptible to the other children's diseases often epidemic in the village. The peasant, despite his stolid, heavy-footed ways, had the animal sensitivity to be aware his daughter Olivia was different than others. He knew she was off-centered in some way.

And as Olivia Gracchi grew older, others noticed it as well. Her own brothers and sisters paid her difference the ultimate compliment of not being as cruel to her as they were to each other in children's fashion. Her appearance threw a pall over their games. They moved away. Others did too. Ciu-Ciu and his wife, noticing these things, thought uneasily of them, yet never discussed them. Speech those days after the war was limited to food, whether there was enough firewood, whether the roof leaked.

Inevitably, Olivia's difference became a matter of village discussion, especially among the women. La Rocca was a small, medieval village, not yet caught up with the twentieth century. Superstition was a major preoccupation, not just casually believed in. It didn't just happen that women went barren, cows dried up, love affairs soured. And before long the name *fiore del diavolo*, flower of the devil, came to be associated with her, and with it the child, ten years of age now, became more and more isolated. It became common practice, if the child passed a group of women on a street or in the piazza, for them to point their fingers at her in the sign of the devil's horns, *le corna*. The tradition was for the men to scratch their balls. A new rumor spread. An ancient word revived. A word out of the Dark Ages. Soon La Rocca was to have an *"iettatrice,"* one who could cast the *malocchio*, the Evil Eye.

One hot July day, the *iettatrice* came of age.

As was the custom, Olivia at noontime would go into the fields bringing her father his bread and wine. At one point she lifted her flour-sack shift and squatted to pee, unaware there was a young field hand nearby. He watched in fascination. Later he swore on the soul of his dead mother that the child had between her legs the dense bush of a full-grown woman. As she continued on her way he followed, his head spinning. He caught up with her, threw her to the ground, and in a moment was into her. He later swore that not only didn't she struggle, but she had responded with a passion and skill new to him. His words in the office of the *maresciallo dei carabinieri* stunned everyone.

"It was how I dreamed it should be but never was," he cried. "Her cunt was a flame. A hot furnace with a life of its own. I couldn't stop if my life depended on it."

A midwife, examining Olivia, found her to be a normal ten-year-old virgin, with certainly no growth of hair. The young man was found next morning in his jail cell hanging from a strip of blanket.

Obviously, they said, he had been seeing things.

The mayor and the secretary of the *comune*, now that the principessa was gone, had risen from their seats and were exchanging insults. The prince looked down, quietly turning a fruit knife in his hands, wondering who would be at Montecatini where he and the principessa would shortly be. Other thoughts stealthily intruded. Thoughts to do with a flame-headed young woman, his daughter, at last a guest in his house. "Drives like a lunatic, I've heard. I hope she's careful."

The mayor was saying, "Your Grace, excuse what I say, please, but this—this rat of a secretary is a disaster for La Rocca. God could better have given us another earthquake."

Not even this roused Don Ettore from his reverie. That dream. That memory relived again and again, as once he had read and reread his Thomas Aquinas until the pages fell out of the volume. Would this page ever disappear from his memory? That memory of eighteen years ago . . .

It had been just another sunny September morning. The mists were still low and the white gashes of the old quarries gleamed ghostlike on the distant mountainsides, terrible wounds never healing. His old housekeeper hadn't come that morning and he had prepared his own breakfast of some melon, coffee and a slice of bread smeared with the delicious apricot preserves regularly handed to him by Rosa, the postman's wife who knew of his weakness for sweets. He had sworn to her time and again her *fritti di ricòtta* assured her a place in heaven. The radio was crackling the news of the outside world, and he was wondering how the turbulence in Rome could be used in Sunday's sermon. No, he had decided, they were as tired of that as they were of man's inhumanity to man. The world burns and the Church talks on. Where was the professed moral force, or was his voice a cry in the wind? This Sunday's sermon needed local—better still, personal—application, he had decided, when there was an urgent knocking at the door.

The classroom of the elementary school, a few hundred yards away from the rectory, was in turmoil. He entered, flushed and sweating from the exertion of the hasty climb. Olivia Gracchi was the center of a great commotion. The nun teacher stood over her at one side; on the other was the mother superior herself. Both were exhorting the child to clasp her hands in prayer. The child stared ahead, her face even whiter than usual, her mouth a grim line. She said nothing, but it was clear to the priest she was stubbornly refusing. He strode forward and instructed the sister to clear the room of the other children. He already knew Olivia's name from the recent incident with the field worker.

"Now what have we here, Olivia?" he had quietly said, even a note of humor in his voice. The mother superior began to explain, but without glancing up he had raised his hand to silence her. "Olivia?" he went on.

The child stared straight ahead, as if her attention were fixed upon some distant place. Her hands remained at her side.

It took an effort but his voice had remained gentle. Patient. "Olivia—child, look at me." There was no response. Despite himself, he felt his patience slipping away. Wayward stubbornness was intolerable. The mother superior was a woman of strict discipline. He mustn't show any weakness, he realized. "In order to pray to Our Lord, we clasp our hands. Like this, Olivia—look up at me. I would like you to do this. Everyone does this. There are no exceptions. Even I do this when I pray."

He let a moment—two—pass. Still there was no response. He recalled his irritation, his reaching over and grasping the child's two hands by the wrists. He had raised them up and brought them together so that they would be clasped. A remarkable thing then had happened. The child's arms flew apart. He had been so surprised, he didn't attempt to stop the motion. Now—angry—he again, more forcibly now, had grasped the two frail wrists to repeat the process. But again the hands flew apart, and he had become aware of a strength—certainly not a child's strength—which had shocked him. He hadn't seen the mother superior step back and cross herself as if she had found herself in an unholy presence. He didn't attempt it another time.

Shaken, he had said sternly, "Come with me." He then had turned to leave the room. At the threshold, he again had turned to look back. The child was still seated, rigid as a statue. "Come," he had called. Olivia Gracchi had risen and quietly followed him, the mother superior stepping aside as if the child were anathema.

He had entered his rectory study first. Not a word had been exchanged during the short walk. When she had entered the room, for some unexplainable reason, he now recalled, he had bolted the door . . .

Sitting now in the prince's dining room, lost in the memory, he realized the room of his study hadn't changed at all through the years. There was still the mosaic marble floor, which during the chill months now gave his rheumatism trouble. The furniture was somber old oak, and there was the still serviceable radio left behind by the liberating American troops. Above his marquetry desk, the only decent bit of furniture in the house, which a Roman antique dealer had once offered him a tidy sum for, there was the large wooden crucifix, the crude product of a local artist, who had seen to it that the Lord's agony was graphic and bloody.

He recalled speaking gently to the child. "Don't be frightened," he had said. He explained he knew she had been having troubles lately, but now together they would work them out. "You would like that," he said.

"Yes," she replied, almost to his surprise.

"Sit here," he then said, indicating an old couch with a fading needlepoint of a Moorish garden inhabited with childishly innocent beasts who clearly meant no harm. It was customary for Don Ettore, when hearing children's confessions, to seat them on his lap so that they could whisper their secrets into his ear. He recalled having qualms about this in Olivia's case. Something about her made him uneasy; then too there was that recent scandal involving her. As for the talk of *iettatrice*, he knew the threads of dark superstition woven into the social fabric of the village, a subculture inhabited by demons, devils and witches—*iettatrici*. He had long since given up his struggle against them, choosing even to insinuate them into the gospel, despite the fact he was perpetuating the myths. He was also giving credibility to his own message.

He sat beside her on the couch. "There now," he had said reassuringly. "Would you like a lemonade?"

She smiled at him. *"No, grazie,* padre." Recalling that smile—that fair, lovely face, the large eyes, he thought of a Botticelli cherub he had once seen in the Palazzo Pitti.

It's all a terrible mistake—this child, he recalled thinking. He knew what envy could do, a rumor starting, growing. A village could be an insidious place.

Then—even as he was thinking this—Olivia did a strange thing, which for a moment startled him. She took his large hand into her own tiny one, and she brought it to her lap. How often had he relived the moment. The shock at first, annoyance at her boldness. But those eyes were smiling into his own, and all the bad thoughts just blew away.

It had then happened.

Slowly she had turned his hand about and held it down to her lap. This was a child, he had thought frantically. A *child*. But then some awareness—a realization—came to him. Something unnatural was there. He was feeling—actually feeling a protuberance where none had any right to be. He had tried to draw his hand away, but again there was that incredible strength in the tiny hand holding his hand where it was. There was no doubt any longer. What reason had rejected was forced on him. It was a penis. A growing, throbbing penis. A sound came from him. A moan, a gasp for air. He could only recollect it as rooted in his soul. A detachment settled over him. A sense of himself splitting. A part of him stood off—watching with, incredibly, no repulsion. No horror. Not even judging. He was watching as a will not his own enveloped and took him over. It made his fingers wrap themselves about what he knew it was, and close about it gently. Holding it, he felt its life and the fibers of his being resonate with its pulse. He remembered something far off— deep down within him saying this was illusion. He was being deceived by his senses. No such thing could possibly be happening. His bad eyes were up to their old tricks. This was but another instance. He could do only one thing, and he did it. He snatched at the coarse material of the child's shift and threw it up.

Between those two frail, childish legs was a shaft, with its pinkish head already starting to protrude from the foreskin. His eyes—he couldn't take them from the spectacle. He had once seen the Hellenistic Hermaphrodite in Rome's Villa Borghese. Could this be La Rocca's freak? No, nor did it matter. Nothing else mattered. If San Eustacchio himself, in green hunting garb and bow and quiver, strode into the room, he could not have taken his eyes away.

His hand came down to it again, unaided this time. The organ of a man attached to a child, a girl child. Beyond reason, yes, but he was beyond reason. This was the magic of the *iettatrice* enjoying her newfound powers...or a man swept overboard by his intolerable fantasies?

A thunderbolt struck, he felt the wet warmth spreading beneath his cassock. And turning his face to the child's, he thought he saw through his befogged lenses that she was smiling, a knowing smile. Then, with a childish laugh, she was off the couch. She straightened her shift, ran across the room, unbolted the door and was gone.

CHAPTER FIVE

Dan Crespi found Dave in his office one day begrimed and staring at the Webendorfer press, which had been disassembled. Old Leo, the pressman, sat nearby, his feet on the desk. What he found was of intense interest, more certainly than his employer's problem.

Although Dave had given no indication he was aware of Dan's entrance into the shop, he said, "Mind getting two beers out of the refrig?"

The two men sat drinking their beers, peering out through the unwashed store window to the deserted street. It was midday. Pojoaque was baking. Their thoughts turned inward; neither man spoke for a long while.

"If you know where I can get a four-inch cast rocker-arm for a forty-two Webendorfer, this week's edition of the *Double-Dealer* can maybe get out," Dave finally said, more to himself. He turned his head to his friend. "Do you, Dan?"

"Nope."

"In that case no one'll know a pair of hookers have set up shop at Millie's Truck Stop; that Harvey Hayden's girl was elected Arizona State's pom-pom girl of the year."

"That'd be awful."

Dave nodded. "Yeah," he said. His thoughts went to the night before. Restless and unable to sleep, he had slipped on his old flannel robe and stepped out of his room to the parking area. The bright neons of the office were off, making more visible the incredible spectacle of the overhead sky with its panoply of stars. He searched in vain for an arrangement—a constellation—resembling the trident. Once or twice he thought he had it, but no.

He stood there in the cold night wondering what in God's name was he getting himself into? He'd uprooted himself from what most people would consider an enviable life. And for what? Searching the stars on a bleak desert floor for some asshole sign an obsessed Indian thought had cosmic importance? Crespi was probably drinking beer somewhere, balling some blond into the Indian scene. And here he was with this . . . Why couldn't he turn it off? And even as he asked himself he knew he couldn't. Something about it . . . about the trident . . . resonated with something inside him? He couldn't say what . . . it was beyond explanation, even rationalization . . . Nothing in his experience called for this—and then the chilling recollection came . . . the last evening he'd seen Janet there'd been that weird, eerie sensation as he was talking bullshit, as though he were somehow being pulled, guided . . . He looked into the sky. Who the hell are you . . . And then an eighteen-wheeler was whooshing by on the nearby road—and he was back. Or was he?

"Not very important, is it, Dan?" he said. It was the following morning. "I mean whether the *Double-Dealer* comes out or not. Today, next week or the week after. I've a feeling not even the subscribers would care, not to speak of the advertisers. They pay and don't care."

Dan said, "You care."

Dave considered this for a moment, then said, "It's trivial bullshit."

The Indian swigged a long draft, then said, "What isn't?"

Dave's words were careful. Thoughtful. "What you showed me back up there maybe isn't."

"The trident—"

"The stupid, goddamned thing!" Dave exploded. "I'm hooked into it!"

"I'm sorry, Dave."

"The hell you are!"

"Why not forget it?"

"Now you tell me!"

"The paper's important to us," the Indian pointed out. "It says what we feel. Want. It's a small voice, I grant you. But without it, there'd be silence."

Dave thoughtfully nodded. He had considered that, yet somehow wasn't satisfied. "I somehow feel," he said, "the paper's just been a step along the way for me."

"To what?"

"That's what I want to find out. I never felt anything like this inside me before." Even as he spoke, he thought of the sequence of recent events. Each seemed to have some motive in his life. "Even this fucking broken rocker-arm," he observed aloud.

"How will you go about it?"

"I don't know?"

"What *do* you know?"

"All I know," David said, "is why a woman goes into a supermarket and buys a package of Twinkies. Maybe I'm telling myself life should be a little more than that. So why not a trident search? It's as good a start as any. What's my line? I hunt tridents."

"You've apparently learned that the trident heralds an impending disaster to a people."

"Maybe it's reversible. Remember, I'm a Western barbarian. I'm foolish enough to hope . . . to think anything is possible . . . even finding a trident—"

"If it exists."

"If it exists . . . You want to help me, Dan?"

"I'll try."

"I need a quick indoctrination, a crash course. Where would be a starting point? Names of people, places . . ."

The *Double-Dealer* had about exhausted his funds, so he called New York. "Cliff, I'm off to Europe," he said to the head of the agency he had left.

"A lady?"

Dave ignored it. "I need money," he said, and went on to mention a number of the firm's stock options he'd received as Christmas bonuses.

"How much you want for them, Dave?"

"Fifteen thousand?"

And so, picking up that amount in traveler's checks at an Albuquerque bank, he began what he had wryly come to think of as his odyssey.

At the Bodleian Library of Oxford he met with several archaeologists recommended to him by Dan Crespi. Time and again the Mediterranean region was mentioned. A recurring theme. He set out for Athens, where he found the trident an almost commonplace symbol among the ancient ruins and artifacts. It was of course associated with Poseidon, brother of Jupiter, god of the sea, usually represented as seated in a chariot drawn by brazen-hoofed horses, attended by Tritons and nymphs, and holding a trident in his hand. But this wasn't what Dave Turrell sought. On the island of Crete, he made his first significant find. In the museum at Heraklion, close by Knossos, the site of the palace of King Minos, his attention was drawn to a bronze disk, green with the patina of thirty-five centuries. On it had been etched rows of cuneiform symbols. There among them was the trident! Arranging a meeting with the museum's curator, and with the aid of an interpreter, his excitement grew as he listened to the Linear B translation of the disk's symbols. Before that, however, he was given a brief résumé of the Cretan civilization of the Minoan period, when the island had been a center of culture predating the Greek mainland's importance.

Dave impatiently interrupted the lecture. "I'm particularly interested in the trident symbol."

It was explained that the entire disk was a fable of the Bronze Age when goddesses had been worshipped as fertility symbols throughout the Cyclades . . . "It has to do with King Minos's wife, the queen. She had been taking a bath. You've been to the excavated palace?"

"Yes."

"Then you've seen her tub in her quarters."

Dave said he had. The group was standing before the disk behind glass, looking down at the object as the curator went on. "One day a serving maid to the queen noted aloud that she bore an odd mark on her body."

Dave felt the little hairs at the back of his neck stand erect. He tried to keep his voice matter-of-fact. "It says that? Actually?"

"About the bath?" the curator said. He seemed offended. "My dear fellow," he said through the interpreter, "the Minoans understood astronomy, they had toilets which flushed."

"Of course," Dave hurriedly said. "Please go on."

"The maid apparently was a Hebrew slave from Canaan and she pointed out to the queen there was a similar sign among her people. It was the first letter of the unutterable name of their one God."

"What happened then?" Dave asked.

"To the maid?"

"To Crete."

"Well, it's been reasonably established that sometime during Minos's reign the great earthquake struck."

"And?"

The curator shrugged. "Crete as a world power, such as it was . . . a center of trade and culture . . . simply vanished. Literally perhaps, beneath the sea. One minute to the next—*poof.*"

CHAPTER SIX

"The child can be your salvation, principessa. It is God's response to our prayers."

It had been several days later. Don Ettore and the principessa had been walking in the villa's garden. He had sent a message that an audience with her was imperative. The invitation was, of course, immediate. Now—eighteen years later—sitting at the prince's table, he visualized the scene easily . . . They had been walking slowly. It was the golden moment of sunset, and there was that pause in nature before the day surrendered to night. The Roman statuary had gleamed white, and he recalled averting his eyes as usual from the life-sized Bacchus, that obscene priapus mocking him.

"It would be a very serious business, wouldn't it?" the principessa said at last, breaking the silence. He recalled the tension he awaited her words with. Life-giving words. If the child were gone from the village, there would be hope for him. Otherwise—he had visualized the body of the youth hanging in the jail cell to which he had been hurriedly summoned. He also recalled his rationale. It was for the child's sake. Unquestionably she was an *iettatrice* who could cast spells. The women of the village were probably even at that moment stoking the fires of their superstitions. Something awful would happen to Olivia Gracchi . . . unless she was gone. Here was another reason for putting his plan to work, one less disturbing. One he could deal with.

"She's a child of rare beauty," he had said. "With proper training at this age, she could one day make you—the prince—proud. The sisters in the school say she's beyond her years in intelligence."

The principessa had tossed her cigarette away. He knew she had come to a decision. "Can it be arranged?" she had said.

"I believe so."

"Discreetly?"

"Your Grace, I should like to point out another interesting point." Her dark, anxiety-filled eyes had looked into his. "As a girl child," he had continued, "there would be no problem with His Grace's relatives."

"Problem?"

"The matter of His Grace's titles. Their being passed on."

"Ah, yes . . ."

He knew she hadn't thought of that possible complication. Her thoughts were busy with her own position, visualizing her husband's return to her arms with the establishment of a family, however artificial. . . .

One Sunday morning after mass Ciu-ciu Gracchi, wearing his one good black suit and black greased boots, had let his daughter Olivia ride the *asino* up to the villa so she wouldn't muddy her high-laced shoes and white stockings. They were brought to the prince and the principessa, who were breakfasting on the terrace. Don Ettore, waiting with the royal couple, recalled his excitement at the sight of the child, who did not once glance at him, for which he was grateful.

There was a long silence as the prince and principessa looked at the child who smiled demurely, curtsied awkwardly and kept her eyes modestly down.

Don Ettore recalled thinking, God, what a performance. That sweet innocence . . .

The principessa spoke first. She had asked the child simple questions, after first insisting she accept some cakes which Olivia had been hungrily eyeing. Olivia's response to the questions were, the priest thought, disingenuous, artful. The couple was pleased and impressed. The principessa then took the child aside, happily showing her various features of the terrace. Don Ettore recalled listening as the prince, not deigning to bargain, offered the peasant the land that he worked and the money to pay off his debts. Ciu-Ciu carefully and respectfully made a magnificent show of deep affection for the child, her value to him and what her loss would mean. The prince allowed the man to play out his charade and produced a few gold pieces, which miraculously healed the man's grief, cut off the heartrending wails of misery and guilt.

A short while later, the peasant and the child gone, the prince had asked Don Ettore if a legal adoption was indeed possible.

"A simple matter, Your Grace," the priest had said. "I've already looked through the village's official birth registry. As is often the case when peasants cannot read or write, the entry was never made."

"Your baptism book?" the prince casually inquired.

"I perceive it as God's will," Don Ettore recalled saying, his eyes fixed boldly on the prince's, for once feeling on equal footing, "that a few strokes of the pen could forever dissociate her from the Gracchi family and all that represents. As for a properly legal adoption—"

"My lawyers can attend to that."

"Yes, I'm sure, Your Grace."

"Padre, I'd like you to know this pleases my wife—and me of course—very much."

Don Ettore suddenly had realized that the prince wanted the child for entirely different reasons from his wife's. It would busy her so that he could more easily pursue his other interests, and perhaps he also thought of himself as kind, solicitous of her feelings. One liked to think well of himself, and of the reasons for his actions.

Don Ettore could well identify with such thinking.

* * *

Beatrice Amontaldi di Donati, having left her luncheon guests, was now in her bedroom, a blend of Renaissance, baroque and Italian modern, blending together well since each piece and the richness of the room's fabrics and wall covering were in superb taste. She stood nude before her full-length miror, which cast back her reflection from three different angles. It was siesta time, and the shutters and drapes had been drawn against the light and heat of the day. Powerful lights were arranged about the mirrors.

In her youth Beatrice, daughter of the Marchese Grisoldi, had been a rare beauty, raven-haired, her skin in alabaster contrast. She had the fine bones and features, with the clear, strong lines considered a photographer's delight. But now, at forty-two, there were the terrors peculiar to a woman noted for her beauty and lacking the other resources to survive without it. She was standing before the mirror now, appraising herself, taking stock as a miser would, seeing his wealth diminish.

With an expert's scrutiny, she went over her facial features one by one. Her fingers probed the texture of her skin, testing its resilience, its smoothness. Her body was given special attention. Although her breasts might have been the envy of a woman years younger, she apparently perceived an imperceptible loss of firmness. Her fingers played lightly with the nipples, which almost instantaneously responded. The good feeling coursing through her body, appeased her somewhat. She drew her breath in, and watched her stomach muscles tense. Hardly any sag there, she noted with satisfaction. Her glance went to the bold hip bones, that flaring parenthesis of sensuality of her thighs and its dark triangle. Unaccountably she sighed, perhaps as an expression of the neglect of that proud, tufted concentration of her entire self. Snapping off the lights, she threw on a negligee and lay down upon the chaise.

Her eyes didn't close. There would be no sleep, she knew. There hadn't been sleep since Olivia—her daughter—had come into the house several days ago. All the years, since Olivia was a child, she had succeeded in keeping her at a distance. There were those nagging fears that the tragedies associated with her at a succession of schools were somehow more than oblique suspicions. She understood the reluctance to come straight out with it. "Your daughter is bewitched." She thought back to the time the adoption had been finalized. It had been decided between the prince and herself that the child would have to leave La Rocca immediately. Training and education were to begin at once. A convent school outside Firenze had been chosen as the best—the most convenient—place. It was in fact the very school which the principessa herself had attended as a child.

Almost at once, a disquieting report came to them while they were taking the waters at Montecatini. Olivia was proving a problem to the nuns, and no less a one to herself in relation to the other children.

In Paris more serious news arrived which appalled them both and for the time made the principessa certain a terrible mistake had been made. She had already suspected that the adoption had been a miscalculation. It hadn't brought her husband closer. His interest in other women continued. The spark of love certainly hadn't been rekindled, nor was it aided by her obsession with her appearance. The hours each day spent in body and facial care—the painful exercises, the diets, fads—all to no avail. Her father had settled a trust fund in her favor. She had even borrowed against it to pay the couturiers', the jewelers' and furriers' bills rather than ask her husband, who she knew was preoccupied with taxes. Compliments rained on her; the fashion editors and photographers gave her no peace. No social affair in Paris, London, Monte Carlo or Rome was considered "A" class unless the Prince and Principessa Amontaldi di Donati were there. And yet she would have surrendered this tiresome, shallow existence if once—just once—her gracious and well-mannered husband opened her bedroom door, came in and lay beside her, something she was too proud to ask of him; and so on and on she went, in the empty hope he would see her as others saw her.

It was in Paris, while guests of the Rothschilds, that the lengthy report had come from Firenze. Olivia had been seen entering a barn with a local youth. When he came out, he had started to cross a field when a bull charged and killed him. An examination was immediately made. Olivia was found to be *intatta,* a virgin. The only physical anomaly found was a strange birthmark within her inner left thigh. This in itself was considered of no consequence; however, her behavior was. The youth had been known by the school administrators for years. He was the son of the gardener, and was absolutely trusted. It was carefully broached in the letter to the prince that it was just possible Olivia may have enticed him into the barn. The letter also alluded to several "bizarre" incidents associated with the child, incidents which the new mother superior obviously had difficulty expressing. She went on to explain her recent, new elevation. Her predecessor was dead. Killed in an automobile accident. It seemed that she had summoned her monsignor for the investigation of the incident. Baffled, the monsignor had consulted with his bishop in Firenze. The latter had asked to see the child. Preparations had been made and the journey undertaken by the monsignor, the mother superior and Olivia—a journey never concluded since the auto had apparently gone out of control on a steep mountain grade, crashed through an abutment, killing everyone. Except the child. Miraculous, the police had said. The child had survived without so much as a scratch.

The principessa had left Paris immediately for La Rocca, where she at once summoned Don Ettore. Her greeting in the prince's study had been cold. She remained standing, and there was no invitation for him to sit. She at once came to the point.

"I've heard things about Olivia," she had said.

"Very disturbing things."

Watching him closely, she had wondered if she hadn't perceived a tensing. A pale hand had come up to finger his silver crucifix. His thick glasses, however, had masked any secrets his eyes might have betrayed. But the nose. There had been the telltale twitch.

"I don't know what you may have heard, Your Grace," he had said.

"She's been associated with"—she now recalled hesitating at the words "sorcery, witchcraft."

"Ahh." His hands had made a deprecating Latin gesture.

"It's true."

"A child, Your Grace."

"She's apparently more than a child."

"Unusual, yes."

"Too unusual." By now she had felt certain he was dissembling.

"A beautiful—a gifted child," he had said. "It isn't good to be different in an Abruzzi village."

She had wanted to say, "Don Ettore, whom do you confess to when you lie?" but she didn't. Besides, she of course had known of the region's dark ways and superstitions, from which, she had to acknowledge, even a child wasn't safe.

After Don Ettore, she had turned to others, starting with Don Giulio, their estate manager who knew everything that went on in the village. She had been struck by the man's reaction to her inquiries. She had recognized that stoniness—that obdurate curtain which descended over the peasantry when confronted by an unpleasant situation—but it was unusual in Don Giulio, the sunny-dispositioned, loyal employee of many years who in the worst of times identified himself with the prince's interests.

"A child, Your Grace," he had muttered. "You know how it is with us. Television in every house. Alfas and Fiats in front, yet the mind is back in the old times, especially—you will excuse me, Your Grace—the women."

And she had gone to the women. The servants in the house first, and they too said more by their grim taciturnity than by anything they might have put into words. One word did somehow emerge. It had been said almost as a whisper. She couldn't even be certain that she had heard it. It was—it had sounded to her like, *"iettatrice."* It had been easy enough to ask what an *iettatrice* was, and the reply had put a chill over her. Her own religious convictions—her belief in the devil and his hell—these resonated with what she heard. Credibility was no problem. The situation obviously was.

The prince subsequently had been asked with tact and regrets to remove his daughter from the Firenze school. A Swiss academy had quickly agreed to accept the daughter of the distinguished family. But in a very few months, more disquieting reports had been received. And finally came the request: their daughter was undoubtedly "special," and it was suggested that perhaps a more specialized institution would be better suited for the child.

"Antonio, it seems we may have made a mistake."

They had been sitting in the small, comfortable room furnished to their taste, since the Committee on Arts and Antiquities had insisted everything in the other rooms of the palazzo remain authentic to its period.

"Mistake?"

"There are things about Olivia—" she had begun.

"Never mind Olivia," he had interrupted, the weariness in his eyes more pronounced. "Perhaps it's our problem, Beatrice. Our differences with which we've lived and said nothing all these years. We see things through different eyes. It seems even our very chemistry is different." His usually casual manner was gone, and he had spoken with a sadness, as if wishing it weren't so.

She, of course, knew he was referring to her devoutness, the fact she was of the black nobility. He had always been patient with the Church, its rituals and hierarchy. But this she knew was more a matter of form than of belief. Conviction. Faith. She even had realized she often made him uncomfortable. He would speak of the priests and their fascination with death. "And you've caught it from them, Beatrice," he had said. "You enter a room as if you were carrying a long candle." And it was true; she had known that deep within her, she had always hoped to win him over. Bring him to the faith.

"You're suggesting now we return the child,"

he had said. "Isn't that so?"

"I know it would be difficult."

"Difficult!" he had exclaimed. "She's our child. Legally." His words now had become coldly precise. He had seemed to her more the prince than ever. "Beatrice, I will explain something," he continued. "We forget sometimes who we are." She had remained silent. Waiting. "We are venerable, archaic and somewhat romantic dinosaurs," he had gone on. "Obsolete, irrelevant class anachronisms. We are guests in our own country. In perhaps the world. Our existence is tolerated as long as we behave ourselves. This very palazzo in which we now sit. For centuries it belonged to my family, as you know. The Borgheses, the Colonnas, the Medici and the Amontaldi di Donatis—at different times—our holdings were Rome itself. Beyond. Now what are we? What do we have? What have we become? Relics. Relics sealed in the glass reliquaries of our brittle society. We even live in museums. That's what our home is now. A museum. We are permitted residence here as part of the mood—the theatricality so part of us Italians in which we are permitted to play roles for which we are eminently suited. The public—anyone—is permitted into our homes once a week and has more rights than we do. You and I have little more importance than the Borromini staircase, the Alberti and Rosetti frescoes. Little more, perhaps even less. They have value, they will be here when we are gone."

"But the child—" she had begun to protest, but

stopped. She could never forget his expression as he got up, forgetting the pain of it.

"Ah, yes, the child," he had said, standing before her. "I will explain another thing, my dear." His voice low, controlled, he then went on to describe the possible consequences should the circumstances of the adoption be exposed. "Our motives would be irrelevant. No one would have the slightest interest in them. Everything would be twisted by those who feel they owe nothing to the past. 'Nobility kidnaps peasant child!' 'Church documents forged by princely family!' This is how the press—especially the socialist press—would put it." He paused for a moment to calm himself, his agitation remarkably not apparent except for his paleness. "The whole Via Veneto would buzz with it over Cinzanos. Paparazzi would hound us, and I don't mean for news of what you'll wear to the Venezia costume ball. I'm not even exaggerating if I say it could become a government scandal. But even worse, Beatrice. Our own people would hate us for bringing attention down on them, since in the public mind we are all one . . . Well, my dear Beatrice, how do you feel now about undoing the adoption?" He had then turned away from her and with trembling fingers removed a pill from one of the many bottles on the nearby table. "There's never mineral water around this damn museum," he had said . . .

The principessa, lying on the chaise in her darkened room, let these old memories replay themselves. She had failed in ousting Olivia from the family, but through the following years she did at least succeed in keeping their daughter entirely away from them. But now—for the first time—Olivia was back. Despite all her efforts and resolutions, Olivia had returned to La Rocca where it all began, and the principessa had an ominous, a well-founded sense of foreboding.

CHAPTER SEVEN

A Sunday in Athens.

Dave Turrell made the compulsory climb to the Acropolis. There, walking amidst the decaying marbles and skirting the German tour group with its shrill-voiced guide disrupting the spell of the place, he found himself in a quiet, rubble-strewn corner overlooking the city. It was coming on toward evening, and there was that magical Athenian twilight so well described by Henry Miller and his friend, Lawrence Durrell. It all helped put him in a reflective mood.

What was this search, this mission, whatever it was, all about? What was he after, really? In his own eyes he was a laid-back, button-downed, uncommitted Presbyterian with no excess of social awareness. At times he regretted this blind spot, as he termed it, in himself. As a student during the stormy sixties he had avoided confrontations as well as issues. Joyce had interested him more than Ginsberg, although he appreciated trendy Tom Wolfe for his way with words and imagery; the message, however, left him unmoved. Che Guevara, he had regarded as a distasteful, swaggering cult figure. And as for anything smacking of the occult and mystic—these he had dumped into his personal trash bin of weirdos along with the Moonies and the outrageous Hare Krishnas. He recalled there had been that Vassar girl—her name forgotten. He had been tantalized by her tits. How they would look, feel, respond. But one day on a friend's sloop on Long Island Sound, she had uncovered not those delectable breasts but her enthusiasm for the Bhagavad-Gita. He even recalled the lines which had moved her so: *"Know me, oh Partha. As the eternal seed of all beings, I am the intelligence of the intelligent, and the splendor of the splendid."* Adolescent bull, he had thought, losing interest in breasts and all.

Now here he was at some far corner of the world pursuing some absurd idea which once he would have called off-the-wall. That damned Indian . . . with the best of intentions he'd involved him in this chimera, in searching for an imaginary monster. No doubt Dan had thought he had been doing him a favor, pushing his nose into a possible Pulitzer, or something. Don't blame Dan, he now thought. He had nothing to do with it— really. You were set up for it, and it grabbed you by the ole cajones because you had no choice. The chilling conviction again touched him. There was a larger purpose to it all. The *Double-Dealer*, the old, broken press, Don Crespi—himself. All accessories—pieces to some puzzle.

So what do I have, he asked himself. A few legends out of ancient times tied together by a common thread. Was he looking for further confirmation? A trident was an interesting archaeological feature to be sure—but leading to what? Did he need more proof that the trident was associated with disaster of a major magnitude? A quantum jump . . .

It came to him that he was now venturing into phase two. Now his search was for a modern manifestation of the trident and its warning. Which led him into new speculations . . . such as, in the unlikely instance he found the symbol on someone, what was he supposed to do about it? Hadn't he prepared sales campaigns for about almost everything? So why not take on—peddle the millennium? "Awake ye! The apocalypse—Armageddon is at hand!" He'd walk a sandwich board down Fifth Avenue—"Repent ye!"

Shula Gorin.

The name came at him from two independent sources. The first was an archaeologist at Athens University who spoke of a brilliant pamphlet written by the Israeli woman on the Messianic view of the Essenes established by certain artifacts and confirmed by the Dead Sea Scrolls. Sitting at a café table on the Syntagma, he had been immersed in a week old *Herald Tribune* to catch up on the world he sometimes felt he had abandoned. On the table, beside his espresso, he had put down a handbook on Greek art loaned him by the curator along with an English translation of the Shula Gorin pamphlet.

"Good stuff," a voice beside him said. He turned to see a blond, bearded young man nodding toward the pamphlet, at first glance one of the countless young backpackers who apparently found Greece an irresistible attraction. The city was filled with them at this time of the year. Many were on their way further east, possibly to India if they could manage the dangerous and inhospitable route through Afghanistan. For many, though, Greece was enough. There were its beautiful Aegean beaches. They had the Plaka, that quarter where food and even a bed could be found within their meager budgets, and above all, perhaps—less hassling by the police than in Italy, where one could no longer bathe in a piazza fountain, or smoke a joint on the Spanish Steps.

"Have you read it?" Dave asked in surprise.

"Several times," the pleasant young man said, adding, "and I've found something new in it each time." Jan Hoogstrater turned out to be an assistant professor in Holland's Leyden University's psychology department. "She says," he went on, "that aspects of Christianity had been practiced long before Christ."

"I'm afraid it's beyond me," Dave said, explaining he wasn't too informed on the subject in spite of the literature in front of him. "I'm strictly an amateur."

Hoogstrater shrugged and pressed on. "Before our recorded history—even before Cro-Magnon or the Neanderthals, there had been other cultures and civilizations. Layers of them. Layers upon layers. A stratified cosmic union of sorts, distinct and unaware of any existence but its own." The Dutch scholar sipped at his drink. "That's Shula Gorin's premise," he went on. "She's into the Kabbala, I suspect. Y'know—Jewish."

It was Dave's first encounter with the word. "Kabbala?"

"The mystic arm of the Jews. The secret, old practices. A poet named Eli Siegel once wrote: 'substance is what remains when everything you can think of is gone.' The Kabbalists were after the inner substance and vision transcending the obvious surface of existence."

Dave found Jerusalem a fascinating and confusing mix of geography, religions and diverse politics. It seemed to him a hopeless tangle of divergences among emotionally volatile peoples, each claiming ancient birthrights with equal passion.

He had found a room in a remnant of colonial Britain. The American Colony Hotel, once a sultan's residence, was now a charming, old establishment superbly run by Swiss management. The employees were mostly Palestinian. It was said, and one could readily believe, that T. E. Lawrence, the legendary English Arabphile, had met here with General Allenby to discuss the Turkish campaign. Now it was the favored place, other than for tour groups, for foreign correspondents and where the United Nation's officers put up their visiting wives.

Dave at once put in calls for Shula Gorin at the Hebrew and Hadassah universities. He was puzzled that they had no knowledge of her. His Athenian curator had armed him with an introduction to the archaeologist in charge of the excavations of the Har Habayit Temple mount just outside the Dung Gate of the old city wall. He visited the Israeli at his dig, and the latter made no secret of his annoyance at the interruption of his work, however, Dave's mention of the name of Shula Gorin elicited a quizzical smile and a grunt—but little more. However, that evening, sitting in the splendid little garden beneath the "Sultan's Room" of the hotel, he had ordered a vodka and tonic. The Palestinian waiter in an impeccable white jacket, had put his drink atop a paper napkin and left. Lifting the glass, he noticed a message scrawled on the napkin. "Be at the front of St. George's cathedral eight tonight."

Surely a mistake, he thought. Mideast political intrigue had nothing to do with him; nevertheless, more out of curiosity and boredom, he followed the instructions.

The street before the cathedral was dark except for the lights of a nearby Moslem coffeehouse. At this hour, traffic on the Nablus thoroughfare was minimal. Eight o'clock. Then eight-fifteen passed. He felt somehow relieved. He'd give it another few minutes then return to the hotel where he had heard a belly dancer was to entertain at poolside. At that moment, a car raced down the street toward him. It pulled to the curb, a door was flung open.

"*In.*" The man at the wheel barked at him in an

accented voice so that it sounded more like *een*. Dave hesitated. He flashed a vision of himself as a hostage of some terrorist group. What was he worth to anyone, he thought. Oh, boy, was someone ever barking up the wrong tree.

"In." The voice was more insistent now.

Even as he entered the car, Dave was calling himself stupid. Headlines can happen to you too, chump.

Dave had done some hairy driving both in Vietnam and in the New Mexico desert, but what he was now experiencing, he recognized as driving in a class by itself. He sat silently, staring ahead as the dark streets ran beneath the headlights, the Mercedes braking abruptly, cutting into alleyways that couldn't possibly accommodate the car's width yet somehow did.

"Where are we going?" he asked, failing, he knew, to sound casual.

The driver said, "Sit back. No problem."

Dave had lived in New York City long enough to know he was in Jewish hands. No problem. How often had he heard an Israeli taxi driver in Manhattan say it to a cursing truck driver. He wasn't altogether reassured, though. He recognized the silhouette of the Montefiore windmill. A few moments later, the car turned into a quiet residential district. The car stopped and the driver got out. Dave was about to follow but was told to stay back. The man stood beside the car for several moments in the darkness. When he was satisfied they hadn't been followed, he opened the door and told Dave to come out.

Shula Gorin was a surprise, if not a shock. For some reason, Dave hadn't even thought of the author of the pamphlet as a female. Even the name was neuter to him. The simple but arcane writing in the esoteric subject was scholarly and original in concept, and somehow he just arbitrarily assumed its author, if not male, was some musty, desiccated woman. He knew he had often behaved like a male chauvinist, had often been called down for it, now here he had done it again. Shula Gorin was a beautiful woman, who, if anything, went to pains to conceal her beauty. In this she failed. Her jeans weren't designer jeans. She wore no makeup, and her hair hadn't seen a hairdresser since her Paris visit—yet such trivia concealed neither the fluid grace of the good, lithe figure nor the classic Semitic features of a Nefertiti.

"I'm Shula Gorin," she said to Dave, extending her hand to him at the door. "Come in. And thank you, Eli," she said to the driver of the car who had escorted him to the apartment.

She smiled and Dave felt he was in love. "You've been pursuing me as though I'm a national treasure," she said when the door had been closed. "Somewhere between the Dead Sea Scrolls and the Benno Elkan menorah."

"Whoever or whatever you are, I'm impressed," he said truthfully.

The comfortable studio had her warmth and unpretentiousness. There was nothing to impress; what one saw was what it was—a place to live, to relax, to remember pleasant experiences. The most significant feature was perhaps the rows of glass shelves holding countless archaeological artifacts belonging to the past cultures of the Mideast going back to the Aramaic times. They were mostly ceramic; however, there was a good sprinkling of bronze and gold treasures which Dave by now could recognize as museum quality.

"You're not an archaeologist, are you, Mr. Turrell?" she asked, pouring him a glass of wine as he surveyed the shelves.

"Not even an amateur," he said.

"You know Dr. Koliakis of the Athens Museum. He wrote me you were coming."

"I am grateful to him, then," he said. Indicating a Luristan bronze bridle bit, he added, "The dealers sell you their best."

"I've dug those myself."

"Oh!"

She laughed lightly. "It's no big thing," she said. "If you know your Bible, you know where to dig."

"I'm curious," he said a while later, mentioning the napkin message, the wild drive to her place.

"A bit of cloak-and-dagger. A nuisance, I admit."

"No one at the universities knew your name."

"They know it," she said. "They just weren't handing out information. You also saw Moishe Landau at the Dung Gate dig. Let me just say I'm being protected, Mr. Turrell."

"From what?"

"In Israel, many of us lead schizoid lives. We'd like to do one thing, but we do another. I would like to dig those things you admire, write articles such as you read."

"How do you know what I've read?"

"I know," she said.

He asked why she did not do as she wanted. A naive, foolish question, he realized almost at once... In the few days he had been in the tiny country, he had seen something of the marvels they had accomplished in a single generation: pushing back not only the desert of millennia, but holding off the threatening human flood on all sides. "I still don't know that other side of you that needs the protecting," he said.

Shula Gorin peered at the attractive young American. It was more than that she was a Mossad agent, which in itself would make her close-mouthed, secretive. She was also an operative with a large price on her head. When the French under de Gaulle had refused to continue supplying Israel with needed Mirage fighter planes it was Shula who had been dispatched to Paris, and in a short time had insinuated herself into a position to help execute a virtually impossible coup. She and her colleagues smuggled out of the country enough blueprints and specifications to fill a freight car, and these eventually resulted in Israel's SFER fighter plane. There had been other exploits, not the least of which was the notorious Scheersberg affair; and later the sabotage of a Marseilles plant making nuclear material destined for Libya. It was inevitable that sooner or later intelligence would report that Shula Gorin was high on a terrorist hit list.

"One day, Mr. Turrell, I may answer your question," she said, "but not just yet. Now would you like to tell me what your burning interest in me is?"

Dave, uneasy with his own doubts and conflicts, had been pretty close-mouthed himself about telling anyone the reasons for his search. Besides, his trident theory no doubt would brand him some kind of obsessed nut with most people. Now, though, for the first time, he felt easy about it. After all, Shula had through her writings shown herself to be a mystic who wouldn't pull back from the arcane, even the incredible. And there was her historic perspective, making her a near-perfect partner for his mission . . . his quest . . . his . . . Without her he felt he'd blunder about haphazardly.

Refilling his glass with the excellent Israeli wine, he spoke about himself—his life—even before his fling at running a newspaper. He spoke about the Pueblo Indian meteorite, and noted her awakened interest. He felt encouraged enough to go on and tell her that he believed, strange as it might be for him to be saying it, that the trident had a fantastic significance . . .

"And now," she said, "you believe somewhere there could be a contemporary manifestation of the trident with all its implications."

"Yes."

"And if there is such an appearance on someone?"

He shrugged. "The message is clear, I guess."

"As a civilization, we too may have reached the end of the line?"

"In a nutshell."

"Mr. Turrell, in Brooklyn, where I was born and spent a good part of my growing up, a remark like that and someone would have said—"

"I was bananas . . . yes, I know. What do *you* think, Dr. Gorin? Am I?"

She laughed in a deliciously throaty way. She got up, her face suddenly solemn, and paced the room. Turning, she took a bit of Roman glass from a shelf and carefully began to dust it. It seemed she was hardly aware of what she was doing. The glass, which was a shard of what two thousand years ago might have been an essence flask belonging to a queen as lovely as the woman now handling it, still glinted with its fiery blues and reds.

She stood before him. Her expression had changed. Hardened. "Mr. Turrell, before you came here," she said, "you'd been checked out, carefully I thought. Much about you is known, but apparently what slipped by is that you're one of those quiet but dangerous lunatics. Tridents, no less! God!" He was confused. This sudden reversal . . . They were standing face to face now. "Now I want you to get out of here at once! The man who brought you is standing outside the door. I could call his name and Eli could break your arm—if necessary, your neck—before you knew it was happening. Will you leave quietly?"

CHAPTER EIGHT

It had been just a few weeks ago. The olives for the most part had been harvested and pressed. Don Giulio had assured the prince that the mists and the hot summer had produced *"Il buon mosto."* A fine, even great, vintage was just possible. Their plans for going to Montecatini had been completed.

They would see old friends, some of whom they hadn't seen since the previous year. Some, of course, wouldn't appear. Would never again appear. But it was unspoken tradition among these elegant survivors of other, better times that there was never to be any mention of death or dying. "The di Soltis are staying on in Cannes," might be said, and everyone knew the lie. The Count di Solti had suffered a stroke and had died that spring. There might be a nod or a murmured word, and their eyes would take on a far-off look, as if gazing inwardly upon their own fragility. Where would they be said to be next year, if—? Antibes? Costa Esmeralda? Corfu? . . .

It had been before one of the usual luncheons in La Rocca with the usual village "dignitaries." A half hour before the others were to arrive, Don Ettore had been unexpectedly announced. He would like an audience with the prince on an urgent matter.

"Be there too, Beatrice," the prince had said. "After all, he's your man."

"It's to do with Olivia," she had said.

"What makes you say that? Ah, yes! Your premonitions."

They both had entered the sitting room together to find the priest awaiting them. After his usual overblown and fustian greeting which never failed to amuse the prince, who thought the man ridiculous yet somehow touching in the way he clung to the fantasy that one day royalty would resume its proper place, the priest had inquired, "And how is Your Grace?"

"Since yesterday you mean, padre?" the prince had replied, deciding to have a bit of sport with him. "Since an hour? Since five minutes ago? These days I measure time in small doses, grateful for Our Lord's patience. There's also, of course, the possibility He doesn't quite know what to do about me yet. I've much against me, I'm sure, yet we must have Him confused what with your fervent prayers in my behalf."

The irony and cynicism hadn't been lost on the priest. Don Ettore was aware how he was regarded by the prince as well as most other men in the village. A priest was all right for certain rituals—birth, marriage and at dying—but otherwise he was a hypocritical scoundrel like the rest of the clergy.

"What is it, padre?" the prince had said. "I sense something. All these years, we should know each other well. I would say you've something on your mind. Something you consider important, such as your church roof again leaking."

The principessa recalled how the priest had deliberately removed his glasses, revealing a rawness on the bridge of his fleshy and restless nose. As he wiped the lens which needed no wiping, she had found herself moving closer to the prince's chair with its comfortable cushion arranged to accommodate his sensitive hip.

"The man called Ciu-ciu died yesterday," Don Ettore said quietly.

The room became very still. In the distance a field hand called to another; a trailer rig on the *autostrada*, miles away, blared its klaxon, the sound echoing among the hills. Neither the prince nor his wife had said anything for several moments. Both were thinking of the peasant with the uncommon name, and the impact he'd had on their lives.

"It was a peaceful passing," the padre went on. "You may have heard the church bell tolling. Tomorrow he's to be buried."

"What concern is this to us?" the principessa had said, "are we expected to attend?"

The priest, ignoring the sarcasm, had replied in an even tone, "People come together on these occasions, sit about. Talk. It's almost as if they would like to remind the blessed St. Peter of certain things in the life of the departed that shouldn't be overlooked."

"Come to the point, please," the prince said.

Don Ettore wet his lips. "Ciu-ciu's children were there last night. The money you had generously given him had apparently been put to good use. Several of them have done quite well. A son is even a pharmacist in Pescara—"

"And?" the principessa impatiently said.

"Their sister's name was mentioned."

"Olivia..." the principessa said.

"Yes, Your Grace."

The day had a chill to it, but that wasn't what prompted the principessa to draw her mohair stole closer about herself.

Don Ettore went on to explain that mention of the name had been forbidden in the house for many years.

The prince cut in. "You told us no one would know about her adoption by us. No one of the village."

"You swore it, Don Ettore," the principessa added quickly.

"And no one does know. Nothing ever came from me. Of course, there's Don Giulio and—"

"Don Giulio would say nothing," the prince

said. "I'll stake my life on it."

"I can only say," Don Ettore told him, "that last night the brothers and sisters came to me—a delegation, you might say. Curious. They wanted to know what I knew about her—"

"Had you been asked before?" the prince put in.

"Once or twice. Obliquely . . . at confessions, after mass. There was no great concern. I even had the impression they were glad she was out of the way, since she darkened their own reputations."

"And what was your reply?" the principessa had said. "Last night and before?"

"I said that for certain reasons—the times as they were—she'd been given for adoption to an agency in L'Aquila. I promised I would investigate if they wished. Make inquiries, learn if I could where she had been given."

The principessa, glancing at her husband, had wondered what he was thinking. From the very start of the nasty business, they had put themselves in Don Ettore's power. He had lied for them. Forged documents. It was unthinkable he would exploit his position.

"Why do you come to us with this, padre?" the prince had then said.

What had followed was one of the priest's unctuous recitals of his loyalty and interest in behalf of the prince and principessa.

"Yes, yes," the prince had interrupted. "And I believe I've also been loyal and generous."

"Oh, yes, Your Grace."

"Then please come to the point, Don Ettore.

What is it you want?" the principessa had put in.

"I believe it is in everyone's interest that the daughter be told of her father's death."

The principessa's voice had been harsh. "Why?"

The priest then had gone on to explain that a mere visit to the grave site would be adequate. When, didn't matter. The word would come down to the village. "Nothing happens in La Rocca which isn't at once known."

"In the course of which she would stay here," the principessa then had said. "In this house."

"Naturally."

"And word of that? It wouldn't reach the village?"

Don Ettore's reply was quick. "The relationship with you would not be known," he said. "Who would dare ask you? Would Olivia say anything? I doubt it. Besides, I could have a word with her advising her against it. The point is: it would stop all talk, especially the family's. They would have to rest content she has done well and wishes to keep apart from them. In light of the past, that would be understandable. She would be your guest, nothing more, and the matter would be dropped."

The principessa recalled her fears at the time. That woman in the same house with her filled her superstitious soul with dread. "It's dangerous," she had said. "I can foresee all sorts of unpleasant consequences."

"Would it be less dangerous, Your Grace," the priest pointed out, "if Olivia herself should hear about it sometime later and wonder why she hadn't been informed? After all, the man was her father. Wouldn't it be the Christian thing to do?"

"Christian!" the principessa blurted out. "You utter that word in connection with her?"

Don Ettore went on, undaunted. "What if the brothers and sisters continue their curiosity—their questioning? Put some lawyer on to it? It seems to me the lesser of evils to have her here briefly."

No immediate decision was made; and yet for several days, the matter hung like a pall over the villa, both aware the other was preoccupied with the problem. One morning, the principessa was at her writing desk when her husband entered the room. By the set of his jaw, she at once knew whom they would be discussing. Olivia, in fact, had been the only subject of open contention between them. All else, she had often thought, was like an old-fashioned gavotte or minuet. Stylized good manners, an occasional, the briefest of touching, then off to somewhere—someone else.

"Beatrice—" he said, "I want an end to this farce."

"Olivia—"

"Yes, Olivia. I've indulged you these years—"

"Indulged, Antonio?"

"That nonsense out of the Dark Ages. She's our daughter, like it or not. When I think of the ridiculous stories we've had to give out where she is— what she's about. Our daughter. We don't even exchange Christmas cards."

"I've never considered her my child, Antonio."

"Better you face it, Beatrice," he said. "Through all the years—how long has it been—seventeen? Eighteen? What have we heard to confirm those absurd tales?"

"They weren't just tales—"

"Village talk. My God, do you know they still hang bridal sheets from the balconies to see the bloodstains?"

"I seem to recall things from outside the village. People have died—"

"Her connection with them was entirely unproven." He went on to explain that his lawyer in Rome knew Olivia was skiing in Peru. "And I've had him wire her news of her father's death. I've also invited her to come here."

"To the villa?"

"Yes."

"I see," she said quietly. She knew it would be futile to argue further. She was aware of a momentary sense of panic, even the impulse to run away, but this was absurd, she quickly realized. It would be the worst of all possible actions—leaving Antonio and that woman together—alone.

"Antonio," she said, "I understand your feelings. Certainly she can stay here, as you wish. But is there any reason we must be here as well? It seems if she wishes to pay her respects to her father—"

"Beatrice, you haven't heard me."

"I was only thinking we could go on to Montecatini. We could leave the house open. The servants on. The place would be hers—"

"You still haven't understood me. I don't give a damn about that peasant out there somewhere. I am her father. You had planned, arranged the adoption. It was your idea. And before it's too late I mean to play the role of papa. Who knows? It may be my last pleasure."

CHAPTER NINE

The powerful Ferrari—tires screeching, fighting for traction, gears slamming back and forth, braking, accelerating—became a scourge of the local roads. Neighboring towns and villages even complained, and the carabinieri seemed helpless to cope against the wild young woman with red hair who made the mountain roads a hazardous place to be. The old-timers of La Rocca remembered, and their whispering started up. The *iettatrice* was back. More prosperous evidently, and why not? More beautiful, certainly, but then there had always been the promise of that, it was recalled. Now she was even a guest of the prince. The women who saw her speed by crossed themselves once more. The younger men, instead of scratching their balls, merely cursed and made obscene gestures at the car.

The car and its speed were a comfort to Olivia,

caught in the boredom of the place. It was also the continuation of an old process with her. She found in pure physical survival a continuing affirmation of her existence and its purpose.

Speed was solace for her. Speed or any life-threatening activity. Each victory over death confirmed her identity, enabling her to continue her swathe of destruction. There were its costs—the isolation. The loneliness. Several times in her life, she had been haunted by a nagging doubt—even a fleeting shadow of humanity. Standing at her father's grave, she had reflected, probing deeply within herself. Where was the grief she knew others felt? Why didn't she feel it? She sifted among childhood memories for recollections of love, tenderness, and found only ashes and bitterness. She had been a burden, a shame. An object of scorn and fear.

At what point in time had she comprehended her difference, become conscious of some special role? That was all vague to her. The accumulation of rebuffs compounded—came together in a synergistic effect—she was different. She was paying a terrible price for something. All that was lacking was what that something was.

At ten years of age, she knew. It came with the peasant youth who had thrown himself upon her in the fields. At first, she had felt the normal terror of a girl about to be raped. She was about to cry out. Struggle. But then—at that moment, for the first time it came to her—that overwhelming sense of purpose. Her fears vanished even as she was about to resist the assault. Her body seemed taken over, and a cool detachment—fearlessness with it—came over her. Another will—a force—became operative, and it made her demonic. She could do wicked things, not only with no moral restraint but nothing in her experience to give her guidance.

Through the years that followed, pity, remorse, certainly revulsion at what she visited on others simply became alien emotions. She felt nothing, not even a morbid sense of gratification at her powers. The only feeling she came away with was the sense that each of these incidents in some way brought her closer to some ultimate realization.

The incident with Don Ettore in his study had given her the first glimmering of a purpose. Immediately after, with the almost incredible adoption by the prince and princess, she sensed the emerging pattern. The die had been cast, the thrust of her life set. Soliciting neither love nor affection, doubts didn't come to her when she was very young. The very meaning of love evaded her. Contact, possessing, belonging to someone . . . those were gaps in her life she accepted, finding consolation in the excitement she was able to create about herself.

By her teens, Olivia had become accustomed to her role. The disasters in her wake left her unaffected; then, too, there was not only her emergence as a mature, stunning beauty, but along with it an appropriate style and sophistication. In every sense, she was a woman to be noticed.

Moving about the Continent—France, Spain, England—gave her a facility with languages as well as a perception of different peoples. The prince's bank in Rome paid her bills; other than that, there was no contact with her parents. Still, she did nothing to embarrass them or to thrust herself on them. It was altogether a tacitly understood wish for mutual avoidance. She knew her beginnings, and that through the years of schooling the prince and principessa had been aware of the deeds associated with her. Olivia suspected it was for their own sakes they had protected her, enrolling her in one school after another when situations became untenable. Arrangements were made without protest; and never once was an explanation from her requested. Which suggested to Olivia that her foster parents had reconciled themselves to the bad bargain they had made in adopting her.

By her mid-twenties Olivia, formally known as Her Grace, the Princess Amontaldi di Donati, had become a notorious personality in certain elite circles of the world where fashionable thrill-seekers gathered for this or that season, or special event. Olivia became a popular, if not notorious, figure at the more exclusive ski slopes, the mountains that offered the most hazardous climbs, water with the most exciting scuba-diving, world-class auto races. Olivia not only excelled at all these sports, but her reputation had grown to such proportions there were those who refused to compete against what was perceived as her foolhardiness. There were, not surprisingly, sharp differences of opinion about her. Some thought she was indestructible; others that she had a will for self-destruction which sooner or later would catch up with her. Some even secretly wished it.

There were, of course, a series of lovers. It could even be said she was rarely without one. But none had any lasting effect. They were, for her, merely helping to pass the time pleasantly; and because of this, perhaps, none of these men suffered the penalty of being another rung to her ladder.

All but one, that is.

Tony Koblenzer was a forty-year-old millionaire industrialist at home in the chic places of the world. Attractive as he was restless, he seemed possessed with his own demon—the need to compete and to win. The acquisition of money and power had long since left him bored and disinterested in conventional pursuits.

Hearing of the by now almost legendary Olivia Amontaldi di Donati, he made it his business to be in the Italian resort of Cortina d'Ampezzo when he heard she would be there. They met at a party, skied the slopes, and were married two weeks later in a local church. His proposal had been a breathless one, literally. They had made an almost impossibly difficult ski run down the mountain. One short stretch remained, the most difficult. She had turned to him. "Tony, I just can't."

He had lifted her goggles, smiled and said, "Marry me."

Marriage was an extension of the contest his life was. Even the intensity of their lovemaking would step up as Tony Koblenzer came at it as if to prove something more about himself. Feeling, caring—these had little to do with the business at hand.

New sensations were sought as a gourmet turning gourmand would track down some new, exotic dish. They followed one on the other, without acknowledgment or careful savoring. They were like scenes from a speeding train passing through a psychedelic landscape. Protracted orgasms were rest stations along the route. And Olivia was the goad, expertly driving her husband on and on to seemingly unattainable extremes, always just a bit beyond his grasp. She seemed inexhaustible, unquenchable—the challenge unspoken but expressed by her inflamed body. At some point, reaching that double helix of pain and pleasure, she would cry out, as if wrung from her, "Enough, Tony. Enough. I can't anymore." And once more Tony Koblenzer had his gratification, his standard had been planted on what he considered for the moment conquered soil. He felt fulfilled, unaware that she was playacting, planning future goals for him. . . .

"Sixty—seventy meters," their fathometers read.
Their yacht was off Paradise Beach in Nassau, and they were diving from it. Looking up through the turquoise waters, they could see the hull of the vessel. Signaling, Olivia pointed down. Their bodies arched, and in graceful sweeps they spiraled downward. The blue of the water changed imperceptibly to deeper hues, their air bubbles meanwhile streaming upward in a slowed-motion phosphorescence. Olivia suddenly stopped the descent. Her husband was close beside her. She pointed to her depth gauge on her wrist and

pointed upward in the accepted signal.

But—and, of course, she knew it—Tony Koblenzer had to go those few fathoms further to establish his superiority. Treading water gently, Olivia remained motionless as she watched him go down, down, down until she could no longer see him.

And so it was that she became independent of her parents' money: a boon to them, and a convenience for herself.

The Principessa Beatrice, lying in the darkened room, reviewed the past several days since Olivia's arrival. Superficially no one would have suspected that the reunion after so many years was anything but the coming together of a well-bred family. There wasn't the slightest hint of emotion or personal feelings, or the mention of the past; nevertheless, the villa was charged with an explosive tension with currents swirling just beneath the surface. Their relationship was cold and guarded, but so very proper that the older woman couldn't fault her daughter.

She had carefully scrutinized Olivia's behavior, sieving it through the fine mesh of her own strict criteria. She had not been able to detect one false note. The very fact Olivia was so impeccable disconcerted her. She believed breeding was inherent, that there was no possible way it could be counterfeited, that the truth of a person's roots would inevitably reveal itself. But she hadn't found the slightest chink—not the subtlest sign that Olivia was anything but "of the blood." One more sign, she was convinced, that the girl had an alliance with the devil himself. Was he not, through the ages, the master of dissembling, of seeming to be what he—and his—was not?

The principessa became aware of still another—even worse—terror. Recalling that Olivia's victims in the past had been males of various ages, the possibility occurred to her that Antonio could become a candidate for her sinister attention if it served her purpose in some way. She indeed had noticed that from the very moment of Olivia's appearance at the villa, unusual changes had come over her husband. He seemed revitalized. More spritely. His aches and pains appeared to have vanished, or at least he didn't complain of them. Once when she had remarked in the girl's presence that he would be straining himself in showing Olivia the old winepress, he had reacted unpleasantly. "Don't fuss over me, Beatrice!" he had said in an unseemly, irritated tone.

The prince himself put an end to the charade one evening at dinner. The principessa, in order to break an awkward silence, had commented on Olivia's dress. "It's a Givenchy, isn't it?" she said, thinking, Holy Mary, I'm sitting here actually admiring the costume of this creature of hell at my table . . .

"It's last season's," Olivia had modestly said, thinking, How she hates me. Of course, she's frightened to death.

"It suits her well, don't you think, Antonio?" the principessa had said, "especially the color. What do you call it, my dear? The color."

"A chartreuse, I suppose."

"Becoming. Most becoming, don't you think, Antonio?"

"What I think," the prince replied, in his even, well-modulated voice, "is that since Olivia's our daughter, we should deal with her as such." He then turned his head to Olivia. "And you might start by calling me father."

"Father..." Olivia had said tentatively.

"I believe I even like the sound of it," he'd said.

Olivia had then turned to the principessa. "And you, Your Grace? I'm to call you mother?"

Mother, she now thought bitterly in the quiet of her bedroom, reaching for a chased silver mirror. Staring at her reflection for several moments, she gently touched the cheekbone beneath an eye. Was this almost imperceptible scratch there yesterday? She couldn't be certain. Putting aside the glass, she settled back. An errant sunbeam had insinuated itself through the blinds, and dust motes danced on the shaft of light. She half closed her eyes, and fell asleep.

Olivia, returning from one of her noonday rides which took her away from the villa during the luncheon when the prince entertained the village people, found the villa quiet and still. It was the inviolable siesta time. Shutters were drawn, the servants in their quarters. Even the dogs were stretched on the warm stones of the terrace. Entering the house, she stopped to listen. All was so very still. Heavy doors everywhere were closed. Her steps as she crossed the hall echoed on the marble mosaic. Along the wide staircase was a collection of centuries-old armor and weapons kept brightly burnished. There was an array of wall trophies hunted at one time or another by various men of the family. A fox, a wolf, a tusked boar—even a fierce eagle with outstretched wings. Its razorlike talons curved in predatory hooks, and its glassy eyes glared defiance.

In her room, Olivia undressed, bathed and put on the sheerest of negligees. Her movements were deliberate and her lovely face expressionless as she brushed her long hair in slow, deliberate strokes. Sitting at her dressing table, staring at her reflection, she was unaware that her eyes took on that inward-looking remoteness that occurred whenever she was about to launch some mischief. It was almost as if she opened herself to her control, saying, I am yours.

The Prince Antonio Amontaldi di Donati lay beneath a light coverlet in his enormous four-poster bed. It was the bed in which he had been born, and in which he felt he would one day die. He wasn't asleep. He slept little, day or night. His thoughts now were kaleidoscopic snatches of memories with a common hedonistic thread. . . .

The best bouillabaisse he had ever tasted had been in a disreputable Marseilles waterfront place frequented by the local fishermen. Then had come a *frutti di mare*—incomparable. The scene shifted as memory brought him back to a Benghazi casbah. A smoky hall filled with the uniforms of Rommel's men, as well as a sprinkling of Italians. Most were drunk, and the place was a bedlam as some sort of sweepstakes was about to get under way. Wagers flew back and forth, odds shifted. A whistle blew a shrill blast. The place stilled. The small stage lit as five nude women paraded out. White women, obviously whores. Each wore on her arm a bit of colored cloth on which a large number on paper had been pinned. One—two—three—four—five. They smiled their seductive smiles at the men in the audience. Next, from the wings came a Sudanese, stripped except for a loincloth, exposing a monstrous erection. The master of ceremonies, an Arab, blew his whistle, and the man set to work servicing each of the women in turn. Two minutes exactly, the whistle would be blown, and the man would withdraw to repeat the process in the next woman. The excitement in the hall grew. Shouts of encouragement, whistles. The man had gone once through the five and was repeating the process when—in number two—his pace noticeably quickened and his face lapsed into a silly grin. The woman increased her own motions. Thirty-eight seconds to go when he plunged once, twice, and withdrew to display proof of his success. "Number two," the emcee shouted in acknowledgment about the din . . . This memory was now crowded out by another, a moment at the Spoleto festival, the prince reliving the magnificence of the entire Haydn E-flat major divertimento. He strained to recall when it had been. '73? '74? In his concentration he did not hear the door open, and he sensed more than saw the movement beside the bed.

"Beatrice?"

"No," a voice said.

He sat upright. Olivia, standing still in the gloom, seemed an apparition. He thought he recognized a fragrance.

"Olivia?" he said unnecessarily.

"Yes."

Something very strange then happened, or at least seemed to happen, to Prince Antonio Amontaldi di Donati. He felt himself enveloped in a warm miasma, a euphoria came over him. He hadn't felt this way in years, not in Marseilles, not in Bênghazi, not, as a matter of fact, anywhere . . .

The vision beside his bed drifted closer. The gossamer over her body seemed liquid. He made out the buds of pink nipples, felt the irresistible urge to reach out to them.

"Antonio . . ." She whispered his name, and he'd never heard a sound as enchanting.

Her hand reached out and grasped the edge of the light coverlet. She flicked it away as a magician would flick his silk scarf to reveal some illusion. But surely this was no illusion, he thought. It seemed too real, too overpowering.

His penis had burst through the opening of his pajamas, a sudden, unexpected encounter with an old friend long thought to be dead. Disbelief was followed by a joy. He was hardly aware Olivia's fingers were busy stripping away his garments, stripping him bare.

"Lay back now," she was saying as she completed the disrobing. "Now look, Antonio, my dear."

He looked down, Chest—thighs—an old man's

thin haunches—varicosed pale legs—all gone. As though they had never happened. He was young again.

Her negligee was now at her feet, like the froth of some enchanted sea. She leaned forward, her fingers playing over his body. Her mouth now . . . her tongue . . . her tumbling hair all over him. He reached for her.

"No, Antonio, not yet."

He would not escape so easily.

The principessa awoke with a start. There wasn't even that disoriented moment between waking and sleeping, the gathering of awareness. Her nightmare did not end, it went on and on. It held the image of Antonio, her husband, and Olivia, entwined together on his bed.

It was Antonio, she was certain, though it was surely not the Antonio she knew . . . his lovemaking was nothing she recalled in long, parched memory. She lay still, her eyes wide—playing the voyeur to what seemed to be happening now, at this moment. It was an instant replay of her worst fears. There was not even surprise that her husband—her frail, formerly ailing husband—could even go through these exercises with the tireless energy she was watching. The impact of it left no room for doubt or question . . . She was in a time warp. A half hour, an hour she lay on her chaise—motionless, eyes wide. The spectacle had long since vanished; what was left was a residue, a backwash of—nothing. Emptiness. A wild tide had gone out, leaving the shore stripped of all but a barren bleakness.

Finally she rose, and now she could feel hatred, anger. She had to leave the villa at once. Passing along the corridor, she resisted the impulse to snatch a weapon from the wall. Breeding—good manners—these all had fled. Never had she felt such hatred. It was a poisonous thing, an effluence of the wronged—the injured innocent. There was the need to strike—to hurt. Consequence had absolutely no meaning. It was as if it had been stricken from the lexicon of anger, bitterness—and overflowing hurt. Her feelings were black and physical. Only in some violence could there be relief.

Finding herself before Olivia's door, she flung it open. Whatever happened would happen. At the threshold, she stopped short. Across the room was Olivia, leaning over a suitcase, folding things into it.

"Olivia."

The young woman apparently didn't hear, deliberately continuing her chore.

"Olivia!" the principessa now almost shouted, moving into the room.

Olivia straightened up and turned slowly to confront her. Olivia? It was no longer Olivia. Olivia had become what Beatrice Amontaldi di Donati remembered as herself at the height of her youth and beauty. Raven-haired, luminous dark eyes—her skin pale, almost translucent. There she stood, smiling—a terrible vision.

Doubt? Skepticism? Suspicion she was somehow enthralled by a remarkably clever illusionist?

Such thoughts never occurred to the principessa. The trap snapped shut on her without any of those rational reserves that might have restrained her. She was in total acceptance, as had been every one of Olivia's victims. It was in the compulsive nature of their fantasies to believe. They cooperated in the magic.

The principessa walked slowly toward the apparition of herself. The transformed Olivia stood smiling. Expectantly. And Beatrice, enthralled as Narcissus, stood before Olivia, peering at the softened mirror image of herself.

"Me," she said softly. It wasn't even a question. "You."

The principessa's arms reached out slowly. Olivia came into them, and the arms closed about her. The two faces—one face—came together.

CHAPTER TEN

That night Shula Gorin slept fitfully.

Damn him, just when she believed her life was in some sort of order, the old conflicts resolved. She could look at her old trowel without a nostalgic longing to use it. She had turned down the professorship at the university, and except for a few letters, her typewriter hadn't been used. She had even discovered her reference books were breeding silverfish. The toys had been stowed away, and she had faced her responsibility. She was "on ice," waiting her next assignment, despite the price the lunatic Qaddafi had put on her life. Not very flattering, she had said, when she had learned it translated to a mere one hundred thousand dollars. Was that the measure of her worth?

Now this damned Turrell character had to enter her life with his cockamamy theory, which she found she couldn't turn off. She lay awake.

Tossing. And with each interminable hour, the theory became somehow less incredulous. Her own fundamentally mystic nature resonated with its possibilities, and the tentacles of its logic wrapped themselves about her, squeezing out objections and resolves.

Why him? she asked herself. How could this naive goy have come upon such a staggering concept? Of all the unlikely people to have stumbled on to such a revelation, Dave Turrell seemed to her the unlikeliest. The way she perceived him, he belonged on Madison Avenue. He suited the role perfectly—pushing Toyotas or whatever other garbage he dealt in. The desert newspaper was stretching it somewhat, nevertheless it was more appropriate than this trident business. In that he neither belonged, nor had any business.

About five in the morning, the phone beside Dave's bed rang. A half hour earlier, he had listened to the recorded voice of the muezzin atop the nearby minaret calling the faithful to the first of the daily prayers. "Allah il Akbar Allah—"

This land of a single God and many prophets had an unreality to him. It was history compressed—and man—the individual, himself, was compressed along with it, becoming a minuscule fragment of the process. A participant watching the cavalcade pass.

Lying in bed, he speculated upon the trident and its meaning. Was it perhaps no more than God's reminder that Man was little more than a transient passing quickly through time? Jerusalem induced these ruminations, with its strata upon strata of ancient peoples in everlasting strife. Conquerors in turn conquered. The place seemed one historical arena. A flash point. And the debris of what had been things of beauty and pride and accomplishment, bore witness.

The phone rang, startling him.

"Hullo—"

"Get your tokus out of bed, Mr. Turrell," Shula Gorin said. "I'm taking you for a ride into the country."

For Dave, it was an unforgettable experience, riding north in an old Buick badly in need of repairs, as the sun rose over the Galilean hills. The scent of citrus, as they passed the groves of several kibbutzim, was intoxicating. For a long while after they had left Jerusalem, they sat silently. She drove well, he thought, getting the most out of the reluctant engine. At one point, she reached down and handed him a thermos.

"Coffee? Have some, then pour me a cup."

"You mind telling me where we're going?" he said.

"To see my father. He can help us. I don't suppose you speak Hebrew—or Yiddish?"

"No."

"His English was never very good, and what he knew of it he's mostly forgotten. But don't worry. I'll translate. He'll be interested in your trident, even if he thinks your theory is nonsense—as I do."

"How would he know?"

In the growing light, and although she was looking straight ahead, he could see her faint smile. "I'll also ask him should I get involved, even though I have no doubt what he'll say."

"And what's that?"

"Do nothing. Wait."

"Wait—"

"Yes."

"For what?"

"For the Messiah," she said. "That's what they all live and pray for. My father and his few cronies that are still alive. 'Read the Gomorah, the Gametria, they say—and wait.' They're even against fighting the bastards who would drive us into the sea. 'Let them,' they say. 'What difference does it make—another war? Why protect yourself? Have no army. Don't fight back. The Messiah will come all the sooner.' Mind you, my mother—his wife—had been machine-gunned in 1967 by a nineteen-year-old Arab. Mr. Turrell, you'll be good news to my father. He and his Hasidim will be overjoyed. You'll be as welcome as the goy prophet."

"You don't agree with him."

She laughed. "If I agreed, we'd all be dead. This road would be a camel path, the city we left still another ruin on top of the last. Those farms there—look. They'd be desert."

Dave felt confused. "Then why do we go to him?" he asked.

"I told you. He'll know if your trident story is nonsense."

"And if it isn't?" Dave said.

"Then we'll see," she said grimly. "One day, Mr. Turrell, I may tell you what I do. Then you'll understand the difference between my father and myself. Where we parted company. He's a philosopher. A society should be able to afford philosophers. The question is can Israel survive if the West perishes? We're of the West, you know. What do you know of the Kabbala?" The question was a surprise to him. "You never even heard the word," she said with a chuckle.

"I've heard it."

"But you don't know what it means."

"No."

For the next half hour he was given a lecture on that esoteric Jewish doctrine, the system of religious philosophy prevalent among mystics for hundreds of years. Some believed it had been taught by God himself to a select group of angels, who after the Fall disobediently had passed the knowledge on to man in order to return him to his pristine innocence. Noah had passed it on to Abraham, who brought it to Egypt, where Moses had been initiated into the mysteries. He in turn had passed it over to seventy of the elders in order to maintain order among the dissidents and idol-worshipers during the difficult wilderness wanderings.

She cut through the abstruse complexities about the nature and attributes of the Supreme Being, the creation and destiny of angels, demons and elementals, as well as the revealed law, the transcendental meaning of numerals and Hebrew letters.

"There's beauty in the Kabbala," she said. "So much of it depends on harmony—an equilibrium throughout the universe. It stands dead center—at the central point of opposing forces, good and evil. Matter—form—can be described as the equilibrium between light and shade. Life itself—good life, good health—owes a debt to that truce, that subtle balance."

"Is it a separate religion?" Dave asked. "Something at odds with the mainstream?"

"Not really. Call it the mystic arm of Judaism. Its focus is on the same God the Kabbalists say is unknowable, indefinable, since the Absolute can't be defined. Because even as you define it, it slips from your grasp, becomes the abstraction of all existence. That's why His very name is ineffable, not to be uttered. It only expresses the human ideal of His existence . . ."

"I surrender, professor. I don't understand—"

Shula laughed. "Who really does? The Kabbalists spend a lifetime trying to understand. How do you handle, "The reason for existence is existence itself,' or 'Existence exists since it presupposes there is existence prior to existence.' Or how about Scholem's, 'The true language can never be spoken.'" She chuckled in appreciation of how ridiculous this Hasidic sophistry must sound to him.

"You mentioned something about angels and demons," he said.

"Yes . . . during the reign of chaos—or imbalance in the universe, as they would put it—demons poured out of the seven hells. They were primal forces. The minions of Satan, or Prince Samael, as he was called. Some think of him as the great dragon, the leviathan of Job, the executor of Judgment and the centripetal force always trying to regain entrance into paradise. This will amuse you. They say his tail is within his head—in his mouth so that he can form a circle. He tries to gain entry into holiness, insinuating himself everywhere."

Dave was hearing no more. The sun was high up. He was thinking of the Pueblo Indian kiva and its stone with its scary message burned into it. The Mayan stele and the Minoan disk. Tail within its mouth . . . damn it, the circle seemed to be forming and he was beginning to sense a pattern. . . .

The town of Safed in some ways reminded Dave of Albuquerque. Small cottages in a lush, semitropical oasis surrounded by arid, forbidding country. Add in that Safed had the serenity of artists and writers living and working there. It was also, he learned, the center of that remnant of Judaism—the practicing Kabbalists; not the scholars of whom there were many, headed by the prestigious and remarkable Gershom Scholem, but those few old men who lived and probed its mysteries in endless investigations.

Dave had expected an austere, patriarchal old man of the Chagall type he had seen in the Mea Shearim district of Jerusalem, wearing beaver hats, beards and the other accoutrements of the devout Jew. Hillel Gorin turned out to be a short, jolly old man with nearsighted eyes bright with humor. Dave's immediate reaction was: give him a bell, a pot and a red suit and he wouldn't be out of place in front of Saks Fifth Avenue during Christmas. The Clement Clarke Moore verse came to mind:

> "He had a broad face and a little round belly,
> That shook when he laughed, like a bowl full of jelly."

Hillel Gorin wore a white short-sleeved shirt open at the neck. Not even a yarmulke proclaimed his orthodoxy. Reprimanded for this by his dwindling colleagues, he would say, "God hasn't enough to worry Him, He should worry Hillel Gorin's head is bare? I have His word it's all right."

The small house was sunny, bright and overrun with books that filled every room. The old scholar had lived alone here since Shula's mother had been killed during the '67 War in a terrorist attack. His needs were meager, and he managed well enough, turning aside Shula's urging he come to Jerusalem, where she could be sure he was cared for properly.

Popping one of his ever-present chocolates into his mouth as they were introduced, the old man studied Dave quizzically. Dave somehow had guessed the question addressed to his daughter in Hebrew, "Is he a Jew?" Shula had laughed and made some quick reply which didn't put off the old man's doubts about his guest in his house, possibly a suitor for his daughter's hand.

They sat in the small well-kept garden in the shade of a lemon tree heavy with fruit. Shula was in the kitchen preparing an early lunch. Dave and the old man sat in light aluminum chairs with colorful plastic webbing, facing each other. Because of the language barrier there was no exchange; yet in some strange way, words seemed unnecessary. Neither felt awkward, discomforted. Dave had the uncanny feeling that the old man was peering right into him; and as for himself, he felt certain he was in the presence of a truly *good* man. A kind of holiness seemed to emanate from the tousled white head . . . at least that was his deep impression . . .

Shula returned with a tray of things, scolding her father for the state of the kitchen, the refrigerator in particular. Hillel Gorin said something in Hebrew—something apparently irrelevant—which took her by surprise.

She turned to scrutinize Dave in what he thought was a new way, as if she was seeing him in a new light. Dave ate his lunch of fruit, cheese and bread, pretending to be very absorbed in it as father and daughter spoke in Hebrew. He realized he was the topic of discussion, and while the old man maintained his equanimity, Shula seemed agitated. She appeared to protest and argue with her father's conviction, in which he remained immovable in his gentle way. After lunch the old man popped more chocolates into his mouth. . . .

"Papa liked you."

Shula and he were riding back to Jerusalem. He saw she hadn't recovered her composure. Those were the first words she had said since they had left, and they were said begrudgingly. Dave thought of her words earlier that day. Balance, equilibrium. He recognized that whatever it was that was exchanged between Shula and her father, it had thrown *her* off balance. And apparently he was the cause of it.

"I know why he liked me," he replied.

"Why?" she snapped back.

"Because for a goy I'm not bad."

Her laugh was involuntary, and the tension between them relaxed.

"I know something else," he said. "He believes in the trident."

She nodded grimly, staring ahead as she drove; he hoped she was seeing the road.

"What else did he say?" he continued.

"Rome."

"What?"

"Rome. You should go to the Vatican," she said. "He believes if anyone knows anything about the trident, they'll know."

"Strange—"

"My father pushing the Vatican? Yes. Yet why not? One of the greatest scholars of the Kabbala was the nineteenth-century German Catholic, Franz Joseph Molitor."

They rode in silence for several moments. "I would go with you," she said, "but I work."

"I understand."

"You don't understand!" she angrily said. "You don't understand a damned thing!" After several moments, she said, "He said another thing."

"Yes?"

She hesitated before her next words. "He said you were chosen."

"For what?"

"What you're doing."

"By whom?"

She glanced at him quickly, but said nothing. He couldn't explain it but he recalled her earlier words having to do with an ineffable name, not to be uttered.

CHAPTER ELEVEN

Antonio Amontaldi di Donati hadn't felt so fine in years, and it was all due to the beautiful young woman sitting opposite him on the terrace having breakfast. His daughter? How could he think of her as a daughter? Ridiculous. The notion of incest bothered him, but, he reminded himself, she was his daughter only by grace of a few pen strokes. Nothing was going to detract from his euphoria. He was the old Antonio again. Not the old. The new old Antonio, the image of himself he clung to, which had nothing to do with the gaunt, aching body that had looked back at him from mirrors. Even the limp was gone.

Olivia raised her cup to her lips, smiling her knowing smile. "You look well, Antonio," she said, ever so slightly stressing the Antonio. The father-daughter relationship was gone forever.

"I am wonderful," he told her.

"As they say; what love can do." She smiled almost demurely.

He reached for the glass of champagne he was determined to have that morning. Raising it, he said, "To love."

"To love," she replied, raising her own glass.

Beatrice, upstairs in her bed, stirred and came awake. She smiled in recollection of the day before. The day and night. Her body was feeling aglow. Alive. It had been so long, she had almost forgotten the feeling.

Where was the guilt she should be feeling, she wondered? Those dark, morbid thoughts her soul was too accustomed to? She stretched languorously. If Don Ettore only knew. Mischievously she would arrange one more confession. She would tell him straight out, and watch his expression. To see that pious face go into shock, she would elaborate—go into the details of her behavior with . . . Olivia. Yes, Olivia, though at the moment it had seemed with the image of her youthful self. She almost giggled as she contemplated the scene. "Not even my good husband Antonio gave me such joy—not even in our best days. I have sinned, father, haven't I? Grievously, wouldn't you say? Tell me my penance . . . But if I have sinned, padre," she would say, "so have you, since it was you who brought her into our lives."

She kicked the covers from her, looked down at her body and shuddered with the memories of the delight it had offered her.

* * *

"What shall we do today?" Olivia said. "Shall we drive somewhere?"

The prince was in a reflective mood, his thoughts elsewhere. Grim, yet strangely exciting and pleasurable—with the overriding determination that nothing must interfere with what he was now enjoying. Not even his wife.

She smiled across the table. "What are you thinking, my dear?"

His eyes moved to hers and he smiled.

Throwing a light robe about herself, the principessa crossed the room to draw back the heavy drapes. Looking down to the terrace, she saw her husband and Olivia, but she wasn't disturbed. A few moments later, in her bath, she thought, Dear girl, it won't be easy for her concealing from Antonio where her true affections are. She lay back thinking how to carry on the deception. She became so involved, the sound she heard in the bedroom meant nothing to her. It became louder. More insistent. Was a maid thrashing the bedclothes? But it was now at the open bathroom door. She looked about, and froze. A large bird . . . it *was* a bird, wasn't it? . . . was flying about the bedroom, in a frenzy . . . why did she feel so strange, dizzy, faint . . . ?

Scrambling out of the tub, she threw her light robe about herself and reached to slam the door shut. The creature came at her in a single, blurred motion . . . She fell back, covering her face as best she could against the bared talons reaching for her, talons that looked for a moment like fingers . . .

could they be hers...? The cries from her throat...from the bird's...blended into one awful sound...

Antonio was laughing as he now filled Olivia's glass. The scene was idyllic: white linen, gleaming silver and two elegant people at breakfast on a warm September morning. "I wouldn't dream of telling you my thoughts."

"Such thoughts should remain secret," she said.

"Yes," he said.

Beatrice had somehow escaped into the bedroom, her face bloody, the light robe torn by the attack. Somehow she found herself at the door to the hallway. Opening it wide, she found herself confronted by the old suit of armor that had been stationed at the head of the staircase but was now, unaccountably, directly in front of her. It was... she was sure of it...and yet how could she be...? She stopped short. Stunned. Her mind was no longer able to cope with the nightmare she was into.

The burnished metal gleamed in the morning light. Its visor was a mirror which reflected back her own unrecognizable face distorted and torn. This wasn't herself, she thought. Not the Principessa Beatrice Amontaldi di Donati. What would *Harper's, Vogue* and *Paris Match* say if they could see her now? And even this horror had its limits. The ghastly tableau ended. She was about to fall back into her room when two arms...arms of the grisly robot...? clamped shut about her. She stared into the visor. At her own face reflected back. She was incapable of appreciating the irony as a narcissistic embrace of steel . . . of herself . . . tightened about her, the fingers digging deftly into her throat. Her face twisted. In a short while her eyes, staring up to the frescoed ceiling, saw nothing.

Below, on the terrace, the prince sat idly toying with a breadstick. He had fallen into the pleasant euphoria of his thoughts. Olivia sat silent in her own thoughts, as if aware of what was happening a short distance away. Suddenly the breadstick snapped in half. Surprised, he laughed. He looked up. Olivia was laughing too.

The principessa lay still on the threshold to her room. There was no movement. No life. A short distance away, a full suit of old armor stood glistening at the head of the stairs in its accustomed place. Further below, among the other trophies, a great eagle hung from the wall, its wings outstretched and its yellow eyes staring into a glassy eternity.

PART TWO

CHAPTER TWELVE

The Hotel Caprice, just off Rome's Via Veneto, was a dark, dingy establishment little better than a *pensione*. At night the din of a basement disco, added to that of the traffic in the narrow street below, made insomniacs of the hardiest and weariest travelers. One could, of course, shut the windows and heavy wooden shutters and switch on the air conditioner, the charge for which was automatically billed; this, however, would prove an exercise in futility, despite the formidable network of pipes, vents and grilles, promising sufficient cool air to intimidate the worst of heat waves. This, after all, was Rome, with its flair for theatrical illusion in which little ever was as it appeared to be.

It was a hot, spring night; and Dave Turrell had enough on his mind to keep him awake without the aid of revved Lambrettas, honking auto horns and disco music.

Shula had admitted that shadowy part of her life in the small lounge of Lod Airport outside Tel Aviv. As she had come toward him, according to plan, she was hardly recognizable. Clad in a smart, loose cotton outfit, she appeared to him New York chic, even to the large Gucci handbag. Things had been done to her dark hair, and a generously applied tanning lotion gave her the look of an American tourist on her way home from snorkeling at Elat. Greeting Dave, she handed him an expensive Japanese 35 mm camera, telling him to drape it about his neck. Sending their hand luggage through the conveyor belt of the X-ray machine, he noticed that the Gucci bag was somehow excluded from examination. He knew this couldn't be an accident in the terminal where security was probably the best in the world. He could only surmise that she had been recognized, and the bag held a weapon. A short while later, in the embarkation area, she approached a scruffy young man who, after a brief exchange, melted into the crowd. Taking Dave's arm, they followed the youth to a small, private lounge where shaloms were said, and their guide left them. Latching the door behind them, she turned to Dave.

"Before we're up to our necks in your *mishegoss*," she said, "I should warn you."

"Of what?"

"I may be more than the scholar—the writer you imagine I am."

"I've had my suspicions even before we met."

"Yes," she said.

"I've read Le Carré, and I've been paid for creative thinking."

"What does your creative thinking tell you?"

"Writers and archaeologists don't get the care—the protection you get. You're special."

Her laugh was ironic. "To the extent someone's put a price of a hundred thousand dollars on my head."

Regarding her for a moment, he was about to comment it wasn't enough; instead he said, "Who's so generous?"

"Mr. Qaddafi," she said, opening her bag to take out a hand mirror to see her face.

"Dead or alive?"

"Dead—if I have a preference."

"It's a risk, your leaving Israel."

"Yes," she said unhesitantly, then crossed the room, parted the slats of a blind to peer out to the field where a busload of arriving passengers were disembarking. He examined the workings of the camera. Neither, of course, were actually seeing what they appeared to be looking at. Thoughts turned inward, questions were asked of themselves. Why? Why were they undertaking this unpromising foolhardy adventure? Curiosity? It certainly had to be more than that. Whatever it was, it eluded them, and yet they knew somehow it had to be done.

"You dropped everything," she said without turning, "your newspaper—your life—to chase this myth."

"On the vaguest of possibilities it's more than

myth," he replied. "I'll ask you a question since you're probably more sophisticated in world affairs than I am."

"Pragmatism is one of our cottage industries," she said, turning. "Y'know, like Jaffa oranges."

"Six months ago," he said, "if I was told I'd be into this, I'd have said, 'flaky.' We are a couple of lunatics, aren't we?"

"Are you asking or telling me?"

"Suppose—just suppose—we do somehow find another trident somewhere. What then? What would you think? Would you believe?"

"What?"

"What your father apparently believes."

"I'm here," she said.

"Proving?"

"Tell me," she said, "are you having trouble handling it?"

"Aren't you?"

"I'm only having trouble with your indecisiveness. I could find you walking away for the wrong reasons. You have doubts."

"Who wouldn't?"

"An integral part of belief is to doubt," she said. Changing the subject, she explained that the man to whom she was responsible in her work disapproved strongly of her leaving the country. "You should have heard him. Hebrew profanity can make a sailor blush."

"You didn't tell him about the trident!" he said.

She smiled. "He'd have had me locked up. If you're crazy, I can only be slightly less." Reaching out a hand, which he took, she continued, "I'll give you a few days in Rome. I know someone who could be helpful. After that—" She shrugged. She asked if he could pretend they were tourists. "We met at the Club Med or somewhere. Can you manage it?"

"I wouldn't be surprised," he said. Her sharp look told him they weren't into some frivolous game.

The El Al Flight went well enough, during which he had no difficulty playing the agreeable role. "Don't get carried away, Mr. Turrell," she warned on one occasion.

At the passport control of Rome's Leonardo da Vinci Airport he had noticed her green-bound passport. "American?"

"I was born there, or didn't I mention it?" she said.

At the desk of the Hotel Caprice, where she had to surrender it, he noted she had registered under the name of Harriet Perry and assumed her passport had been doctored. She took charge not only in the selection of rooms on different floors; he watched with admiration as she examined the doors, their locks, what the windows overlooked, even the access to exits. A lousy way to live, he thought. In the brief time he'd been in Israel he had observed an entire nation surviving by just that caution . . . Skeptical about what others said or promised, not even expecting the best of presumed friends who one day might give higher priority to expedience.

Jammed tightly together in the ridiculously tiny elevator, he was aware of the Gucci bag which she now held between them, obviously to avoid contact. He had noted that it was usually in a readily accessible position. By now he had no doubts about its contents.

"Your floor," she said as the elevator lurched to a stop. She held up the large key tag for him to see the number. "If you go out, let me know."

Breakfast the following morning of brioches, coffee and a bit of jelly wrapped in impossible plastic packets was in the small dining room just off the dingy lobby. He spied her at a small table to one side facing the entrance, having her coffee. As he approached, he glanced at the Gucci bag, easily accessible, and thought of its contents. She wore a less informal dress and a silk foulard scarf with a Hermès label. For the benefit of the German couple at the adjacent table, he asked what she had planned for the morning. "Trajan's Column or the Coliseum?"

She smiled in appreciation of his caution. "Father Martenius at the Vatican expects us," she said.

Once again he was made aware of history, and his own totally different American perception of it: what was new, what was old. Entering the St. Anna Gate of Vatican City, he realized he had entered an independent principality which required them to show passports and go through other entry procedures. He was at once struck by the stolid, businesslike appearance of the administration buildings ringing the vast courtyard, so different from the baroque theatricality of the nearby St. Peter's Square, the basilica and the gardens, public facilities calculated to awe and impress, make more credible its accessibility to God.

Father Jan Martenius had been born in Rotterdam, the son of a prosperous optometrist. He was a pleasant-looking giant of a man in his early thirties with a crown of reddish yellow hair. His bulk and physicality might easily have fitted him into a Brueghel pastoral; however, by temperament there was nothing of the cliché Dutch stolidity. His boiling point was low and he didn't suffer fools and knaves easily. He admitted to being a born extremist afflicted with humanist feelings. The latter had led him into the Church but there he encountered frustrations and disaffections which left him isolated and often embittered. His deep-rooted faith came into conflict with Church policies and directives which he considered not in the best interests of either Church or mankind in general. What was worse, the young priest was quick to speak his mind; and for this grievous fault, he was often disciplined. He was subsequently sent to Rome, where it was felt the fires in him would be dampened within the bosom of Mother Church. This was a miscalculation. Here again he locked horns with a hierarchy whose vision of Christ was so different from his own. The young hothead was relegated to a post where it was thought he would be safely removed from controversy. In a tiny basement office, attached to the Congregation of Cardinals, he was given the dull task of indexing reports of miracles and petitions for beatification flowing in from all parts of the world.

Jan Martenius and Shula had met during a Christmas pilgrimage to the Holy Land. His studies in mysticism and hermetics, required by his work, brought him in contact with her writings. She had been teaching at the Hebrew University, and he had called upon her. Respecting and liking each other, they became friends, maintaining a regular correspondence.

The three now were sitting in the priest's windowless basement office furnished in the tackiness of a second-floor bail bondsman. Old metal shelves and a desk and chair appeared to have been salvaged from some warehouse. The room's sole decoration consisted of a large photoprint of the Holy Father smiling benignly down upon the clutter of countless folders of overstuffed manila bound with twine. The only personal feature was a rack of smoking pipes atop the desk, and each pipe's well-chewed stem bore witness to the inner tensions of its owner.

Jan Martenius attentively listened as Dave gave his unembellished story of the trident and its apocalyptic history, which he presented in a quiet yet impressive fashion. Even as he spoke, Dave flashed to those Madison Avenue days when he pitched campaigns to clients. A separate part of himself imagined the words: "—and the trident logo has been market tested producing a ninety-eight percent product identification." When he was first introduced to the priest by Shula, he had evaluated him as a tough nut to crack. She had warned him Jan Martenius would see through bullshit. She was right, he now knew.

Ending with his finding of the bronze disk at Heraklion, he summed up his theory in even more temperate and measured tones. He implied that western civilization had had it. The precise when and how were all that remained unsettled. Q.E.D. *Quod erat demonstrandum.*

A silence settled over the room. Shula concentrated upon the ash of her cigarette as it grew longer. Father Martenius, leaning back in his chair, sucked upon an unlit old briar. His ill-cut, black gown gave Dave the impression of a judicial robe. The only sound was from an adjacent room which Dave recognized as a copying machine in operation. Thank God, it's a miracle, he thought.

Jan Martenius rose slowly, his chair making a harsh sound on the stone floor. Lips compressed in a grim line, Dave found nothing reassuring in his expression. Looking down at Dave, he said, "I'm expected to swallow that, eh? What kind of fool you think I am? Such a story!"

"What does that mean?" Shula said.

The young Dutch priest glared at her. "What you think it means!" Whirling about to face the crowded shelves of documents, the sleeves of his loose gown flying, Dave could only think of the wings of some great, black bird.

"There!" the priest said, pointing, "there's what I call the oriental section. Cambodia, Japan, Malaysia—the lot. My Asian correspondents. Just below's Latin America. Mexico, Central America and south—that part of the enlightened continent. A lot of fantasy mixed with Indian lore. Very active contributors. Your United States of America? This we keep special, here. Le dernier cri. The last word in everything, eh? And fertile, oh yes. But then the whole world is fertile with miracles. People with drab, impotent lives wishing to believe in the supernatural. The bizarre. The unexplainable. I couldn't begin to tell you of the places where the image of the Holy Virgin has appeared. It's all there, some attested to even by bishops. From inside teacups to garage doors. Usually there are cures involved. Cures for eczema to fallen arches to cancer." He took two great strides to another group of shelves. "This I keep strictly for stigmata. My God! When I think of where the agony of the Lord has reenacted itself. On what sort of people. Ah! But my favorite shelf is this one. You've heard of the well-known Shroud of Turin? Here, my friends. Shrouds of Turin galore! The Lord's image appearing on Sheraton Hotel bedsheets to you-name-it. One here we've been asked to believe is from a NATO tank driver. Belgian, I believe. The hot exhaust from his tanks had burned a Christ image on the metal which won't come off. Are the people involved in these charlatans—frauds? No. No more than I think either of you is a charlatan—a fraud."

Dave was now standing. He could feel his temper rising. "Just hysterical, say it," he said grimly.

"You go further than these poor, deluded people," Jan Martenius went on, ignoring Dave's remark. "I congratulate you for the added fillip of your delusion. Its social context. You're afraid for the world, as everyone should be." He turned to Shula, disapproval in his face. "I'm surprised at you," he went on. "To be sure, metaphysics strains at science, coming in as it were through the back door, pleading for belief. But even as an intellectual exercise, there are limits."

"And the trident is beyond those limits," Shula said.

"Yes," was the reply.

"It's odd," Dave said. "This is one place I thought would have interest in the human condition. And what do I find? Tombs. A morbid fascination for tombs." He looked about the windowless room, tomblike itself. "Who's buried deeper—St. Peter or you?"

Shula had also risen to her feet. The air soured. Only the pope in his photo continued smiling.

"You're right, absolutely right," Dave went on. "This is the last place I should have come to." He turned to leave the room. At the door he waited as Shula was saying to Jan Martenius, "I remember your saying, 'Reality often offers the greater mystery.' For whose benefit was that?" With that she turned to join Dave.

"Wait! Wait please." Jan Martenius strode to his desk. Holding out a pencil he said, "Draw it for me—your trident."

Dave glanced at Shula, then returned to accept the invitation.

They left Vatican City, crossing the great square without exchanging a word. Threading their way through parked tourist buses on the street outside, they found a small café. Sitting at a small, outside table, they sipped espressos. Glancing at her, he wondered if she was into the same miserable thoughts he was.

Once again that uncertainty had nailed him. Was he indeed an hysteric? It had been his own word, his own description of himself. That priest had made him feel a romantic Don Quixote launched on a hopeless quest. Tilting at tridents. What was he really pursuing, or—whatever it was—was it pursuing him?

Shula spoke first. "You ever wonder how it is," she said, "Italy, which grows no coffee, still makes the best cup of it in the world?" Her hand reached out and took his. "You ever seen Trajan's Column?"

His juices settled. Smiling, he said, "Nor the Coliseum."

Holding her hand, he thought it cool and soft. Well, why shouldn't it be, idiot! he thought. Glancing towards the Gucci bag and its contents, he sorted out those thoughts. He imagined those long, tapering fingers aiming a gun at someone, pulling a trigger. The conjured image clashed with another. She seemed to him, despite her warm, dark loveliness, essentially strong, capable of dealing with things. A take-charge kind of person. A memory flashed. Connecticut in winter, years ago. His pet collie was involved, the dog-above-all-dogs he had had in succession. This one would even pull him on his Flexible Flyer. Then, one day it was killed by a car before his eyes. His mother—a woman cool and austere, who rarely showed affection or even laughed—had taken him in her arms and said, "Cry. Let the poison out." He recalled she had said it as if she herself wished she could let out the poison in her own life. He thought of her now, and in his heart mourned a little. How much more of her didn't he know or suspect?

For a long while Father Jan Martenius sat contemplating the trident crudely executed by Dave. He realized if he had any sense, he should have crumpled it, thrown it away. So what if it had come, endorsed, as it were, by Shula Gorin, whom he respected? He thought of their correspondence—their talks in the past. The transcendental had been accepted between them, as she had said. It was in fact the bond between them, their common tie. Had that American fellow spotted what was happening to him? His bitterness and frustration. Was it blinding him? Closing off his normally inquisitive mind, putting him in the role he decried to others? A pious hypocrite? The American had spoken of St. Peter. St. Peter *in vinculi*—bound, chained upside down. He was indeed becoming chained—bound upside down.

Overcome with a bleak despair, not liking himself very much, he ripped the page from the small pad. Thrusting it into a pocket, he rose and left the room. At an upper floor, he emerged from the building to cross the great courtyard and entered another building.

Monsignor John Campo was a fragile-looking, seventy-year-old scholar with silvery hair. His warm, dark eyes, behind horn-rimmed spectacles, reflected a patient philosophy and understanding appropriate to the head archivist of the Vatican, a man who had read profoundly secret things, shared by few others.

The dimensions of the white-painted, high-ceilinged room made the aged priest seem even more diminutive. His desk beneath the ever-present engraving of His Holiness was an antique Spanish refectory table, and the room's other furniture and appointments were no less starkly austere.

Jan Martenius had no trouble gaining an interview with the monsignor since a special relationship existed between them, one the young priest didn't entirely comprehend. He thought the old man was merely kind and compassionate, having heard of his isolation in the hierarchy. The fact was the monsignor had indeed happened to hear about the brash, young priest with his reprehensible ways. This touched something in the prelate who was reminded of himself—or rather what he had been. In his youth, during his early training in the seminary in Bologna, and even for a brief while later, he had envisioned a different, more militant Church that would take up the struggle of the poor and oppressed, somehow correct the grinding poverty he himself had come out of, battle against social inequities throughout the world.

For a while, like Jan Martenius, he had stood up for his principles, had even spoken his mind publicly despite the displeasure of superiors. Pressure inevitably followed. Humility, discipline and respect were taught him, and he had been put to work in the archives; and in time, by reason of his unusual intelligence and scholarliness, he became head of that important section; and with each promotion more guilt was forgotten, the fiery ideas leached away, their remains buried under the weighty history of the Church.

Monsignor Campo studied the drawing of the trident for a long while. Jan Martenius sat motionless, watching the white-haired old man bent over the paper. He wondered if he hadn't gone too far, wasting the important man's time and energy in such trivial nonsense. There! He had done it again, he thought. Gone over his superior's head with some wild idea even he regarded with contempt. Then why had he done it, he asked himself. What had prompted him? Why hadn't he just thrown it into a trash basket? Buried it among the other innumerable appeals for credibility?

"Who gave you this?" Monsignor Campo said in his high-pitched voice, looking up. At this point there was nothing in his manner to suggest any undue interest or concern to the younger priest.

"An American," Jan Martenius said, going on to describe his relationship with Shula Gorin who had brought Dave Turrell to him. He pointed out that he considered the Israeli woman a serious and respected scholar in his field.

The old man, holding the paper in his hand,

suggested it could be a simplified hieroglyph called a demotic. Also it was reminiscent of the Hebrew letter *shin*. There was also a resemblance to the Greek letter *psi*. Jan Martenius was puzzled when the archivist rose and asked him to follow him.

The giant of a man trying to adjust his steps to a much smaller, older man, both in their long, loose vestments, made for a bizarre spectacle as they traversed the long corridor to enter a room equipped with modern copiers and microfilm viewers. In one corner a young priest was at a computer terminal studying the design of the triple-crowned tiara worn by Innocent III at his invocation rites.

Passing through large double doors, they entered the archive itself. This narrow hall was of such length one could hardly see its end. It was occupied entirely by carefully indexed and labeled shelves of large volumes of bound, mostly handwritten documents dealing with the minutiae of Catholic life down through the centuries. Below this cavernous room, on other floors, were three similar chambers, above ground level, and below that three more stories, in all encompassing one hundred continuous miles of written documentation.

Jan Martenius followed the older man down an aisle to a section dealing with the reign of the recent Pope John. The monsignor pointed to a volume beyond his reach. The young priest brought it down, and was then directed to place it upon a small metal table. He stood back while the archivist delicately riffled the pages until he found what he was looking for.

"There," the old man said in his high-pitched voice, stepping back to make room for Jan Martenius. The latter saw what appeared to be a letter bearing the seal of the bishop of Firenze. Jan Martenius read an account of a girl in a seminary accused of involvement in a series of inexplicable, tragic events in which a supernatural connection was suspected. His attention was drawn from the fine, almost illegible handwriting to the bottom of the page. The trident. Crudely drawn, but unmistakably the trident. He continued reading details of a physical examination of the child which revealed no abnormality other than the fine birthmark on her inner left thigh.

Jan Martenius was, frankly, stunned. He could only stare at the page of finely executed writing. As if seeking some sort of confirmation, he turned his head, about to look down at the old man beside him. The latter's face was aglow, and Jan Martenius realized the man wasn't concerned with the incidents depicted or the people involved. He was simply proud that after all these years, he had recalled the matter. His powers as a librarian were undiminished. This was confirmed when Monsignor Campo said, "Of course, I wasn't in charge here then. It merely passed through my hands."

The possibility of coincidence crossed Jan Martenius's mind. One couldn't accept the connection that easily.

"It wasn't investigated?" he said. "It went no further?"

Monsignor Campo smiled. "You didn't notice the name of the child? Her mother—by adoption apparently—was the Principessa Beatrice Amontaldi di Donati."

No more was said, nor needed to be.

CHAPTER THIRTEEN

Olivia had taken a large step. Her title of principessa was hers alone—unchallenged; more importantly she had the prince enthralled. Father and daughter attended the high mass said for Beatrice in the thirteenth-century church of Santa Croce, called the Florentine pantheon, where the devout noblewoman was paid the singular honor of being buried under the pavement of the impressive cruciform structure with its beamed ceilings and Ghiberti windows. Sitting among the Grisoldis, holding each other's hands, they gave the appearance of grieving relatives; the fact was: grief and solace were farthest from their thoughts. Hand touching hand, their proximity: these were affirmations for him of his newfound happiness which he often found difficult to believe. In the contact he found reassurance there would be even more delights for him. His eyes didn't see the splendor of the old church, but rather a replay of the sexual fantasies in which he had played a major role. As the choir's *Gloriam Dei Laudamus* swept over them in sonorous waves, Antonio could only think of the night before, and shuddered.

Guests of Beatrice's people, they had been given adjacent rooms in the magnificent Renaissance palazzo overlooking the Arno. Lying in bed, he had projected his will. Olivia must come. She must come to him at once. *Now*. He had said to himself he would count to ten. By then she would appear. He began. He was at—seven—eight—nine—no. He decided he would make it twenty-five. He began again—slower now. As the count progressed, he could feel the strain, the concentration of the essence of his being projected out to the woman who in so short a time had returned to him the miracle of youth, those vigors he experienced only as warm memories.

Finally she did appear. Not within the twenty-five, nor even another twenty-five, but in her own well-calculated time. At one point he had been about to toss the covers from him, burst into her room; but princely pride, strained to the utmost, enabled him to endure the agony for just a while longer. Finally—his resolve about to give way—it was then he was aware the door to his room was opening slowly. His heart pounding, he strained to see through the darkness of the room. What seemed an apparition was gliding toward his bed. There was a sound, and the blur of a garment swirling through the air. The paleness of that beloved body was now beside him—within reach;

yet somehow he didn't move. He waited. He knew she preferred it that way. He was to remain passive, be a spectator—a voyeur of his own pleasure. Not a word had been exchanged. That transaction too had been made. Words were empty—meaningless for these transcendental moments between them. And this, too, enhanced the effect that what was happening was somehow unreal. His body shivered with expectancy. He hardly dared breathe lest the spell be shattered and illusion become gross reality which hovered behind him like the specter of death. He now felt the slight sagging of the mattress as she came to him in the bed.

Each night it had been different. Olivia would bring out from her limitless repertoire another treasure—another delight, new in itself yet somehow familiar. It was as if she poked about among old memories; and finding one still alive, breathed new life into it. This night, for example, that exquisite fragrance he associated with her was gone. Instead was a sweetish, fruity odor, familiar somehow, yet defying his best effort to identify it. For some obscure reason he had to know what it was. It became obsessive. Like a hound pursuing a scent, he sniffed hungrily at her neck. Down he went, nuzzling her breasts now. He dallied at the pert, hardened nipples to tongue, suck at them. Somewhere—from some distance—he could hear her sharp intake of breath. He visualized her eyes rolled up in her head, those lips loosening. Opening. The navel was given a moment, then down further he went as the scent grew stronger. He was at the entrance to that temple he worshiped at—the odor stronger—when recollection struck. He remembered.

He saw every detail of the gloomy cellar in La Rocca where apples had been stored. As growing boys, it was here he and a cousin, a cadet of the family, would come with an illustrated copy of de Maupassant's short stories filched from the library upstairs. Over the photoengraving of a nude woman, buxom in the fashion of the century, who was apparently awaiting the arrival of her lover at the edge of her huge four-poster bed in a candlelit room, the two would stare at that shadowy place between her thick thighs and ponder the wondrous secrets beyond. The moment would come. Trousers were unbuttoned and boyish cocks came out erect and eager, facing each other like diminutive tournament lances. Eyes on the Parisian succuba, fantasies rampant, hands reached out, took their holds and the mutual masturbation would begin.

One afternoon, more adventurous than usual, the daring suggestion was made to take it in the ass. It had been made in all innocence. It was their own discovery since neither of them had heard of such a thing before. What the woman in the photo had, perhaps they too had in facsimile. It was at least in the same general region. But whose ass, was the problem. Who would do it to whom? They resorted to the finger game of scissors, paper and stone to decide. Antonio had won, in the sense he was to slip it to his cousin. It was done—or partly done since it was all very awkward and required the aid of the juice of crushed, withered apples.

Antonio had recalled there was no particular pleasure in it, and his cousin—in the midst of it—had jerked himself away to run from the room in shame and guilt with some instinctive awareness that this could never be told in the confessional.

With a sigh of pleasure at recognition of the odor—a homecoming—Antonio buried his face in those soft hairs, reached with his tongue for those moist, frayed, yielding lips. The door was found and opened.

The Princess Olivia became the *regina del mondo*—queen of the world—certainly of Rome.

She simply took over an important part of its social life. Her inherited interest in the widespread Koblenzer Industries refurbished the family palazzo in the city, returning it to its pristine splendor. Influence had been applied in the proper place, and it was taken out of the category of municipal museum, dependent upon a disinterested committee of antiquities. The gatekeeper too had his pride restored. With ill-concealed satisfaction, he turned away the tourist guides and their busloads of herded aliens whom he wholeheartedly hated.

Olivia entertained lavishly; her wit, personality and intelligence—not to mention beauty—making the palazzo the nerve center of the city's political, artistic and intellectual life. She had created a salon in the old sense of the word. Invitations were sought by the shakers and movers of Roman affairs, and it wasn't long before the name of Amontaldi di Donati was burnished anew, as brightly as ever. And of course her father, the prince, couldn't have been happier as he was swept along in her popularity. For him it was a wondrous, exhilarating experience—he had been given that rarest of all gifts—new life in the Faustian sense, another chance. With his finely honed sensibilities, the idea often intruded that his presence among her friends was endured rather than enjoyed. There was that subtle patronizing that he refused to acknowledge. Could he permit such thoughts to sour his new life?

One morning, he came into her bright sitting room, and found her at work at her desk.

"You slept well, dear?" she said with a pasted-on smile. He bitterly thought he might have replied, Not a wink. I had trouble with nightmares. Ghouls, monsters—terrible, and she wouldn't have heard, or cared.

Making a correction in a dinner menu for the following evening, she crossed out *escallopes de veau chasseur* for *gigot du pré salé rôti*, murmuring, "You'll be going to the Jockey Club today I suppose."

"No," he said, and when she looked up in surprise, he wondered if she suspected this cooling down of his interest in old friends, those reminders of his recent painful life from which he had managed to escape with her help. "The Jockey Club has become a bore," he said with that elegant insouciance he could affect.

Her eyes moved over him, and he knew she had noticed his new tailoring. He couldn't suppress a glow of excitement. It was as if mama was approving his new tweed jacket, gray slacks and soft black loafers. "Very nice, Antonio," she said.

"Paolo Capobianca mentioned his tailor one evening." He laughed nervously. "To be altogether truthful, I asked his name. Paolo, I mean. Paolo has a knack with clothes, don't you think?" He was hoping she would notice his new hairstyle as well. Actually she was wishing he'd leave. Nevertheless her tight little smile encouraged him to continue. "I was thinking of lunch," he said. "You and I, Olivia. Just the two of us. There's that new trattoria in Eur." His eyes went up, his head waggled in an Italian gesture of sublime ecstasy. Prattling on about *calamari*, stuffed artichokes and the excellence of a superb Frascati vintage, he knew how ridiculous—how absurd—he must be sounding; yet he was unable to stop. The phone rang, and he was relieved.

There was that intimacy in her voice that suggested to him she was speaking to a man. Humiliation rose in him. She was behaving as if he weren't there. How could she have such small regard for his feelings? How needlessly cruel to put him through this. He could easily have killed the fellow at the other end, no matter who it was. He wanted to leave the room. It would have been the thing to do, yet he couldn't. Finally she hung up.

"What were you saying, Antonio?" she asked lightly.

"I was suggesting lunch."

"Today?"

"Yes."

"But that was Carlo Sylvestri," she said. "I said I

would lunch with him. He has that new Lancia Medusa he wants me to look at." She rose and stroked his cheek. "Go to your club," she continued. "It may not be boring today. After all, they are your friends."

"I doubt it."

"I understand," she said, turning away to make a note of something in her appointment book.

"What do you understand? What can you possibly understand?"

"Beatrice," she said, turning again to him. "It's to do with Beatrice."

"What about Beatrice?" There was an apprehensive note in his voice. A new circumspection.

"They never really accepted the findings of the carabinieri and the doctor. About her death, I mean. The circumstances."

"It was an accident."

"Of course," she said quickly. He wished she wouldn't smile so. That mocking smile.

"How could anyone think otherwise?"

"I can't imagine," she said, now very seriously. Too seriously. "And yet they're such wise old owls. They understand everything—politics, money. They certainly talk as if they do. Sometimes I worry about it."

"About what?"

"Their talk. It could be dangerous, you know. What they might be saying about us. Our relationship."

"That's nonsense!" he cried. "Absolute nonsense!"

"I've thought of it, Antonio, mightn't it be wise

if you saw other women?"

"Other—"

"Oh, you know what I mean," she said. "Not that it will ever be different between us—but you're so attractive. So—princely. There's no better word for it. After a proper time, of course, I seriously believe you should consider marriage."

He was struck by the irony of it. Once, in just this way, he had persuaded Beatrice to seek other interests so that he could more easily pursue his women. Here was repayment in kind. He wondered if it was possible Beatrice had known, as he now knew, what Olivia was about. The thought of it distressed him, that he had thought at the time how clever he was.

"I love you," he blurted out like a schoolboy.

She smiled again, patted his cheek, almost as if she were the parent, he the child. "I love you too," she replied, and even as she did so, she was considering—weighing his future worth. How much more mileage could she expect out of him.

After she had left, he looked about the bright sunny room with its new Provencal wallpaper and its new furnishings and decor. How different it had been when it had been Beatrice's. Then it had been as somber and gloomy as her life. He reflected on the comparison. A chiaroscuro of black and white. Olivia had brought him into the light, leaving behind his prejudices, the class snobbery. Lifted him from one point in time to another. It was a new life, a renewed life, and she had done it even as she took the chill from his bones at night. But behind it all—lurking behind his happiness like some vague specter which he refused to acknowledge—was that awareness of how poorly he fitted into her life. He was an appendage, dragged along in her popularity. He knew full well what the guests in the palazzo—the other men especially—what they thought of him. How often had he at one time or another played the same role: pretending friendship and warmth for some man whose wife he was sleeping with. And Olivia wasn't even his wife. The bitterness in him was agony, and the thought occurred to him that for the first time in his life he was experiencing what was called the pangs of love. How unbecoming— even unseemly—for someone his age, someone in his position.

Later that same day he found himself in a Trastevere *caffè*, sitting at the counter having his third cup of espresso. It was a vantage point from which he could peer through the grimy window, across the narrow street, clogged with parked cars, to the entrance to the shabby building into which Olivia had gone. Like its neighbors, a century ago the building might once have been a brilliant terra cotta. Now it was just muddy and dilapidated. At one side, cut into an upper part of the wall, was a tiny niche encasing a faded effigy of the Holy Mother bestowing Her blessings.

Antonio wondered what had impelled him to follow Olivia as she left the palazzo. Even as he was doing it, he knew he was behaving like some pathetic Pagliaccio. How unlike him it was. How alien to his style. Yet, even knowing this, he was hopelessly caught up in something he couldn't stop. Today it was Carlo Sylvestri. Tomorrow it would be someone else, as it was yesterday. But at the moment Sylvestri served perfectly as a target for his anger and hatred. An entrepreneur in oil bragging about Arab sheik friends and money. Everything was money; he couldn't utter a sentence without some reference to it. There were times, he reflected, when he would have dealt with that sort as he would have a sleazy maitre d'—an actor of minor rank. Yet here he was now—elevated to the rank of adversary. Helping him with his car, he thought bitterly. A lame, ridiculous excuse. A lie, obviously.

When she had parked her car in the piazza near the Church of St. Maria in Trastevere, he had paid off the taxi in which he had followed. He had then followed her through the bleak, curving alleys of one of the city's most rundown sections. At first he had been puzzled. Sylvestri would normally never hang out in such a section. He was no less paranoid than others with money and influence, living a siege mentality, avoiding public ostentation of wealth. Sylvestri, he had thought, might well have been spawned in such a district, but would have thereafter avoided it like the plague.

Antonio had followed Olivia with considerable difficulty since there was not only his bad hip, but the stress of the situation putting an added burden on his heart. She had walked, he had noted, with that furtive air of someone who didn't wish to be seen. Coming to the house, he couldn't help but sense, she was familiar with it. As she paused in front of it, a young man had materialized. A few words had been exchanged, and she had been allowed to enter. Antonio could only surmise that Sylvestri had a bodyguard, if only to acquire some status in talking about it.

What should he do? He speculated on several options. Burst in on them? The satisfaction of that would only be brief, and besides, he was in no condition for any physical confrontation. He finally decided he would just wait until they came out. He would stow the incident away along with others. It could one day be useful. Be honest, Antonio, be honest . . . you just don't want to upset things. If this is the only way you can have her, well then . . . all right. You're not, after all, what you once were. Forget those old days when you could afford the grand gesture. Know who you are and come to terms with it.

Luigi Compo had been a promising engineering student, but then he became political— "political" meaning the leader of a notorious terrorist group known as the Prima Linea. In a short while, the former student—a product of a middle-class family that knew neither want nor poverty— became a dedicated Marxist, wanted for murder, kidnapping and an assortment of bank robberies. Prima Linea was well organized into small cells which had no knowledge of other similar units, yet it was a sinister force in every city of the country, with Compo himself evolving into a charismatic folk hero because of his attacks on the rich and powerful—the government itself.

Luigi Compo looked the role. Of medium

stature, his dark saturnine features reflected a brooding, suspicious nature—if not cruel, certainly indifferent to human consequences. His eyes had the intensity of the zealot, withering to those on whom he fixed them.

Olivia sat across from him, a chipped enameled kitchen table between them. The apartment had the appearance of a fortress, automatic weapons and cartridge boxes everywhere. Windows were shuttered tight, and one or two soiled mattresses on the floor suggested they were intended primarily for barricades. A television set, a telephone and a late model Olivetti typewriter seemed incongruous amid the litter indifferently scattered about. A cupboard of dishes and a pair of gilt-framed enlarged photos of a stiffly posed Italian peasant couple with fierce mustachios and a black-shawled woman suggested a family had once occupied the premises. In one corner, as if abandoned hurriedly, was a stuffed teddy bear with one arm.

They were not strangers. Olivia had been here before and had dealt with the terrorist; nevertheless, his suspicions toward her had never diminished. Her own air was characteristically self-assured and relaxed, and this too disconcerted him. Luigi Compo depended on fear in his relationships.

"You still don't trust me, do you, Luigi?" she said. "It would be much easier if you did, you know." She went on to remind him of her value to him, that there had been no betrayal of trust. "How many has it been now?" she went on. "Five—six? How many hundreds of million lire has that added up to? And have I ever asked you for a single lire of it? So say something, please. Don't just glower at me."

"Why? Why are you doing this?"

"What difference does it make?"

"I must know."

"You might not understand," she said quietly.

"Let me judge. I must know who I deal with. My life depends on it." He was leaning forward, half out of his seat.

"People don't understand you either, Luigi. Some say you're a common criminal, a member of the Camorra even. But I know better. Leave it at that. Don't try to understand me either. Follow my directions and be grateful. Simple enough? It's all I ask."

He lit another cigarette from the one he was smoking. He moved about the room like a caged animal whose cage was too small. From time to time he would cast a sideways glance at Olivia. "All right," he finally said. "What have you this time?"

"Carlo Sylvestri," she said.

"Who's he?"

She shrugged. "A nobody, but very rich. He keeps millions in cash about for his deals—"

"If he's nobody—"

Olivia understood. Publicity was as important as money to this man. "He'll get you headlines," she said. She drew a small notebook from her bag. "You'll destroy this when I leave. This is where he has his office. This is the license number of his old Critroën, but don't be deceived. It is armored and with bulletproof glass. His driver is a professional. On Mondays he travels to his office by way of Via Pinciana. Tuesdays he takes Via Nomentana."

"He carries a gun?"

She smiled. "He's a sleek worm, he jumps when he hears a backfire."

Luigo Compo who lived and survived by his instincts found the woman baffling. His eyes narrowed, his face hard, he again studied her for several moments.

"What is it now?" she asked.

"There isn't a member of Prima Linea—I don't care which city . . . Rome, Naples, Bologna—that I can't tell you what moves him."

"Does *him* mean her too?"

"Don't be funny with me."

"You keep on with this hard-nosed suspicion."

"I keep on."

"Pandora lost everything looking into the box," she said quietly.

"Don't play games with me." He was pounding at the metal table. Olivia, startled by the outburst, involuntarily moved away from him. At that moment there was a commotion outside the apartment followed by a heavy hammering at the door. Luigi went to it, snatching up a weapon.

"Who is it?"

An urgent voice outside said something hurriedly. Luigi crossed the room to unbolt and open the door. The youth who had accosted Olivia a short while ago rushed inside.

"Someone's across the street with an eye on this

place," he said, going on to explain that the information came from the proprietor of the *caffè*. "Vincenzo said he came in just after *she* got here."

Olivia stood frozen, for the first time in her life knowing fear. Both men were also still. Bland, expressionless faces except for the eyes, which were fixed on her. The Prima Linea were not rightists, the neo-fascists of the Italian Social Movement whose signature was bombing, indiscriminate killing. The Prima Linea, like the Brigate Rosse, singled out their victims with no particular personal animus. It was simply war. Betrayal, treachery, however, was another matter. This was the ultimate, the most unforgivable sin for which there could be only one punishment.

"Outside," Luigi Compo said, gesturing with his head, not taking his eyes from Olivia, who had backed against the wall nearest the cupboard. His comrade hesitated. "Out!"

"What about the one down there?"

"Keep an eye on him. No more."

The youth left. Luigi bolted the door behind him. He turned again to face Olivia.

"Luigi," she said, "I didn't know I was followed. I swear it. I can take care of it, you're in no danger. I know who it might be."

"Now I understand, huh?"

"No, no, you *don't!*"

He came toward her slowly. Not in a single, direct course, but in a series of arclike movements, ever closer. Olivia tensed. She was not deceived by his apparent relaxing. She understood what was going on within the man, the coiling of the steel spring. The tension building. Although the room had weapons scattered about, she also understood her death had to satisfy something infinitely more primitive in him. It had to be by his own hands, not even by a knife. The restlessness in the hands, the fingers splayed, ever so slightly quivering as if in expectation of the part they were to play, held her attention. Closer now. He had only to reach out—

Then it happened.

The incredible became real. Her patron, protective force, dormant for so long it had almost been forgotten, came into play in a fashion that no less confounded and astonished her than its victim. Luigi Compo found his arms immobilized in an iron grip. He was spun about and flung across the room. He came against the kitchen table, which collapsed under him. Olivia, using these few moments, grabbed up an UZI automatic rifle which she brought up as the terrorist scrambled to his feet, collected his wits, and like a raging bull came at her again. The weapon was being raised and pointed at him when—whatever *it* was—*it* struck again. He was jerked aloft, his body suspended in the air by no visible means—then all at once it was propelled away from her. Shutters and windows shattered as he went through them. Arms and legs flailing the air, he fell the four stories, his one continual shriek cut short by the damp cobblestones of the street below.

The body lay still in that unnatural attitude of death, as if it had come as a rude surprise. A trickle of blood fought its way among the dusty crevices of the stones, picking up bits of refuse along its way. The busy thoroughfare had become strangely still, as if shock had cut off its vitality, waiting for realization to catch up. People then began to move forward slowly toward the body, somehow afraid, peering at it from shop doorways, from behind parked vehicles as if there remained in it a potential for harming them. No one knew who it was. It didn't matter. It was death—and a violent one at that. The stillness was shattered by the slamming of heavy shutters on both sides of the street. A shop's metal gate clattered down. A woman's shrill voice cut through the air . . . "Em—man—uell—e." The child she was seeking was among the first to ring the body.

Prince Antonio Amontaldi di Donati looked anything but nobility as, ignoring his limp, he scurried from the *caffè*, passed the crowd, gathering to feast on the curiosity of the dead. He disappeared into the dark doorway through which Olivia had gone, instinctively feeling that the body in the street had something to do with her. He climbed several flights of the poorly lit, graffiti-scarred staircase painted in that universal color of poverty, a bright reptilish green. Hearing the clatter of steps above him, he looked up to see Olivia coming down toward him.

She was several steps above, and what he saw in her face stunned him. There was a raw hatred there such as he had never before seen, in war—anywhere. It was only momentary, but the effect was lasting. As she continued on down, he moved aside for her to pass.

Skirting the excitement in the street—the crowd milling about the body, the police trying to disengage the congealed traffic blasting its horns—he somehow managed to return to where Olivia had parked her car in time to see her speed off.

He found her at home.

He was directed by one of the servants to the *salone da ballo,* an enormous formal room, perhaps the largest in the palazzo, decorated in baroque gilt, gigantic crystal chandeliers and wall sconces and a frescoed ceiling by the renowned Renaissance artist, Guercino.

She stood stiffly in the center of the great room, her head slightly cocked as if listening to some distant voice. Struck by the surreal aspects of the scene, he paused for a moment at the threshold. She seemed unaware, indifferent to his presence, even after he had approached her. His steps on the marble mosaic floor had seemed to him deafening, drowning out the sound of his blood rushing through his head.

"Olivia—Olivia, we should talk . . ." He forced his voice to be calm, his words carefully measured.

Turning her head toward him, he was struck by the . . . dead look in her eyes. She blinked once or twice, as if gathering awareness. For some reason he now thought of Beatrice and her morbid warnings about Olivia. He tried to brush them away, as he more and more often brushed away other unpleasant thoughts and happenings.

"Come," he said. "We'll go to another room." He wanted more than anything else to sit. This exertion and excitement, he thought, wasn't for one his age. He wasn't feeling at all well.

"Wasn't this the room where your family once handed down their judgments?" she said.

"No."

"What's your judgment, Your Grace?" she said.

He didn't like this. He didn't like it at all. She was here, yet she wasn't. "What nonsense," he said. "Come."

"Say it now, Antonio."

If only that roaring in his head would go away, he thought. "You don't thoroughly understand the role of your title," he said, realizing even as he said it how obsolete it sounded. An echo of another age which he had been trying to quit.

"Princesses don't mess around, is that what you mean, Antonio," she said. "Certainly not with someone the likes of Carlo Sylvestri."

"No, no," he protested, waving his hand as if he would fend off that slangy talk.

"You think Carlo and I were lying in some mattress in that miserable flat, don't you?"

"Olivia, stop it—"

"And if not Carlo, it was someone else. Ah, of course! Some well-hung truck driver with a strong back. But then who am I? Where did I come from? You forgot, but the real principessa didn't, eh? Isn't that so, Antonio? Your wife, Beatrice, she knew about this peasant whose father could eat and pick his nose at the same time."

"I won't listen to this," he said more quietly, turning to leave.

"Listen to me, Antonio," she called after him. "You've heard nothing yet. Listen." He stopped, but did not turn. Her words seemed to echo in the empty ballroom. "Carlo Sylvestri is nothing. Nothing. Not that I haven't slept with him. But there were others too, I mean since our intimate relationship began. Yes they too were nothing."

He turned about slowly. His eyes were wide, his voice incredulous. "Nothing?"

She shook her head. "You give too much importance to it, Antonio. I say again—nothing, not in the larger scheme of things."

"I don't know what you're talking about," he said.

"I'm sure you don't," she said almost sadly, her eyes on a blue vein snaking along his temple. His paleness made it more prominent. "The body you saw in the street was Luigi Compo's." There was a flicker of recognition in the prince's eyes. It was a familiar name, conjuring different images to different people. To Antonio and his class it was anathema. "Luigi Compo and I have known each other for some time," she went on. "We had, you might say, a professional relationship. A business, he would call it."

"Business?"

"Very simple. I'd pass on to him someone's name and certain other information, and in a short while that person would simply disappear for a while."

The lean, fragile-looking man before her began to have trouble applying her words, associating them with anything that had meaning. Her words were only sounds that played like little hammers on his nerve ends. Then they abruptly quit, went unheard as overloaded circuits cut out the present for the more pleasant past . . . the best days of his life were his flying days. His attention fixed on those. This made sense. Even the bullets and explosives shot at him, in recollection had a certain nonthreatening beauty.

"I was with Luigi Compo to explain to him how best to kidnap Carlo Sylvestri." She laughed lightly. "You thought it was for making love. Oh, you Italian men. And my father—a prince among them."

. . . the billowing cumulus piled up in mountainous heaps, slipping, climbing among them, dropping into their pockets and fighting the controls against the turbulence, it was all so good, a joy. His head lolled side to side as if following the angle of banking . . .

"Before Sylvestri there had been Rico Stozzi and Maurizio Cianelli, men we've entertained here. Foolish man, Maurizio. His stubbornness cost him two fingers and an ear."

"Money," he said, his voice a whisper. He had no idea why he said it, his thoughts certainly weren't on it.

"Money had nothing to do with it. Publicity was the thing. The important element. Publicity planting the terror. The fear. The disorganization. Christian Democrats, Socialists, Social Democrats—everyone squabbling—what to do—what to do. The fascists coming up. The communists. The beginning of the end when it all comes down. You do understand now, Antonio. You do, don't you?"

Beatrice... his lips said without a sound. His head ached terribly and the light from the chandeliers bothered him. Rays in colors of the rainbow shot out from myriad faces to mix with what was going on in back of his eyes... arrows of hurting light. With what was a great effort he just managed to get out a single word which rang through the room... *"Iettatrice!"*

It was the last word Prince Antonio Amontaldi di Donati would utter. As if all the bones had been at once removed from his body, he sagged to the floor and lay still. His eyes... life still in them... stared up to the frescoed ceiling where the cherubs among the billowing clouds of heaven blew their golden trumpets in silence. Perhaps he was privileged to hear them. No living person would ever know.

CHAPTER FOURTEEN

They were no exception.

The spell of the Roman spring fell over Dave and Shula, banishing all thoughts but of each other. The trident matter was no match for the lacy pines of the Pincio at sunset. Even the mad Qaddafi's bounty was forgotten, and the weapon she carried about was left behind somewhere. Something new broke through the crust of cautious reserve in their relationship.

"I should be getting back to Jerusalem," she said one evening at dinner in a small *osteria* overlooking the sluggish Tiber. He nodded thoughtfully. "What are your plans," she continued. "Where do you go from here?"

He hadn't thought of it. The trident had been pushed aside . . . in part because he had no clear purpose. The Vatican priest had cooled them both with his unequivocal rejection of the trident theory, and they had little or nothing to refute the supposed expert in these matters. Dave, in pulling back, tried to take a cool, dispassionate view of himself and his embrace of the nightmarish vision. What an ego trip, he thought. Where did he get off giving himself this role? How was he so different from the next guy caught up in everyday life—dealing with job, romantic hassles and keeping his hair? What made him any different except some crazy need? Chosen indeed ... he thought, recalling the old Jew's opinion of him. So what was he reaching for? Uniqueness? Some nuts found importance, attention—even a twisted form of love—in shooting down celebrities. He remembered the recent words of a dying playwright who said of course everyone has to die sooner or later, but he thought he was an exception. Was the trident his stake-out to the exceptional? *Chosen* ... what a crock—

"Dave," Shula said, "what are you thinking?"

"That you'll go back to something worthwhile," he said. "Something important to you."

"Necessary ..."

"Me," he said. "My future's filled with detergents and underarm sprays."

"You could go back to your newspaper.

He laughed. "The *Double-Dealer?* I was double dealt—except for one thing."

"Yes?"

"You. It led me to you."

She smiled, turned serious. "Are you giving up on it, Dave?" It was as though she'd been reading his mind.

"You think I shouldn't?"

She nodded firmly.

"Any suggestions how to start again? Where to go?"

"What does the mystic in you suggest?"

He was startled. "Mystic! Me?"

"Everyone has it," she observed. "Some more than others. Civilization dulls it. We Jews have an extra share of it, perhaps as part of our survival kit." She reached for his hand across the table. "Come to Jerusalem," she said. "Another refugee won't matter."

"Refugee?"

"From detergents. Underarm sprays."

He had played with the idea of he and Shula making half-Jewish babies for the next Holocaust—the last, non-sectarian one. "You come to America," he said. "You were born there. Come back."

"I couldn't," she said, and he understood. She needed commitment as much as he did—the difference being: she had hers. But at least he sensed that the logjam holding back their feelings about each other had finally been broken. The games—the bullshit, as he termed it—were done with.

The meal was finished in silence, the bill paid. Returning to the hotel, aptly named if only because of its elevator which ran capriciously, their tension and expectancy grew as they rode up. It seemed tacitly understood what was the next order of business. He knew she had noticed that on entering the elevator he had pushed the button for her floor, not his.

Their coming together was all he'd dared hope it would be, and he had every good reason to believe it was the same for Shula. Her tall, lithe body, surprisingly full-breasted, became a vibrant instrument, evoking pleasures which had no restraints, no coy holding back, no suggestion of shame or self-consciousness. Making it possible for two becoming one, and—when it became most unendurable—pain and pleasure fusing in their coming together. Then, lying in each other's arms in damp exhaustion, both were aware that some search had been ended. The groping among other bodies was somehow finished. Was it love? Who could say, but it was surely close enough . . .

At two in the morning the Via Veneto was almost deserted. The shops were darkened and the ranks of café tables lining both sides of the noted thoroughfare were surrounded by upended chairs waiting for the next day's uninterrupted lines of assorted behinds. The corner kiosks, which in a few hours would be bursting with international periodicals, were dark and shrouded, and even the usually busy maw of the Excelsior Hotel was free of traffic. The last of the prostitutes left her post in the shadows of the side street to shuffle wearily homeward. No longer peddling her body, her walk became relaxed, just like any woman's. It was only her feet that hurt, but it had been a good, a profitable night. A convention of American orthodontists was in Rome to exchange views, and chalk up a tax-deductible fling abroad.

A couple came out of the Via Liguria to enter the Via Veneto . . . hand in hand, Dave and Shula, fresh out of bed, gave off all the indications of a couple in love, wrapped as they were in their own intimacy. They were in search of a hamburger and a cup of coffee, no easy task in late-night Rome. They talked lovers' nonsense, and laughed at each other's responses. It was their world, their's alone—

And then, as they walked the street between the empty café tables and the buildings, the sudden scream of tires, a car sweeping around the corner from the darkened mass which was the American embassy. It took several moments for Dave and Shula to come out of themselves to realize what was happening. The car braked. Two men carrying wicked-looking AK-47, jumped from it as it was still moving. Shula, in charge of herself again, took herself away from Dave toward the questionable protection of the forest of metal chairs and tables. Dave, disbelieving, saw a weapon raised and aimed at Shula. With a near-instantaneous reflex action, he grabbed a chair and threw it at the man a dozen paces away, upsetting his aim. Gunfire flashed, the reports echoing in the canyon of buildings. The other man pointed his weapon at Dave, who spun himself away with a reflex honed during his Nam days. Bullets ricocheted about him in a metallic clatter. Other dark figures materialized out of the shadows, running toward the scene, handguns firing. But their attack was diverted from Dave and Shula; the former, crouched low, burrowing his way among overturned tables and chairs, many of which had been punctured and torn apart by the fusillade. Now shots came from the car, which had stopped, but the three young men who had diverted the attack were now firing and moving, firing and moving with professional expertise.

As quickly as it had started, it ended. The car was driven between the combatants, and the bodies of their wounded accomplices scooped up. The car then sped off toward an old wall at the end of the Via Veneto, disappearing into the darkness of the Borghese Gardens. Police sirens could now be heard in the distance. Two of the three young men who had, as it seemed, miraculously appeared to help them disappeared into the night. The third came to where Dave was still shielding Shula with his body.

"Get up and get out of here! Quick!" he said in Hebrew.

Shula looked up at the young man in disbelief. "Ari..."

Dave grabbed Shula's arm, and the two fled into a side street even as the blue lights of the carabinieri car flashed into view, followed by another converging from another direction.

They were again in her hotel room with its high terra cotta walls and tall wardrobe. She sat at the edge of the disheveled bed that only a short while ago had carried them from reality. Shock was still etched upon her face, the pupils of her blue eyes still unnaturally wide. She spoke to her hands loosely clasped in her lap. "It's what hanging around me will mean. Here—in Israel—anywhere. More of same and no place safe." She raised her eyes to Dave standing at the dresser contemplating the Gucci bag. She watched as he reached for it, opened it and took out a 9 mm Belgian automatic pistol.

"What are you doing?" she said.

He didn't reply. His thoughts had gone back to a rice paddy outside a village called Bhu Dop. It had been the last time he had held a weapon in his hands. He hadn't realized it, but the war experience had left him scarred. With a new cynicism some might call maturing, he simply had been turned off by the politicians' speeches, distrusting the grand words and extravagant promises. You've come a ways, he thought—you the original campus jock. The gun in his hand triggered the old memories of too many body bags filled with the mangled pieces of younger men, some of whom he'd known and liked. Could this maybe have been what had been behind the trident business from the very start, a subconscious drive to hold back the fingers from those red buttons unleashing a destruction far worse than what had struck the Mayans, the Cretans—the whole cavalcade of dead cultures and civilizations remembered now only as footnotes in the history of man?

He replaced the weapon in the bag, saying, "You're going back to Jerusalem. Tomorrow, the first thing."

"And you?"

The question was answered for him by the telephone's ring. It was after four in the morning, and they looked at each other in surprise. She lifted the instrument, listened to what was said at the other end, then replaced it.

"That was Father Martenius," she said. "He wants to see us."

Father Jan Martenius had appeared at the gate of the palazzo Amontaldi di Donati. The gatekeeper there was accustomed to the frequent visits of the clergy, especially when the Principessa Beatrice was alive. Jan Martenius had lied. He had claimed to be a Vatican specialist in Roman history in which the palazzo's residents and their family held a distinguished place.

"His Grace—I'm sure—will give me an interview—" he had begun.

The gatekeeper had snorted. "I'd like to see that," he had said, turning away to enter his small lodge beside the large iron gates with the elaborate scrollwork and a sophisticated new lock. There too was the enameled seal of the Amontaldi di Donatis with its *corona chiusa*. Jan Martenius had followed the man inside. Glancing about, he had seen an old overstuffed chair of an indeterminate color, a telephone to the palazzo itself and a one-burner electric heating coil on which rested a chipped coffee pot with a blue and white floral design. On the wall there was an old photoengraving of the Lord whose bountiful heart was graphically exposed. Between the photo and the wall had been stuck a frond of palm from last year's Easter, now dust dry and yellowed.

"Excuse me," Jan Martenius had said. "I didn't

understand you. I was hoping for a few words with His Grace."

The old man had turned his rheumy eyes toward the young priest. "Hope!" he had grumbled. "He can use all you got."

The priest finally had drawn from the man the fact that the prince was dying in a clinic. The gatekeeper's bitterness then had overflowed. Martenius had been unable to leave before hearing the man's woe. "My father—my father before him—we tended this gate. It was something then, believe me. Dukes—the king himself—three times I myself opened it for Il Duce. *Il Duce!* You hear that?"

"Yes."

"There was respect here then. Respect! No one got in or out if Giovanni Festa didn't say okay. I had responsibility from both ends. The family for me, me for the family, right, eh? Where's the responsibility now? What if he dies? The prince, I mean. What then? That new young principessa? She and that crowd! Ha!"

Father Martenius wanted desperately to get away. He had learned what clinic the prince was in. But the old gatekeeper had had him literally cornered. "You think my sons want any part of this? I can just hear them saying with respect in their voices: 'Good morning, Your Grace. Good evening, Excellency.' Respect is inside a man. These days, ha! Not even these walls keep the scum out. What happens to me, father? I mean, if he— bless his soul—goes? What happens to me?"

Jan Martenius had been struck by the whiteness

of the clinic room. Everything: walls—ceiling—floors—all were of such a whiteness that it was impossible to determine where one began, the other ended. Even the white curtains over the window sucked the color from the daylight beyond. If it hadn't been for the single red rose in the small crystal vase on the bed table, that and the priest in his cope, alb and surplice administering the last rites, Jan Martenius would have been disorientated by the whiteness, cast on a white sea with no horizon.

At last came the—*in nomine Patri*—and the priest's hypnotic droning had ended. A nursing sister—in white, white too—glided past him like a wound-up toy to straighten a nonexistent wrinkle on the bed's white counterpane.

The visitor had crossed the white vinyl floor and came to the foot of the bed as the priest was stowing away his paraphernalia in his black bag. The latter had looked up in surprise at the sight of another cleric.

"The family priest, father?" the latter had asked, softly volunteering a confession was unobtainable.

Jan Martenius hadn't taken his eyes from the prince's still, almost rigid form. Was he alive yet, he had wondered.

"Father—" the other priest had repeated.

Jan Martenius turned to him and muttered a few words. *"Collegium cardinalis,"* he had said.

"Ah!" had been the reply. And with no further questions, he had disappeared.

"Sister—" Jan Martenius had said. And she too

vanished, white into white.

Jan Martenius had peered down at the sharp, pallid features that eloquently bespoke their patrician lineage, even more so now. In his mind's eye he could see the face molded in marble atop a crypt, arms crossed, the warrior's vestments and the great stone sword to hack his way through eternity. Leaning down, he had said softly, "Your Grace—your Grace, it's most important you hear me." He then went on to describe himself as a priest attached to the Vatican. He had had no indication he was being heard. He couldn't even be certain the man was still alive, the breathing was that shallow. He had paused a moment before saying the all-important thing. "Your Grace, I'm interested in your daughter, Olivia. Your adopted daughter. There's a letter I've seen. A very old letter. It was written by the bishop of Firenze to Rome. It's about your daughter Olivia. It suggests she was involved in supernatural incidents. Several of them. Several people even died." Once more he hesitated—pausing before saying those words which could have such a dread effect upon the world. "Your Grace," he had gone on, "there was mention of a birthmark on her body. Would you know of it?" He had deliberately avoided any prompting, any suggestion of the trident.

The head on the pillow had shown no life. And yet Jan Martenius had perceived—or had thought he did—a movement of the thin, fragile hand on the counterpane. He had leaned forward. A tear—a single tear showed in the corner of one closed eye. It had come loose and began a hesitant course downward along the aquiline nose. Jan Martenius could only think of a first raindrop on a dry, dusty window.

"Your Grace, you do hear me!" he had said. "You've heard what I've said!" He had stared at the hand that had moved. There! Once more it moved. Again! Jan Martenius had hoped he understood. Rummaging in an inside pocket, he had produced a ball-point pen and a small notebook. He had positioned the pen in the prince's hand with some difficulty. He put the notebook beneath. "Write, please! Write!" he had urged.

The hand, with the pen in it, remained still for several moments. Jan Martenius had closed his eyes and prayed. "God in heaven," he had thought. "If ever you can prove your love of man, it is now. Now is the time. This moment. If evil—the devil is afoot, let me know. Give this sign."

He had opened his eyes. The hand was moving—jerkily, erratically to be sure—but something was being drawn upon the paper. Abruptly it had stopped. The pen had fallen from the waxy fingers. Martenius had looked up. The tear had come loose and had fallen to the pillow.

Father Jan Martenius found Dave and Shula at an outdoor table at a *caffè* on the Piazza Barberini. He at once sensed a difference in them, but didn't comment on it. He realized they were anxious to hear what he had to say, but for his own reasons he held back. Ordering an enormous breakfast, he apologized, explaining that his large size required it. "Not that I wish to be a Falstaff with a turned-around collar, but actually it's the opposite. My body is my standard. It advertises my cause."

"Which is?" Dave asked. He still smarted from their last confrontation.

"The way to God is through the stomach. There, I've summed up my politics," the priest said, going on to explain that he wasn't one of the blessed-are-the-poor school. "Which of course gets me in no end of trouble."

"You said you had something important to tell us," Shula said impatiently.

Wiping his lips with his napkin, then loosening his collar, Father Martenius proceeded to tell his story of the bishop's letter in the archives. How, still unconvinced, he'd visited the palazzo, then the clinic. "The prince obviously had little time left. I could only pray he could hear me. I worried that I was talking to myself, but I asked whether the Principessa Olivia had a birthmark. Somehow, with one last effort, he drew this." He handed Shula the opened notebook. Dave leaned across— to see a crude, but unmistakable, trident.

"The princess—" Dave began.

"Amontaldi di Donati," the priest finished. "A lady—if that's the word—of considerable influence in the city, and of talent and beauty, so I've been told."

"And she has the trident on her body," Dave said, finding it nearly incredible that of all the people in the world he'd come to the right place. It wasn't a large step from here to believing it had somehow been prearranged. Planned . . .

"So says the man who was her father by adoption," Jan Martenius was saying. He read the question in their eyes. Her father? How would he have known? "It would suggest," he continued dryly, "that theirs was a rather more intimate relationship than commonly exists between father and daughter . . ."

Dave had nearly written off the trident as a bizarre consequence of a process whereby reality was somehow created out of illusion, convenience, need . . . and bonded together by the latent mysticism Shula had identified in him. Now—all at once—disbelief, doubts, were driven off.

"The princess then . . ." Dave began, finding it difficult to say the words.

Jan Martenius again finished his thought. "She's apparently an historic harbinger of things to come—"

"You're convinced?" Shula said.

"Yes," Jan Martenius said, choosing to ignore her pointed irony.

"Is she more than you can handle?" Dave said.

"I'm not sure I know what you mean."

"You say you're convinced . . ."

The priest nodded.

"So put it before your bishops and cardinals. Who better than your church to speak out about this? Perhaps the Holy Father himself . . ."

For several moments no one spoke. All about them the piazza was coming alive with its morning traffic, the magnificent dolphin fountain at the center spraying its pattern of water, indifferent to the concerns of the milling people. And meanwhile a woman and two men, one a priest, sat at a small table beneath a striped awning trying to digest the unthinkable, the incredible. An ancient coin had been turned over and the face of Medusa had confronted them.

Shula spoke first. "I'm not going back to Israel—"

"Yes, you are," Dave said.

"And leave you to that ... woman, creature ...?"

"He won't be alone," Jan Martenius told her.

"And what will you do?" she asked. "What can you do? Stage an exorcism? This isn't Hollywood."

The priest glowered at her like a great pink bear. She didn't flinch. She knew Dave was right, she had to leave. She had used up the time granted to her; and besides, once the Arab terrorists recovered from the preceding night, they would come after her again with redoubled effort, and as she had said to him ... she was a threat to everyone around her.

"But if the lady is, well, merely the messenger," Dave was saying, "can it maybe be turned around? I mean ... this sentence or whatever it is that's been passed?"

"By whom?" the priest asked.

"Isn't that your department?" Dave said. "Go to your bishops and cardinals. You seem to be convinced. Put it in front of them. Perhaps the pope himself, why not? Or don't you think it's that important?"

"I may not be the best man," the priest said, looking off across the piazza. "I could hurt more than help."

Shula said, "What do you mean?"

Father Martenius explained that aside from the fact his own position at the Vatican was a shaky one, most Dutchmen weren't enjoying favor at the moment. "We've got the reputation of being a rebellious lot. And I'm not even a Hans Küng or a Father Schillebeeck, who although questioning papal doctrines and even gospel, have their constituency and are treated at least respectfully. I've nothing. Nothing, you understand?"

The conversation lapsed into the general area of the most likely form of worldwide catastrophe, and it was agreed that the nuclear was mankind's greatest threat.

"All men to be cremated equal," Dave said, recalling some black humor he had once heard, adding, "Technology, history seem out of control."

"In this nuclear age," Jan Martenius said, "everything moves quickly. And it's at the heart of my problem with my church. Our vision is a thousand years off, and so we amble." He turned to Dave. "You're not Catholic."

"No," Dave replied. "Don't comfort me now by assuring me Armageddon will be nonsectarian."

"Word games!" Shula burst out angrily. She was about to get up but Dave put his hand on her arm. "Sit down."

"Then talk about what can be done," she said. "Everything you've said suggests the enemy is invincible."

"At least invisible," Father Martenius added. Turning to Dave, he went on, "And as you said, things seem out of hand. Nothing seems to make any difference. Unless we can change human nature so that there'll no longer be human conflict, wars. All we need to do is arrange that. That's all . . ."

A pall of depressed silence came over them. A few yards away the spray of the metal dolphins caught the sun's rays, and a false rainbow curved over a busload of Japanese tourists being disgorged from their German vehicle, putting cameras to work.

It was more pageant than funeral. A special high mass for the Prince Antonio Amontaldi di Donati was said in the minor basilica of Sant'-Agnese fuori le Mura built in 342 A.D., its subterranean catacombs and fourteen antique columns of *breccia* and *pavonazetto* intact. The bust of Christ, attributed to Michelangelo and the Byzantine mosaics seemed appropriate to the pomp and panoply of the occasion. The mourners included members of the noble family gathered from all parts of the Continent, a contingent of scarlet robed cardinals, other ecclesiasts lending color along with a few survivors from the prince's military days, old, creaky men whose uniforms and medals were brought out solely for these occasions. The rest were mainly friends and acquaintances who magnanimously forgave the deceased for his recent desertion of their ranks, but who wouldn't have missed his funeral for anything since the affair had achieved the status of event in the upper social hierarchy of the city.

Olivia sat in the very front pew, somewhat separate from the others, clad entirely in mourning black including a heavy veil. Far back, sitting on the aisle, was Dave who had gained entrance with the aid of Father Martenius who sat beside him. Dave, new to such rituals, was awed both by the milieu and the theatrical solemnity for which it had been intended. He had come to see the principessa, and he assumed the tall, slender figure at the very front was she, but there was little more to see until the end of the service.

The bronze casket was carried up the aisle to a waiting hearse that would carry it to the family crypt in La Rocca. The procession of mourners followed, led by Olivia.

It was then it happened.

The heavily veiled figure had already passed Dave and Jan Martenius, standing as were the rest in the church. Suddenly she stopped. It was as if she recollected she had left something behind. It created some confusion since the mourners behind her, family members mostly, had to stop too. Slowly she turned toward Dave, and took a step closer to him. With both hands she lifted her veil, and he saw her face for the first time. His thoughts were awhirl. Confused. That she was strikingly beautiful, he was certain, but only vaguely. It was her eyes that diffused all else. Eyes that looked into his with recognition. He felt now totally alone with her.

PART THREE

CHAPTER FIFTEEN

Dave couldn't deny he wasn't looking forward to a confrontation with the Princess Olivia. "I'm scared, father."

"And I don't blame you one bit," Jan Martenius said, shaking his large head gloomily. "Checking into her past—as far as I could—there hasn't been a man who's crossed her path who didn't end up dead—and usually violently."

"It isn't even that," Dave said.

The priest regarded him quizzically.

"*La belle dame sans merci*, is one thing," he continued. "It's stepping into the dark where you *know* there's a deep, black pit."

"How can I help?"

"I guess you can't."

"In another time," the priest observed, "she'd have been a prime candidate for burning."

"Which brings up a question, Jan." They had

reached a first name intimacy after, among other things, learning they shared a preference for a good Lowenbrau over Italian wine and neither liked life in a groove.

They had been strolling through the side of the old Roman Forum. They were now atop the Palatine Hill from which they could look down over the excavated ruins of what had been the heart of the ancient empire that had proved itself somewhat less than eternal. Tumbled marble columns were everywhere. In the distance could be seen the weed-strewn remnants of the stadium where gladiators had fought. He imagined he could hear the cheers, the chanting of the excited multitude, the clatter of iron-rimmed wheels on rough paving stones. Decayed monuments to a monumental dream. The home of Augustus lay below. What had been the great Caesar's palace was now the refuge of abandoned cats.

It was now several days since the incident in the basilica. Questions ate at Dave. How in the world had she known him? (In the world, or out of it?) What did she know? What was it *he* had sensed in her in that briefest of moments? He had come away from the encounter truly shaken, that he *knew*. Subsequent nights had been sleepless, haunted by that face of classic beauty, the almost translucent complexion framed by thick, black mourning veils. Yet the face had been somehow blurred. He had difficulty recollecting its details. Only her eyes . . . eyes fixing on his, had burned their way into the depths of him, putting all else out of focus. He thought and thought about the brief, wordless exchange. What message had her look, her eyes carried? What was intended to be evoked in him? Hard as he tried, answers were as evanescent, as shrouded in mystery, as the woman herself.

At one point his thoughts went to an experience he'd had in Tokyo during his war days. He had been taken to see a sumo match, where he had been struck by the ritualized formality of the oiled behemoths coming out from their corners— bowing, paying homage to the tradition. Was this the sort of thing he'd seen, felt in her eyes? Acknowledgment of something... primordial, something old as time, created by a larger design? Was it possible the Princess Olivia was somehow archetypal... if not her, would there be others like her to follow?

All right, high-flown thoughts. Melodramatic thoughts. But the building evidence tended increasingly to ground them in scary reality. The dying prince had, after all, confirmed that Olivia's birthmark was a trident... he'd drawn it... the priest has said so...

Dave and Jan Martenius had also spent several days learning what there was to know about the woman. Dave's brief stint at journalism, his ability to make contact with wire service people at the *Time* and *Life* bureau in Rome, together with the priest's Vatican resources, enabled them to create a composite of the woman's background. They had agreed that if it weren't for the overtones of the supernatural—the seemingly demonic forces behind her—she might easily have been mistaken for just another remarkable woman whose ambitions and amorality brushed aside all human cost and consequence in its relentless upward thrust. However, what they knew about her, together with historical precedents, made it almost impossible *not* to believe that the Princess Olivia was beyond the pale of normal human criteria. And if her purpose was as dreadful as they were coming to have to accept that it was, then wasn't it their obligation to try to defuse it, in even the remote hope that the chaos associated with her would somehow be put off . . . ?

"I should go to her village in the Abruzzi," Dave said.

"You'd get nowhere," the priest said. "As an alien, an outsider, you'd get nothing. You wouldn't even find a place to sleep."

"I'd like some words with the local priest who handled the birth registry. I'm sure he had a hand in her adoption by the prince."

"Probably."

"So come with me, Jan. Help me. You're right, I couldn't get anywhere alone. I don't even speak the language."

"What good will it do? How much more do we have to know about her before—"

"Before we do something? Say it. Do we take it on ourselves? Who passed this judgment on her, on us? God? That's your department. What do you say?"

When Martenius didn't answer, Dave went on, "Well, I guess we can at least say that knowing her is knowing more about the nature of what's called evil, something you and your people have been at a long time without noticeable results."

"Because we accept it—I mean good *and* evil."

"You mean a creature like her—?"

"The point is, and it's not exactly original with me, there can be no God without His counterpart. Good without evil would, I'm afraid, have no meaning."

"But in the conflict, good has got to survive," Dave said, and instantly thought, How pretentious can I get . . . it's beyond conceit, it's a megalomania. Still, damn it, it's my world too . . . and as some philosopher once said—without me it'd be nothing. For me, anyway . . . He said aloud, "Shula talked about the rule of chaos. Is this what she meant?"

Dave prowled the outside of the walled park, within which was her palazzo. He would stand at the hotel entrance across the street from the great gate, watching cars enter and leave, speculating on what went on inside. Was it a witch's coven, he dramatically wondered? A place for fiendish cabals, games of dungeons and dragons, the devil's black mass? And yet, the traffic didn't suggest this. Other than the usual service vehicles, there were the taxis of visitors who seemed to Dave the same chic, attractive people he had seen at the prince's funeral service. Among the limousines belonging to important government functionaries were a number of foreign diplomats making condolence calls. One drizzly evening, standing in the shadows and gazing across to the palazzo, his thoughts returned to that day in the basilica—her face—her eyes—the message he saw in them which had affected him so. From his position, a clear view of the palazzo was blocked by the towering wall and the heavy growth of trees and brush within. He could see just a portion of the upper floors. Several windows were lit, and at one point he thought he saw a white curtain move and be held open. A figure—a woman's figure—was silhouetted before the light behind her. Certain it was she, he moved out from the shelter of the building. Peering up, he again felt that inexplicable bond between them.

Father Jan Martenius glanced at his watch. Six-fifteen. His Excellency, the Bishop Strassoni should shortly be appearing for his stroll through the Vatican gardens. Several days' observation had provided Jan with a pattern of the prelate's movements. Now he positioned himself a short distance from the elegant and picturesque Fontana dell' Aquilone. Other ecclesiasts, singly and in pairs—a brace of Carmelite nuns—strolled the meandering path in meditative thought or quiet discussion. The only sound was the crunching of their feet on the white marble gravel against the background of the fountain's splashing. It was coming to that moment in the early dusk when the birds—all nature—seemed to pause. The famous pines of Rome made lacy, sharp patterns of their branches against the darkening turquoise sky.

Father Jan Martenius became alert as the bishop came into view, his heavy head, sunk into his shoulders seemingly by its own weight, bowed in pensive thought. He was short by any standard—yet, somehow, he didn't give the sense of a small man. Following the course of the winding path, he never wavered one iota from dead center appearing to be on invisible tracks. Jan Martenius had at first thought this remarkable, until he decided that the prelate, traversing the same route for years, could undoubtedly do it in his sleep.

The Bishop Peppino Strassoni of Napoli had been the man chosen by Jan Martenius as most suited for his purpose. The gentle, soft-spoken prelate was not only popular, he was considered apolitical and trusted by Vatican conservatives and liberals alike, a man of all factions. What was of particular interest to the young priest was that the scholarly bishop had written some years ago a learned paper entitled: "Mutations and Transmogrifications of the Devil."

Father Martenius, with no illusions about himself or his reputation, realized that were he to present it, his story of the trident—assuming he even could gain access to the cardinals—would in all likelihood at once be shot down. The crazy Dutchman, they would say, was at it again. No, he had decided, it wasn't for him. The matter needed an acceptable advocate, needed to be sponsored by a respected figure. Only then would it have a chance of being passed along the hierarchy for the attention it needed. Deserved.

He maneuvered himself around the fountain so that he and the slow-moving prelate were on a collision course. Pretending preoccupation, he made contact, yet by reaching out for him prevented the older man from falling.

"Oh, my goodness!" the bishop cried out, groping for the steel-rimmed spectacles that had slipped from his large and purple nose. Mumbling profuse apologies, Jan went down on hands and knees in search of the glasses. Finding them, he wiped the lenses clean on his gown before offering them back.

"Ah!" Bishop Strassoni said, replacing them along with his ever-present smile put on in the morning along with his dentures. "Only this morning," he explained, "the same thing happened with a Swiss Guard. The poor fellow's halberd almost guillotined a Coptic cardinal. A fine scandal that would have made, eh?"

The two were about to continue their separate ways when Jan called after the bishop, "Your Excellency . . ." The cleric turned. "I've a most difficult problem," Jan continued. "If I could impose—"

"Walk with me, my son? By all means," was the gracious invitation.

It was a long, slow-paced walk intermittently interrupted as the Vatican prelate stopped to regard Jan Martenius in amazement as Martenius came to some significant point. The story of the trident was told simply, without embellishment. Martenius took pains to handle the matter as if it were a fragile bubble of Murano glass. It's credibility would shatter, he knew, if he slipped into hyperbole or pushed too hard. He didn't fail to mention his own initial doubts and skepticism.

"However," he said, "the letter in the archives from the bishop of Firenze largely dispelled my old doubts. Still, even then, I probed further into it. I'm not altogether inexperienced at that, I may add."

"Your work here—"

"Exactly."

"You say you were with the Prince Amontaldi di Donati when he passed on."

"And I'm convinced, Excellency, the final tear he shed was at least in part a tear of relief that he could warn us."

"You and your American friend."

This time it was Jan who paused in their stroll. Peering down into the face of the bishop, he said, "I mean *all* of us. People everywhere . . . I'm aware how improbable it must sound—"

"If you're impressed, my son, how can I not be?"

"It's for you now, Excellency. In your hands."

"Eh? How's that?" A sudden look of caution had come up in the prelate's eyes.

"The Holy See must act—"

"Ah! And what exactly did you have in mind?" the bishop said, his equanimity apparently recovered.

At moments when Jan Martenius had been most frustrated and discouraged he fought against the heretical thought that his church was part of the problem rather than the solution to the world's ills. But involvement with the trident served at least one good purpose, he thought . . . it proved his basic faith staunch, incorruptible. Now he was convinced that if anything could be done to divert what might otherwise be inevitable, it could best be sponsored by the Church.

"A crusade of some sort, Excellency, I don't know. It's why I've come to you. It's for better minds than my own. Neither my American friend nor myself have the competence. But attention must be given. I've no question about that."

"Yes, yes... indeed." The bishop at least seemed impressed by his younger colleague's sincerity.

"I see it as our responsibility. Otherwise..." Martenius's voice trailed off.

"Otherwise, my son? Please go on."

Jan Martenius shrugged his large shoulders. The sun's last rays made golden orbs of the bishop's eyeglass lenses. The bishop waited, expectant, and Jan felt momentarily hopeful. He had a vision of His Holiness himself becoming involved to carry the message.

"I wonder," the bishop said, more to himself than Martenius, "does our destiny belong to us, or we to our destiny? Ah!"—he laughed abruptly—"a foolish speculation. Father, I must ask you... this trident business will bear investigation?"

Jan Martenius replied that he had facts—material evidence organized. "And I'm certain," he went on, "that the American will be available for questions."

"Good."

Father Martenius's hopes rose a notch further. Just sharing his awesome—awful—secret, which had lately taken over his life, made him feel better. The hope that more experienced, wiser minds would now be involved gave him a sense of relief. At least the burden would be lifted from him ...

"May I make a suggestion?" the bishop asked. (Jan was stunned ... a bishop was asking *him* for permission?) "Who is your direct superior?"

The young priest felt cold. "Monsignor Aiello."

With a paternal gentleness, the bishop went about pointing out why discussing the trident with his superior was the best way to proceed. His own experience had taught him so. "And to whom is the monsignor responsible?"

Jan was no longer listening. He was caught up in a familiar anger and frustration that he tried to keep down. The bishop's words seemed distant. He could only see himself helplessly entangled in the bureaucracy. The question was repeated. Who was above the monsignor?

"Cardinal Heckle."

"Ah! Excellent! I know His Eminence. It couldn't be in finer hands, don't you agree?"

"Oh, yes," Jan said, thinking of Monsignor Francis Aiello, a lean desiccated priest with much neck and little chin, embittered by his own years of frustration. Aiello remembered himself as a sort of wunderkind whose father had once showed off how he could add, subtract, multiply or divide five digits by five digits. He could have been a banker, a physicist even, but mama had said be a priest, and so he had become one. He fitted God into a mathematical formulation, and his long ambition was now to be in the Vatican's finance, even real estate, division. This somehow never came about, leaving an old man wondering how his life had been wasted. A square peg in a round hole. What was worse, those working under him paid a heavy price for his disappointment. And those included Jan Martenius.

Well, he had to give it another try, he thought. It was too important. "Excellency," Martenius said, "your suggestion, as I knew it would be, is splendid. Precisely to the point. Discipline and a sense of order must be maintained. However..." His voice deliberately trailed off and he looked away.

"Yes?"

With utmost tact, Martenius then explained how the monsignor *might* be... well, a stumbling block... "Not, of course, to say that he's not a man of exceedingly strong faith, but the very nature of the trident situation requires a mentality that will accept matters beyond the five senses. What we have here requires that. The monsignor, unfortunately—I hesitate to say it—"

"Say it."

"He is rather a literal-minded person. A good man, undoubtedly," he quickly added, "yet he may not accept the trident's significance—whatever the facts."

"You don't question his faith, you say?"

"Oh, no, *no*, Excellency."

"Then how do you equate his faith with what you have just said—his inability to cope with what is beyond his senses? How can one have one, not the other? Would you say he believes in the immaculate birth?"

"Of course. I'm certain of it!"

"Is that not, in a *sense*, supernatural?"

Jan realized he had been trapped. A bishop didn't become a bishop without cause. That bland Falstaffian appearance masked a formidable intelligence. Yet, the bishop, sensing the young man was becoming upset, had no intention of letting him go off thinking less of him. Making himself likable was second nature to him. First nature. And so he tried to reassure Jan about his own belief in the warning, and that something must indeed be done about... "Yes, my son, I see this as a priority. If you will just put this into channels—"

"Channels!" That word! Anathema to Martenius. The bishop was smiling at him with his beatific smile, a warming bath of good will. He had to get away, he felt. He might say something, do something. That smile—a treacle trap—

"At once! Let us lose no time," the bishop was saying.

"By all means," Jan replied. "I will discuss it with the monsignor."

The Bishop Strassino regarded the young priest moving off into the shadows. A shadow of his smile remained. Poor child, he thought. Still another casualty. Some are just not meant for their vocations. He sighed. He would keep the name in mind. Martenius. Father Jan Martenius. Dutch. Ah, those Dutch. Whatever happened to them? A retreat to some nice quiet place should be just right for the young man. Perhaps Monte Cassino. He would recommend it himself, if he thought of it tomorrow. Trident, indeed! He thought with satisfaction how useful his *arrangiarsi* was—that art of survival by sensibly getting along. That fine Neopolitan art that he had nurtured so carefully. He stooped to pick a rose from a bush. Smelling its fragrance, he turned and made his way back to his dinner, keeping, as always, to the center of the path.

Dave and Father Jan Martenius sat at opposite ends of the small room in the Hotel Caprice. They sat without speaking, looking at a small object lying in the center of the bed's red acrylic coverlet. Although the shutters were closed against the heat of the day, the playing of an electronic organ from the disco below filtered through. Someone, remarkably, was practicing a phrase from a Bach fugue. Over and over again. It was a melancholy sound, appropriate to their thoughts.

The object which held their attention was Shula's 9 mm Belgian handgun, which she had insisted Dave carry with him out of fear that the terrorists might carry their frustration over onto him. He hadn't carried it. He had no intention of doing so, even though he had accepted it, to appease her.

Father Martenius was the first to break the silence. "You suppose you can do it?"

Dave shook his head.

"I understand. Besides, what's a gun against her

kind?" the priest said, adding with a touch of lightness that he felt they both might profit from, "Perhaps a consecrated bullet would be in order," and he started to intone, *"in nomine Patri . . ."*

But Dave was deep in his own reflections, trying to conceive of the moment of confrontation. During the war, in the Engineer Corps, he had pulled triggers, thrown grenades in hand-to-hand combat. As a demolition expert he had destroyed villages, killed he didn't know how many people, their guilt or innocence never determined. It was war. Killing was sanctioned. It had been called duty. And there was always the rationale of kill or be killed. But this was something else, wasn't it? He was thinking of killing a woman—and such a woman—on the basis of his own judgment. If he were, say, arrested, could he truly make a case for himself? "Gentlemen, the lady was a monster. A creature of hell . . ." The best he might hope for was a mental institution for the rest of his life.

"Dave . . . Dave . . ." his friend was gently saying, trying to bring him out of his bleak reverie.

"I'm sorry, Jan. You were saying—"

"Nothing." . . .

The days following he wandered the streets of Rome, observing its aged charm, the minutiae of its life. And as he wandered he had the nerve to ponder whether he was a Jeremiah seeing the fruitful earth as a wilderness, nothing left to mourn and the heavens black. In such a lousy mood he felt a detachment, as if he were somehow apart from it all. He thought of the Atlas figure on Fifth

Avenue, carrying the burden of the world on his shoulders. Oh, come off it, he told himself, you're like a guy come from a doctor's office, told he's got cancer, sees the birds picking seeds out of horseshit and says, "How beautiful! Wow! It's been there my whole life, I never saw it!"

Still, it was true. He wandered among the unwashed young sprawled over the Spanish Steps . . . a guitar plucked here, snatches of conversation there . . . such earthshaking matters—"Hey, the Piazza Navona fountain's okay today for a quick bath, the cops aren't around." Where a bed and some grass were available, cheap. His senses sharpened, giving him a whole new experience of things—even the gasoline fumes, chestnuts roasting, the look and smell of the stand of flowers. Slipping a few hundred lire to a hustling youth from L.A. on a sabbatical—a hiatus between his B.S. and entering medical school—he listened as the young man said he had to once again swim the Aegean before winding up in proctology or something. The bright sun glistened on the polished brass plate denoting John Keats's home. He thought of the poet's "Endymion"—*and there's not a fiercer hell than in the failure of a great object.*

Once or twice, late at night, when he was in his room there were calls from Shula asking if he was all right.

"Of course. And stop being a Jewish mother," he told her. But Shula wasn't to be put off. He offered her vague, unsatisfying explanations of his activities.

"Have you seen her?" she asked.

"For a brief moment, in a church. You're a lot prettier."

"Shut up. Dave, come here. I miss you."

"I miss you too." Only a partial lie. He did, but he also needed to move about without explanations. She asked if there had been any suspicious activities directed at him. "I wouldn't know," he honestly said. "Hell, if the devil doesn't get me, the Arabs will." Some joke.

She ignored this. "Be careful, Dave. Please . . . I'm afraid—"

"No need to be—"

"Especially the woman."

"I survived a war—years on Madison Avenue."

Shula wasn't reassured, or humored, though she appreciated his efforts.

He spent hours across from the gates of the palazzo, peering up at the upper floor window where he had once caught a glimpse of the princess. He had no plans, he had no idea what to expect. When Jan offered to join him in his vigil he refused.

"Don't worry, my friend. Please . . ."

"I do worry, Dave," the priest told him. "When I think of the other men in her life, I have to ask why you should be an exception. I mean, how you come out of an encounter with her. I'm afraid you're heading for it . . ."

"Yes." Dave's voice was flat.

"Where's the gun?"

Dave patted his hip pocket. A lie. The gun was in a bureau drawer, beneath a pair of cotton pajamas.

"Do I say good luck?" Jan asked.

"Don't look so forlorn." Dave laughed. "This is no more than a gothic western, and the white hats always win in the end." . . .

What he was waiting for happened.

Not that he knew—even dreamed—it would be as it came about. Once he simply awoke from a troubled sleep, dressed, slipped on his battered trench coat and went out into a stormy night. It was several blocks to the palazzo. Threading his way among the ranks of parked vehicles, he took his post from which he could peer over the wall to the darkened upper window where he had once caught a glimpse of her.

The rain pelted down in slanting sheets, splashing up from the hoods and roofs of the cars parked at right angles to the street. The din was fierce. The gusting wind had ripped apart the awning of a nearby outdoor restaurant, and the tattered ribbons of colored canvas snapped and fluttered like so many sodden pennants.

Wiping water from his face, he strained to see through the deluge. Across the street, all was dark, slumbering and somehow sinister. The high brick wall glistened in the streetlights like some scaly creature of the deep. The closed gates held back from prying eyes the mystery of what dwelt within. Like most Renaissance structures touched by the baroque, the playfulness was kept for the interior.

Outwardly, it was a stone crust of somber strength warning off those who dared challenge it.

The window lit.

Once again the curtains parted and a figure vaguely appeared. Dave stepped forward, excitement and tension wiping away all else from his mind, the wind, the rain, the discomfort. It was she! It had to be, he thought, seeking to bridge the gap between them by some mind-reach.

For several moments, he stood motionless—transfixed—unaware that his will was hemorrhaging from him. He lost awareness of himself—of time—of the cautions he had promised he would take. All fled before the spell of the Circe singing her muted song.

The small door within the gate opened to his touch. Peering into the gatehouse, he could see the gatekeeper brewing coffee at his one-burner electric heater. Oddly, the buzzer attached to the small door within the gate was sounding but the man didn't appear to hear. Unchallenged, Dave walked up the inclined gravel road which wound to the porte cochere at the opposite side. The trees and heavy foliage glistened and bent in the wind. Sightless Roman senators stood proud and pale, impervious to the water streaming between the folds and pleats of their marble garments.

Dave had never been to this place, but it didn't seem to matter. His steps were remarkably sure. He came to the great doors, pushed, and he was into a small, round foyer. There were several red velvet benches of gilt rococo, and the flocked walls carried portraits of the three Amontaldi di Donatis, known better as vicars of Christ.

There were several doors leading to various parts of the palace, but Dave never hesitated in selecting the one which would take him directly upstairs.

CHAPTER SIXTEEN

Shula hardly listened to the remonstrations of the balding, middle-aged man in a sleeveless open-necked shirt who might have been a harassed shopkeeper. Zev Cohen was, in fact, a commissioned general who headed the famed and respected Israeli Mossad and whose exploits during the British occupation had made him a near-legendary hero. Her back was to him as she peered through the opened blinds of her upper-floor apartment.

"I don't have enough to do," Zev Cohen was scolding, "I must worry about love affairs?" He went on detailing the fallout from the incident of the Via Veneto. The Italian government apparently had protested to the foreign office. "And what I got from the ministry, I won't tell you . . . Shula! I'm talking to you!"

Her gaze had been fixed on the sun glinting off the metal loudspeakers atop a minaret in the Old

City. Anachronisms everywhere, she had been thinking. Old, new—old, new. New life coming out of the old. Jerusalem, womb of both. Troublesome Jerusalem.

She turned. "Yes, Zev. I'm sorry."

"Sorry! Ha! Against my better judgment, I had some boys keep an eye on you. If you and your friends got yourselves shot up, who'd be sorry?"

"I didn't know."

"Does it matter you knew?" He knew he sounded like a querulous father, yet couldn't stop. What was worse, he knew it would do no good. "I raised two children, badly, of course. I am Zev Cohen. So what do I do in my old age? I take on a couple of hundred more. All crazy—suicidal—scattered over the world—"

"Like me."

"Like you!"

"Zev, you'd like some tea?"

"My stomach eats itself, my doctor says. A kosher cannibal."

She came about to pat his few gray hairs. "You shouldn't worry, Zev," she said.

"You didn't listen," he said gloomily. "No one listens."

"I listened."

General Zev Cohen nodded grimly. He knew what love was. He also knew he wished he could take Shula "off ice" and return her to active duty. "That damned Qaddafi!" he muttered. Shula knew what he was thinking. Islam's loose cannon waving his petro-dollars about. "Lucky for you it's Qaddafi," he said. "For Arafat I know a few *yidlach* would be tempted. A hundred thousand American dollars is no small thing. Shula, go back to the university. Teach. A job comes up that needs the one and only Shula Gorin, I'll call you. Who's this American in Rome? What is he up to?"

"Zev Cohen doesn't know something?" she smiled.

"I'm not God. A sparrow can sing somewhere, I'm not that interested. Well?"

"He's got some crackpot idea."

"We need another crackpot," was the wry retort.

At two o'clock that night, she made a phone call to Rome. The room clerk said that Dave's room didn't answer. The panic button in her was pushed; icy fear grabbed her heart.

"When was the last time you saw Mr. Turrell?" she asked. The reply was vague. He might have come in and out. Someone else may have been at the desk.

"The key?"

"It's in the box, signorina."

She sat at the edge of the studio couch considering what to do. Her reputation among her comrades was one of coolness. Depend upon Shula not to blow it. Her quiet resourcefulness had been proven on more than one occasion; but now, for the first time, she felt inadequate, as well as an overwhelming sense of helplessness. She berated herself for having left Rome, whatever the consequences. Recriminations and guilts piled one upon the other in a suffocating profusion. She was about to reach for the phone. Father Jan Martenius would know. He had promised to keep an eye on

Dave. She then realized he wouldn't be in his office until morning.

Without realizing it, she crossed the room to put on a tape of Vivaldi's *"Four Seasons."* In the midst of the last movement, she decided she would return to Rome. First, however, there was something else she must do. It was an unusual step involving folklore and the orthodoxy she had left. She wondered about it. She had to acknowledge that her early training had left its imprint. Mysticism was in her blood, always trying to accommodate the demands of science. How would her father feel about what she was about to do? Undoubtedly he would consider it a triumph of sorts. Good, she thought. Then he wouldn't deny what she intended to ask of him.

Shula took off before daybreak on a bizarre journey. Driving south, she came to the Arab village of Hebron just before Bethlehem. The night was starless and the faintest traces of the pink dawn were showing above the moonscape cliffs toward the east. Parking her car beside an olive grove with its twisted, gnarled trees, she clambered over the rock fences of terraces Christ had known. Finally she came to a dusty clearing flattened by the feet of innumerable visitors. At the center there appeared to be a mass of rubble excavated from the earth.

From out of a canvas shoulder bag she took a spool of kinky red wool she had unraveled from an old sweater before leaving home. Carefully anchoring one end of the string to the excavation, known as Rachel's Tomb, she then wound its entire length three times about the rubble of what had been a small ancient structure. When it was done she looked off to the sun just breaking over the cliff. A good portent, she thought—hoped. She then went about retracing her steps, winding the woolen string back upon the Farber number 2 yellow pencil as if she had been pulling in a kite.

What she had done was perform a ritual ceremony dating back several millennia and observed by generations of the devout. It was a mystic appeal to Rachel, the biblical grieving mother who had protected the Children of Israel during the Diaspora. The red thread wound three times about her tomb was the prescribed procedure whereby the Spirit of God was invoked through Rachel to protect the wearer against the Evil Eye.

Returning to Jerusalem, she first tried in vain to reach Father Martenius in his Vatican office, then went about combing the city for the chocolate-covered cherries, her father's favorite confection, usually reserved for the Passover or Hanukkah. This offering, however, was an exception since she had an exceptional thing to ask of him.

Hillel Gorin's small, white, thick-fingered hands fairly trembled as he tore away the wrappings and opened the box his daughter had brought to Safed. "Chocolate... covered... brandied... cherries!" Each word was uttered slowly, as if relishing it. His hands came together in delight. At that moment, Shula felt the trouble she had gone to, was worth it.

"Enjoy, papa," she said, adding almost casually,

"Papa, I'm going to Rome. To David."

They sat in the shade of the lemon tree in the small, lush garden before the little house. The bees did their business, blossom to blossom, their faint sound drowned out now and again by the thrumming of a hummingbird ... sounds that belonged and didn't bother. The only intrusive sound was the distant heaving and straining of a bulldozer engine.

Shula had told her story of what had happened in Rome, including the discovery of the woman with the sign of the trident on her body. The old man had listened, his head faintly nodding. Remarkably, he showed no disbelief, no doubt. At one point, while she was speaking of the Princess Olivia, Shula thought he'd murmured, *"ain,"* which she remembered as "the negatively existent one," as compared to *ain soph*, the "primal focus of the unknowable one known as God, the Absolute." The single word recalled the days and nights she'd poured over the old books as if she were a boy, a yeshiva bocher.

"You don't need permission to go?" he said.

"Why ask for it?" she replied. "Since I know I won't get it? I'm not deserting; I'm not on active duty." She was glad now she had never told him about the bounty on her life.

"So?" The old man nodded. Tacitly he was inquiring why she was visiting him.

"I'm afraid," she said. "You once taught me about angels, demons, elementals."

He nodded with the recollection.

"There's another thing you taught me," she added.

"Yes?"

"A talisman can give protection." With this she reached into the canvas shoulder bag, drawing from it the spool of red woolen thread, which she gently placed on the white metal table.

"An *aruv*?" he said, his voice low and heavy.

She explained that she had gone that morning to Rachel's Tomb. "You taught me this too, papa."

"That you remember . . ." he said, obviously touched.

"Yes, papa," she said, "but is it enough?"

"Enough?"

"This isn't just a Jew traveling on shabbat. We're dealing with the devil himself. Satan. His wife, Ashtinerum."

"The Gametria," he observed, smiling and nodding his head with pleasure.

"The *aruv* needs more—much more, papa," she said. "It must have in it the power of—"

"*Nu?* Of what?"

"Of God Himself. *Adonai.*"

There was silence except for a bird's staccato hammering at a nearby tree trunk. The sound seemed louder than it was.

Finally the old man spoke, his words heavy with disapproval and not a little apprehension. "You know what you ask?"

"I ask for all the help I can get. If I had to go so far as to prepare an *aruv*, you can imagine how desperate I am. When before, papa—in your lifetime—has there been anything like this confrontation."

But Hillel Gorin was thinking of the handful of men like himself, the few Kabbalists who were left. Either they spent their time warming themselves in the sun or coming together in their synagogue to argue the fine, arcane points in their sacred Zohar. In the old man's eyes, what his daughter was asking was defiance of the tractate Hagigah from the Talmud, which said: *"Seek not things too hard for thee, and search not for things hidden from thee. The things that have been permitted thee, think thereupon; all else, the things that are secret, thou has no business with."* These old men spent their time—harmless hours—seeking the illusive, unattainable *yesh,* the three hundred and ten worlds underlying and sustaining all existence, a synonym for the treasure awaiting the saints in future life.

"Yes, papa," she replied. "I know. I know what I ask."

"We are old. Where does the strength come from?"

"The strength you need is of another kind, and you have it," she replied. "Papa, here is the test of your life."

"I need to prove something?"

"Yes," she said. "You and your Hasidim—what has it been? Word and number games."

"Shula, what do you say!?"

"Word and number games, papa. You sit, you argue how many angels on the head of a pin. Your charts, your commentaries—games."

"No!"

"Unless they have meaning, what else are they? Old men's games. Mystic games afraid of the light—"

"Shula—Shula—"

"If they're not games, papa, prove it. Not to me. To yourself."

CHAPTER SEVENTEEN

Many doors opened on the gallery of the palazzo, but Dave never once hesitated, despite that he had never been there before. Twisting the ornate bronze knob of the mahogany door with its hand-carved acanthus-leaf design, the door effortlessly opened.

He entered his past, a lovely unspoiled part of it . . . The spring dance at the Tau Sigma house was a gala event that emptied out the racks of white tuxes at Charlie's Reasonable Rentals. Many girls were from the university, sophomores and seniors. Others had been imported, but all of them were gussied up appropriately in chiffon, organdy and taffeta. Chaperones were Marge Haevigsen and her husband Max of Phys. Ed. At first everything was a bit self-conscious and formal, the way these affairs generally began. Until it got warmed up, that is.

The Tau Sigma house on Euclid Avenue, a gingerbread Victorian mansion with gables, attics and elaborate fretwork fringing a wide wooden porch, had had its respectability rescued only a year before when a rich alumnus who manufactured heart pacemakers in Framingham, Massachusetts, had bought up the mortgage, which was then ceremoniously burned.

The Marvelettes' fee had about drained the frat treasury. The strains of "Soldier Boy," played in their sedate rock style, drifted into an attic room softly lit by several candles stuck into Ruppert beer bottles. Dormer windows were open and soft laughter could be heard. The nightblooming jasmine almost but not quite overpowered the smell of mildew from the rain that had come in through a small hole in the uncovered slats of the roof, giving the place the appearance of the inside of a whale. Five youths in white jackets stood about a cot in the center of the room while a sixth copulated with a young sophomore, Melissa Wainright, whose ruffled taffeta gown had been thrown up to her waist and whose legs were locked about the youth's back. She stared into his face, waiting for him to come, wondering what he would say or do. She collected such reactions as other girls collected wrist charms. Yet for Melissa it was more than souvenir-hunting, or even clinical curiosity. These were fragile moments of power. Of being in charge of, if not her own life, someone else's. She felt wanted, even essential in something so essential to them. And not to her.

"Hey, Rod, hurry up," one of the voyeurs said.

"Get it off already." The attention span of undergraduates was not measurable.

The door opened. Dave Turrell stood at the threshold for several moments, looking over the scene. His expression showed nothing. As he entered the room, though, a remarkable thing happened. One by one the students seemed to vanish, melted away like the morning mists before the warmth of a new day. One minute they were there, the next—as in a dream—they seemed to dematerialize, the last being the fraternity brother on top of Melissa. He too, drifted off, leaving Melissa's lovely bare legs a parenthesis embracing a void . . .

In the soft glow of the candlelight, memory, nostalgia took over. She herself was vague, harmless. Innocent . . .

"Care to dance, Melissa?" Dave said, holding out his hand.

"Oh, yes, thank you," she said, rising and brushing out the creases in her taffeta. The rustle of it reminded Dave of his beloved grandmother. His father jokingly used to say she needed oiling . . . For a while they danced the Stroll and the Twist. After some refreshments they went out to the porch. She sat on one of the old wicker chairs. He sat before her on the porch railing, a rakish pose with one foot on the floor sustaining his balance. It was quite dark, the glow of their cigarettes stronger than the June bugs' cold illumination. The music inside was playing "Sherry" and he tapped his foot to the beat. Neither of them spoke. Neither had to. It was idyllic and they were at ease with each other.

"David," she said softly after a while, "I could suck you off."

"No, thank you, Melissa."

Her cigarette glowed, and for a moment her pretty face was faintly lit.

"Thank you for inviting me, David. To the dance, I mean."

"Enjoying?"

"Oh, it's been neat."

"Y'know Tau Sig," he said nonchalantly. Henri Jourdan couldn't have been more debonair.

"You were wonderful, Dave. At the game today, I mean."

"My coverage could have been better, I thought."

"Twenty-seven. You were the only one I watched. Twenty-seven," she said.

"I've had my eye on you too," he said.

"Dave, you didn't!"

"You're an English major. Elizabethan lit."

Her surprise and pleasure were genuine. "How did you know?" His shrug suggested mysterious sources. His coolness could have been Jimmy Dean's. Her smile, even in the gloom, seemed radiant. Her cigarette, flipped over the porch balustrade, was a shooting star's parabola. "David, are you sure?" she asked.

"What?"

"The way I do it—they say... I heard it described like you feel the top of your scalp's torn off."

"You won't feel let down if I say no."

"Not at all."

"Thank you, nevertheless." . . .

Olivia, of course, became Melissa Wainwright for Dave, he seeing her through the distortion of a romantic dream. And as a youthful ideal he endowed her with imagined virtues. Glossing over her sexuality wasn't charitable forgiveness. It was a double vision allowing reality and fantasy to exist together. Such was the magic of Olivia—the power to understand her subject's needs, then to insinuate herself and her powers within them. Her triumph—and poison—was their surrender.

But Dave Turrell was a new experience for her, an adventure she didn't come away from unscathed. The sexual odysseys she had undergone with other men had been degraded, bestial. Position, rank or professed moral rectitude had nothing to do with what she could dredge up from the depths of her subjects' psyches. She was as nonjudgmental and cooperative as the most expert and expensive whore. What was almost extraordinary about her—her magic, in fact—was that she didn't have to be prompted. Whatever the esoteric needs, she *knew*. She knew and performed like a harlot of the ages, so that both she and her partner came away from their coupling with appetites appeased, and above all—free of guilt.

With Dave Turrell, it was different. For the first time different in that she had been elevated to some strangely exalted position. Being regarded as beautiful and desirable was nothing unusual for her. It was being endowed with a virtue that confused her, and every effort to drag him down into familiar territory proved futile. He was sincere.

It threw her life into confusion. She found herself trapped in a fantasy she never believed existed. She knew its perils, that she was beclouding her role, that there could even be a reckoning for it. Looking back, she realized she had felt that same confusion at her father's grave. If she was what she was, why had she felt grief? That was a human emotion, as this one was. Was this some vestige of humanity? She didn't altogether belong to the Darkness?

Father Jan Martenius sat in his windowless office contemplating the shelves of material lining the wall. Each paper, each document, was another testimonial of faith, an appeal for confirmation. Thousands upon thousands of them. An accumulation of decades of hopes in a miracle, hope most desperate. He thought of the form letter he would in some cases send out. A tactfully written message, never stripping hope away, because that would leave only despair. Yet there was always the reality he had to deal with. Procrastination became a fine art with him, his Vaticanese way of demurring, never until at the very last suggesting the claim was groundless; even then holding out the possibility of a further review at some future date. The incident with Bishop Strassoni in the Vatican gardens was a test of his own faith. He had to remind himself, as he had done before, that the prelate was a man invested with human frailty. The Monsignor Aiello was another. The few cardinals he observed were no less flawed, and he had no doubt the higher he went in the hierarchy, he would find the same or other weaknesses and deficiencies. But so what? Difficult as it was, frustrating as it could be—at times he literally had to force himself to consider what it was *really* all about... the grand purpose at the very top, beyond the institution itself. That essence of the Church. Christ in His pureness and perfection—unrefined and undefined by His pastors. He was reminded of it by the simplicity of faith in the letters he received. He saw it in the faces of the pilgrims in St. Peter's Basilica. In the black marble effigy of the saint, the centuries of fervent prayers and appeals, its toe worn away by touches and kisses. How could one give up on such an institution, such a receptacle for so much love and faith.

He worried about his friend Dave Turrell. He worried he would do something rash, precipitate. Between his chores, he tried in vain for several days to reach Dave at the Hotel Caprice. Concerned, he visited the hotel.

"The signor hasn't been in his room for three days," the desk clerk said.

"Any phone messages?" Jan Martenius said.

"A few calls from Israel. A woman there. She too asks for the American signor. Before he disappeared, they spoke. She too is worried now."

The priest was glad the desk clerk was summoned by a tourist demanding to know why the bank a few doors away had cashed his traveler's checks at a better rate than the hotel. The French tourist was getting nasty, making insinuations about the rapaciousness of Italian hotelkeepers. The clerk somehow managed to keep his temper in check. He returned to Jan Martenius who had been glad of the interruption. He had written his office phone number on a slip of paper.

"If you hear from Signor Turrell, please call me at once," he said.

"Padre—"

"Yes?"

"The room is needed. The bill has not been paid. Another day and—"

Jan Martenius didn't allow the man to continue. He had no money with him now, but he promised he would come that evening with enough to pay the bill.

"Very good, padre."

Walking toward the palazzo a few blocks away, he felt a strange apprehension. He was aware that a strain of superstition—a fear of the unknown— was a human endowment and condition, however much denied. He was no exception. Preoccupation with the Princess Olivia had built her into a larger-than-life image. It was late afternoon; the streets were almost literally congealed with noisy auto traffic. How difficult to believe, he thought, a devil's handmaiden living just a short distance away. It was an anachronism—the stuff of nightmares and medieval tales.

"I'm looking for a Signor Turrell, an American," he said to the dour gatekeeper, who recalled the priest from his previous visit. "I understand he's here. Visiting."

The gatekeeper shrugged and went into his gatehouse to telephone. The idea of sprinting through to the palazzo occurred to Jan. Let the fellow come after him, he thought. He could handle it; however, he discarded the notion with a certain self-disgust. His impulsiveness was at it again. As if it hadn't put him into enough hot water most of his life. Now at least, he urged himself, be reasonable. Use your head, not that damned, clumsy body better suited to a peasant or an ironworker.

The gatekeeper reappeared. "La Rocca," he muttered in his most surly tone.

"What's that?" Jan said, alarmed. The name of the village was repeated. "What does it mean?"

"How do I know what it means? It's the place in the Abruzzi."

"You mentioned the name I gave you?"

"Turrell! Turrell! I'm not some fool, padre. This is my business."

"Yes. Yes, of course," Jan Martenius said, adding, "May I ask whom you spoke to?"

"Someone in the house, who else?"

"The princess?"

The gatekeeper fixed black suspicious eyes upon the priest as if the latter had uttered an unspeakable blasphemy. He didn't even deign to reply.

"Could I have your permission to use your telephone?" Jan asked with the respect he thought might be helpful. Instead, he was directed across to the hotel.

"They have many telephones there," the gatekeeper said.

The *autostrada* west of the city rivaled the German *autobahns* in every way. It was a marvel of the engineering at which the Italians had excelled since the time of Caesar. The route cut through the country, never faltering or deferring to any natural obstacle until it ended in Pescara on the Adriatic. Ingeniously lit, ventilated tunnels cut through the very hearts of mountains rather than bend to their contours. Martenius had little trouble procuring a vehicle from the Vatican pool, but it was evening by the time he started the journey. He drove fast. Before long, though, he had a problem that grew disproportionately... Fatigue overcame him; more than anything else, he wanted to sleep. All the factors that should have made the two-hour journey fast, easy, safe and comfortable somehow joined to become a nightmare. The smoothness of the road, the lights regularly spaced on the road and in the tunnels, the gentle banking to accommodate the high speed: they had a hypnotic effect, lulling him into the sleep he fought against.

He let the windows down so the blast of air would chill him. He turned up the radio to full volume. Bologna was leading a Yugoslavian soccer team two to one. The very roaring of the partisan crowd became for him like the stormy sea off Zandvoort, where his parents had a cottage. The warmth of the bed, the thickness of the great dike a few hundred yards away, his father's snoring in the next room... how secure he had felt. What a kind, good world it was, that children's world... His eyes ached with his effort to keep them open. He would stop at the next service stop. A cup of coffee, perhaps a little nap. But no! Just a while longer. He would make it. Popoli was just ahead. La Rocca could only be a little further. He turned off the radio, which had almost betrayed him. He sang. It was a song he recalled from those old days. He sang as loud as he could.

The blinking lights cautioned: CONSTRUCTION AHEAD—SLOW. Instinctively he lightened the pressure on the accelerator. Odd, he at first thought without any great alarm. The car didn't seem to slow. He took his foot completely off the pedal. Not only did the car not slow, it actually seemed to be going faster. He glanced at the speedometer. The needle quavered at 130 kilometers—but it was *climbing*—133, 135. He had to swerve to a slower lane to pass traffic in the inner fast lane. He could only glance quickly at the speedometer, but he didn't need to realize he was going still faster—143 kilometers an hour! He was mystified . . . he knew the car was in gear and he wasn't on a down slope. Both hands gripped the steering wheel, the song he had been singing was forgotten. The throttle might be stuck. He jammed his foot down—once—twice—no effect. Braking had even less, and here he knew he had to be careful that the brakes not lock. The lights on either side of the expressway were speeding like fence pickets, though he was only peripherally aware of them. With the thought that his situation could be more than mechanical, he felt his heart race. He raised his view of the road to a further point. His lips were moving rapidly in a silent "Our Father . . ." He flashed memories . . . bits and snatches irrelevant to the moment and each other. Far ahead a huge shadow loomed. A darkness darker than the sky. Coming closer, he realized it was a mountain. The tunnel cutting through it was a sickly green maw. Signs were no longer readable. Everything was blinking, flashing lights. Blasting his horn to warn slower traffic to make way for him, he shot into the tunnel. As he emerged from the other side he had an uneasy sense that a part of the mountain had come away and was flying along just above him. It was no more than a vaguely outlined shadow that attached itself to the car, yet both flew on as one.

Seconds, minutes lost their perspective. They were no more than the lights on either side. His universe was himself and his uninvited escort overhead. Together they plunged ahead.

A constellation of lights of a work crew preparing an off-ramp appeared in the distance. He didn't think of it as a particular hazard until he felt the steering wheel becoming suddenly rigid. It no longer responded to his touch. It had *frozen*.

And he knew—knew with the insight sometimes given to those in their last moments. He knew that even as he was no longer in control of his car, he no longer had control of his life. It was in other hands. He reached to his chest and his fingers closed over the crucifix there. He peered straight ahead, fixing his gaze on the island of lights. The expressway curved away from it, but he knew even before it happened that he would be leaving it—that he would continue on in a straight line. On into infinity.

The short distance was devoured in an instant. The car was lofted through barricades and sailed into the air. Clusters of lights flashed and sputtered with sparks and broken circuits. A cement truck with a revolving drum loomed ahead. The arc of the airborne car was graceful. At the end of the arc was the cement truck. The crash of glass and metal melded into one sound. Car and truck fused.

A chute from the truck disengaged, and the great drum, still revolving, spewed out a torrent of cement engulfing the unrecognizable remains of the small car.

Traffic had stopped on the expressway shoulder. Flares were lit, and people—including the work crew—hurried to the wreckage. They stood silent. Cement, still oozing, had encased the remains of the car. Someone pointed. An arm protruded through the congealing mass. In its hands was a crucifix.

CHAPTER EIGHTEEN

At that moment five old Jews were groping their way on a mountain road overlooking the Hula Valley in north Israel. It was night and they had left their ocher-colored houses of Safed that seemed to jut from the mountains. It had been called a Jewish Shangri-La because of its geography as well as its mystic tradition.

"Careful," their leader called back. "Hold on to each other." The leader was Hillel Gorin, and he felt responsible. "Just a little more," he promised.

It was a muddy, rutted utility road cutting through a citrus grove. The night was moonless. There were five, including Hillel Gorin. He was dressed in a heavy woolen yellow sweater, a white and gold yarmulke and, wondrously, powder blue jogging shoes. His companions wore the traditional broad-brimmed beaver hats, from which their curled forelocks fell; and long, black, shiny alpaca coats. They appeared patriarchs out of a Chagall shtetl who belonged behind their books or in their beds rather than on such an expedition.

"We're crazy," someone in the dark called out between a spasm of coughing. Others, too, were grumbling and complaining. But their leader was too busy searching for the cutoff among the trees to hear. How different it was in the daytime, he was thinking. He had placed a white stone marker on the road. He was so disoriented he wasn't certain whether it had been passed in the darkness.

They stumbled on, clutching at one another for support. Electric torches—even a candle—had been forbidden, out of fear that the jeep patrol might come down on them. Not that they could ever be mistaken for terrorist infiltrators, but they would have been brought in and reprimanded. By their children—and their children's children— they would have been told that old men shouldn't be out at night.

Discomfort, even physical terror, meant little to them. They had experienced the worst of that. Who could do worse? It was a spiritual fear that gripped them . . . at some point during this night they would say awesome words, risking that unspeakable things could happen . . .

For a while the only sound was their labored breathing, that and the incessant rasp of the crickets. A bullfrog was answered somewhere by another. One of the group stopped abruptly. Low voices urged him on, but the bearded old man was adamant. Shifting his small package to another arm, he said, "No, I won't. It's *forbidden*."

Someone called Evon's name, and Evon, handing his own package to another man, came back. The stubborn one was identified. "What is it, Schmuel?" Evon said.

"I go no further. It's forbidden."

"I promise you five minutes more at the most."

"It is forbidden," Schmuel repeated.

"Where? Where is it forbidden?" Gorin demanded. A silence followed, and the others gathered about. Several days before, Hillel Gorin, their spiritual leader, had persuaded them in the synagogue to help protect his daughter, who was about to go on a sacred mission. He answered their arguments, prevailed over their fears—for the time. But the night—the circumstances—the approaching confrontation—coming all together made it seem all very different. They couldn't admit they had lost their courage. They told themselves they had been betrayed by Gorin and his "golden tongue." One of them had later said, "His daughter wants an *aruv*? Let her have an *aruv*, but without the prohibited ritual. No one needs that. The law—even in the Zohar—it says only in the direst need should it be considered. Even then—"

Schmuel now said, "How can you say where it's forbidden? Everywhere!"

"Where it is forbidden to fight the terrible *Samael*? It is our *duty*."

"Are we maggidim?"

"If we are chosen to be maggidim," Hillel Gorin said, "so be it." In the darkness he explained to his followers that as Moses, the true prophet, had oneness with the Absolute at all times, needing neither angels nor intermediaries, they themselves could attain the highest level of *devuketh*, occurring at the fifth stage of the soul. "It's called *yechidah*," he reminded them . . . "the perfect union with the Absolute." He quoted Maimonides, saying for the moment they would become superhuman. "We'll be earth-dwelling angels to fight His eternal battle against the demons of hell." Silence fell over the group. "Come," he said gently, smiling at his own solemnity, "A little longer, I promise."

The white stone was where he had left it, and he led the way off the road into the citrus grove. Following a line of trees, they walked single file for about a hundred meters. The night air was dense with the perfume of oranges and lemons, the fruit vaguely luminous in the dark. They came to a small clearing. The earth was packed hard, and several large stones were scattered about the periphery. What made it ideal for their purpose were the thick-foliaged trees, which like a massive wall shut them off from all but the square of starless sky overhead.

The packages were opened on the stones, and their contents spread out. The heavy white prayer shawls with their fringes and blue stripes were put aside for the moment. Hillel Gorin distributed thick white candles, which he ordered placed in a precise geometrical arrangement, describing a tetragram symbolizing the four Hebrew letters transliterated WHWH, forming the biblical proper name of God. Other candles were placed in a small area at the center. The men at this point took up their tallithim, kissed the fringes, said the appropriate prayer and enshrouded themselves. As he did so each man recalled the Baal Shem Tov, which taught them that to become one with prayer was becoming one with God. The litany was chanted while each took his place before a lighted candle. They were a congregation, and yet in a larger sense they were not. Each man went about losing all sense of his own self, pushing away extraneous thoughts. As practitioners of Kabbala they were accustomed to these meditative practices in their reach for exalted states of consciousness. At one point Hillel Gorin drew out from a draw-stringed pouch of goatskin the red skein of wool given him by Shula. Gently, almost reverently, he placed it in the center of the inner square of candles, precisely equidistant from each.

Their prayers and *gilgulim*, led by their leader, grew louder. Their bowing of the upper body grew more rapid. And as their sense of self vanished, their egos annihilated, their inner selves soared, their vision broke barriers, and with it their human fears and terrors fell away. And even as they did so, they passed through the ranks of angelic hosts, entering that divine state of Nothingness. They were well into their journey. They stood at that peak of spiritual love, journey's end, where human speech dared not intrude. They were at once man and God in His cosmic reflection, the anthropomorphic reflection of the Absolute. The experience buffeted the bodies of these old men, but not their strong spirits. All but Hillel Gorin lay prostrate on the ground, their talliths over their heads. The candles somehow remained lit, and between the flickering light and now flashes of lightning, Hillel Gorin stood erect, his face lifted upward in his ecstasy. His hands were held high, his fingers separated in the manner of the high priest. His voice cried out the words of the ancient Merkabah hymn expressing the ineffable experience of "seeing" God:

O wreathed in splendor, crowned with crowns,
O chorister of Him on high,
Extol the Lord enthroned in flames
For in the presence of the Presence,
In the inmost glory
Of the inmost chambers
You set up your posts.
Your names He distinguished from His servants' name,
The flame surrounds, a leaping fire,
Around Ḥim burning, glowing coals.

His words were drowned. The *aruv* among the candles became a focal point. God had been revealed. A blinding revelation. Then it all receded. They had, they were convinced, been in the radiance of God's presence—the *Shekhinah*. As all again became quiet, still, Hillel Gorin raised himself to his full height. As he reached up his arms, the prayer shawl fell away from his head, and he chanted the ancient words of praise:

Melech avir, melech adir, melech adon,
Melech baruch, melech bachur, melech baruk,

Melech gadol, melech gibor, melech gaavah . . .

through to its alphabetical end of rejoicing.

Five old Jews now walked the muddy, rutted road back to Safed. It was early morning, and the mists still clung to the ground. The five old men walked slowly. Silently. Carrying small packages under their arms. The workers of the kibbutz, young men and women with bronzed faces and arms, on their way to their work in the fields and grove, greeted the old men with laughs and good-natured jokes. The old men did not respond. How could these young people know these old men were certain they had just "seen" God?

CHAPTER NINETEEN

He stood at the threshold to Olivia's sitting room, peering in at a stylized replay of his life two decades past.

"Come in, Signor Turrell," her voice said. It was a voice out of context with what he was witnessing, certainly not the voice of Melissa Wainwright. And at that moment the fragile illusion began to dissipate like a desert mirage with the cool of evening. "Come in, please," she said again warmly. And as he did, the veranda of the Tau Sig house and its two occupants returned to memory.

In hesitantly stepping forward Dave instantly severed himself from past, present and whatever conventions by which he knew himself. His personality fractured into a thousand fragments, leaving another with no apparent relationship to what it had replaced. Physically he seemed no different; but the difference in other respects was profound.

She was sitting at her desk, half turned around. The soft light from the silk-shaded desk lamp whose base was a square Chinese wine vessel of the Shang dynasty made her appear even more beautiful than he had remembered her.

"A high mass for one's father isn't the ideal place for a man and a woman to meet." As she rose to her feet the glints of fire in her red hair played against the green patina of the centuries-old lamp base. His head swam with her beauty. He could think of nothing he wanted to say. It was enough to be just in that presence, bathed in that smile, aware of her as she was of him. "So here we are," she continued, reaching out her hand, which he took. "Finally."

"Finally," he repeated dully.

"Yes." She laughed lightly. "You were in the rain. You're wet."

He looked down at his dripping things and seemed almost surprised. "Nothing." He shrugged.

Her hands moved and in a moment he was at least out of the sodden trench coat.

He remembered her. He even remembered there was something unpleasant involved with her. His thoughts were giving him trouble. What was it? What was it he had come to do? It was as if he had misplaced an idea he knew was important, and it bothered him, not remembering. He felt so damned stupid. Something peculiar was going on. What?

"Won't you sit down?" she said, that smile

insistent, provocative.

"Were you expecting me?" he said for some idiotic reason he couldn't comprehend.

"Of course," she said. "Wasn't this inevitable? Sooner or later?"

"I suppose..."

"You suppose."

Was he being mocked? "You wanted me to come—"

"Yes, David," she said quietly.

And at that moment he knew—impossible as it seemed—that she had willed him to come, and *that* was why he was here.

"Well?" she said. "What does it look like?"

It was a bizarre posture, yet somehow she made it appear graceful. Olivia, nude, was standing atop the foot of the bed. The rumpled satin sheets made it seem as if she were rooted in the free flowing base of a Degas sculpture. Her intent was to expose to Dave the trident birthmark in order to learn what it meant to him.

From his pillows, he studied the mark for several moments without a comment or any significant change in his apathetic expression. "Well, David?" she said impatiently.

"Giselle forgot her tutu," he said indifferently. She laughed and fell to her knees astride him. She leaned down to him, her face still aglow from their lovemaking just a few moments earlier.

"Your *carissima*'s flawed," she said. "I wanted you to see."

"And I'm perfect, of course."

She laughed again. Watching him closely, she said, "Did the mark suggest anything? Anything you remember?"

"Like what?"

"I don't know. A trident, I've been told. It does resemble a trident." The word had no apparent effect. There were only the subtle changes her spell invariably brought upon her victims. A certain vagueness associated with the dissolution of will and character. The vacuity of the bewitched. A pliant softness.

She reached for his hand and brought it to her breast. She peered into his eyes as his thumb gently moved to and fro over a nipple. He watched its hardening as he would have the newest wonder of the world.

"The trident, David," she said softly again.

"I want you," he said rather petulantly.

"David—"

"Kiss me."

"No."

"Who cares about a trident!" He seemed more like a spoiled child denied a whim.

"It's supposed to mean terrible things," she said.

"Ah, sure," he said, pulling her down toward him.

Her face was just above his. "Some even say it's the devil's mark."

"Yeah."

She repeated it slowly. "The devil," she said. "I belong to him."

"You're a guinea cockteaser," he told her, grinning, "and you belong to me, not him . . ."

Her half smile fell away. In a quick motion she was off him. Off the bed. She slipped into a negligee, tossed her mane of hair so that it fell almost to her waist; then stepping across the room, she threw back the heavy drapes, flooding the room with the light of a sunny morning. Lighting a cigarette, she stood peering down through the opened windows to the gardens. Once, just this way, she had stood in front of her father's grave, seeing down through the earth. Her vision now went to what was below the gardens, and she smiled at still another secret.

"Olivia . . . I'm sorry."

"You're vulgar. A pig," she said without turning.

"Hey, principessa," he said mocking. "Your *Grace* . . ."

Laughing softly, she tossed her cigarette down to the white gravel below; then, turning, slipped across the room as lightly as one of the dust motes in the shaft of morning light. Flicking away the sheet over him, her body came to his. It was as bestial as it was aesthetic, communal as solitary. . . .

They lay side by side, spent. "Devil," he breathed. "I believe it."

She turned to him. He was staring up at the bed's damask canopy. "How do you mean that?" she said.

"You destroy—devastate—wipe me out," he said. "I won't argue with you either."

"About what?"

"Your relations with Old Nick."

"So long as you're happy, David."

"Happy?"

"Aren't you?"

"How would I know? I can't grab hold of anything . . . who—what I am . . . I feel batty . . ."

"What are you talking about?"

"I don't know, forget it."

She spoke now with a new voice. It had a far-off, almost distant quality. He listened and learned what he never knew about himself, accepting it without challenge, or questioning how she knew these things. In some disturbing way the conviction grew in him that it was he himself speaking. Saying what he knew to be true. She was putting her finger on secrets he'd never dealt with. They'd been too upsetting . . .

"Success," she was saying, "frightens you, doesn't it, David? It's come too easily? Perhaps you don't even want it? Hasn't the possibility occurred to you?"

The truth . . . victory, success, achievement, what other men broke their asses for—held no special pleasure—no joy for him. He had what someone once called "the right stuff," but he'd never been the killer, the classic American hero as D.H. Lawrence had put it . . . He'd backed away from the agency vice-presidency. Earlier—since high school days—it had been pretty much the same. Honors came easily and envied by those who tried so hard and couldn't cut it. During the war, the guilt about it took refuge in modesty, so that an ass-chewin' captain had to say, "Look, boy, don't give me no humble-pie act. You done good, damn good. Helps the old body count..."

Aware of his thoughts, she said, "You know I'm the one victory you can never have. You do know that, don't you, David?"

She came later into his dressing room with its three tall mirrors that angled him from every side. He stood looking at himself in a new suit, part of the wardrobe made up for him by Olivia. He was preoccupied with himself, as he was supposed to be. Narcissus in Gucci loafers. Olivia stood back, regarding him for several moments until he caught her reflection. He grinned.

"Lovely, David. Just lovely." She moved closer. "Who is a Shula Gorin?"

"The crotch," he said. "It's a little tight—"

"Shula Gorin, David. Who is she?" The name didn't register. "Someone by that name," Olivia continued, "came to the gate and asked about you. Of course she was turned away."

The dome of St. Peter's loomed faintly spectral as it shimmered in the city's haze over the terra cotta roofs. Below traffic pirouetted about the piazza fountain, darting in and out from the narrow streets feeding into the square. Silvano d'Alessandro, formerly a building contractor but now an important Christian Democrat member of the government was having one of his frequent cocktail parties. It was a small relaxed affair on his penthouse terrace; the guests were carefully selected for their influence and usefulness. Most knew each other, and standing about drink in hand, observed a social and political pecking order in a graceful gavotte. Today, however, the main topic of discussion was Rome's sudden importance as the site of a summit conference between the United States and the Soviet Union that had been engineered by the pope himself, heading off what appeared to be a particularly dangerous international crisis. Even at this moment the complicated logistics of the meeting were being arranged before the arrival of the principals.

A group of women, mainly wives of the guests, less interested in the politics of the world, found an exciting diversion in Dave. These lovely and elegant women had him surrounded. He aroused their curiosity, not to mention other emotions. He was the present interest of the Principessa Olivia, whom they enviously regarded as the arch-whore. What could this American have that could satisfy *that* notorious appetite?

"Ah, Signor Turrell! You are a *giornalista*—"

"Surely you know Sergio—"

"Sergio Scarpa."

"Annamaria Cavani is the United Nations correspondent."

"Ah, but you must agree with Oriana Fallacci, who says—"

He stood leaning casually against a geranium planter that once had been the marble sarcophagus of an ancient Roman gentleman. His smile fended off questions that didn't expect replies. He looked into dark eyes heavy with their languorous hungers, their thoughts. He had come with Olivia. They knew who he was, that was clear. And he was enjoying the sensual luxury of his new cashmere jacket. The attentions he drew were an ego trip, heady as their expensive perfumes.

Inside the oak-paneled study with its carefully lit Tintoretto, the attention of a more serious group was fixed upon Olivia, sitting aloof in a suede leather chair. She watched with total absorption as the ash of her cigarette grew, then fell on to the almost priceless Souruk carpet. There was Silvano d'Alessandro, along with three other members of the government, two of them like himself, ministers. The most undistinguished of the group was Arnoldo Luvera, a mere salaried foreign office career man. Olivia was being urged to hostess a dinner to be followed by a reception at her palazzo capping the summit conference; and up to now the idea didn't seem particularly attractive to her.

"The president of the United States and the premier of the Soviet Union will be your guests," the minister of foreign affairs explained, his tone suggesting it was a social coup that any one of their own wives would have envied.

"Why me?" Olivia said demurely. "Why do I deserve this honor?"

Silvano d'Alessandro pointed out that other palazzi had been considered. Larger, more famous ones. "But yours," he said as if it were an offering, "was in everyone's mind as first choice."

"The Borghese, the Villa Wolkonsky, the Colonna—" she mused aloud.

The thin, swarthy foreign office man in the dark suit with slightly shiny elbows cleared his throat noisily. Eyes turned to him. Up to now Arnoldo Luvera had said nothing. As the only professional in the group he had the knack of remaining inconspicuous if not invisible in any gathering of his superiors.

"Yes, Signor Luvera?" a minister said in a tone appropriate for an underling civil servant.

"To answer Her Grace's question," came the reply, careful that it be directed at his superior. "Perhaps it is less the palazzo than who resides in it."

The anxiety in the room suddenly lifted. There were smiles. Nothing like a damned professional! someone thought. Gloomy suspense was replaced by hope.

"Exactly!" another minister enthusiastically cried with Gallic passion. He turned to Olivia. "The man has said it, Olivia."

"So why didn't you, Franco?" she said, then turning to Arnoldo Luvera, added pleasantly, "We are in an army with too many generals, Signor Luvera, even if you are too kind."

She remembered his name! And the compliment! The recognition by the others! Inwardly he sang. Soared. He visualized the nagging of his wife Mafalda cut off as the new dining room set was delivered; their daughter Flavia's teeth would be straightened so she would look less like a werewolf. This would be just the immediate fallout. Arnoldo Luvera saw for himself a new day rising over the horizon.

Silvano d'Alessandro crossed to Olivia on feet small for a man his size. One had the impression he might topple over at any moment, yet he was surprisingly agile, even graceful.

"So it's settled, eh, Olivia?" he said, reaching for her hand. "You as hostess. Rome will be proud."

"Bullshit, Silvano," she replied, and everyone, even Luvera, laughed.

Driving home with Dave beside her slouched down in the seat of the open car, Olivia went through a mental checklist of what would be required for the affair. The dinner would be for a select group, the reception to follow might involve hundreds. There was another problem, she realized; a most delicate one for what she had in mind. It was certain that security until the summit was over would reach huge proportions. She understood the terror of terrorism and the reaction politicians gave to it at times for their own purposes. In this case Rome, being what it was in the eyes of the world, a meeting between the heads of the two superpowers had to inspire grotesque scenarios for their respective security people. She was thinking now not so much of canapes—seating arrangements—other such details. She was ruminating on the surprise she was planning. The excitement was delicious. Even better than sex, she thought. Leave it to an Italian to do the spectacular. She wouldn't disappoint them. They wanted their leaders to come together? Very well, she'd see to it. They'd never be closer than in death.

Dave, watching the branches of the famous pines of Rome fly by over him, was thinking of the dark lady they had called marchesa. She had slipped him a card and told him to call.

"The palazzo will be a busy place, David," Olivia was saying.

How could he think of another woman, he thought. His balls ached even now. Yet somehow he was.

"We're to have a party," she continued. "You can say hello to your president."

Reaching over he took one of her hands from the wheel and drew it to his lap. She laughed at what she discovered there. "The president of the United States, David," she said.

"Make that red light," he muttered.

"The purpose of the summit is to avert a nuclear war."

"Hurry."

"Life and nuclear war are incompatible, the pope has said."

For some reason he was thinking of a penny arcade he knew as a child. Oak Beach on Martha's Vineyard, it was. A penny and you manipulated a tiny claw scoop. You grabbed a colored gum ball, if you were lucky, you had a bonus of a crackerjack toy.

"Mankind could become extinct," she said dreamily. It suddenly occurred to her as she was holding on to the bulge in his trousers, she was excited as he was. "David . . ." she said, "soon you'll know it was no accident."

"Accident?"

"Our meeting. Our coming together."

*   *   *

At the palazzo Olivia lost no time taking Dave by way of the kitchens into the cellars. He felt increasingly uneasy, and at times showed it. He had no interest in this grim place, saw no purpose in the excursion. Olivia, however, seemed too excited to even notice his discomfort. "Come along," she said sharply at one point as he lagged behind.

"You pick a strange time for a tour," he said.

"Be still and follow me."

Bare, low-wattage bulbs covered with grime cast shadows. Shapeless mounds of debris, piled up through the centuries, bristled with legs of chairs and other discarded furniture that had outlived their usefulness. The air became cool and dank with the musty cellar smell of old rot. A rat scampered before them, but Olivia didn't seem to mind. Once again she waited for him to catch up.

"You're not frightened, are you, David?"

"I'm crazy about rats and spiders."

Shortly they came to what appeared to be a wall of mortared stones. There seemed nowhere else to go. Indicating a heavy Biedermeier chest against the wall, she told him to move it aside.

"What are you staring at, David?" she said.

He shook his head. Her face, he noted, had an unnatural pallor, and her eyes had the sort of glow he'd seen in animals at night. The chest of drawers moved more easily than he'd expected, revealing a hatch of several sturdy boards that covered a wall opening. Olivia impatiently stepped forward to help him pull it aside. A cavernous darkness lay ahead. Without hesitation she stepped into it, calling for him to follow.

The sudden glare of an electric torch shone in his face, blinding him so that he had to turn away.

"Like most of Rome, the palazzo is built over ancient catacombs," she was saying. "You're in one now." She swung the light about and he could make out crude tunnels excavated from the brown raw earth. Columns of old bricks and stones gave support to the walls into which niches had been carved. Other passages and chambers opened darkly on all sides.

"Come, David," she said, moving off. He stood motionless. "Will you *come?*" she called back more sharply, her voice echoing.

From the very first he had worried her. A boy—at times an idiot—had been wished on her. How could he be entrusted with the delicate mission that was now just beginning to unfold? How could this have been arranged? Permitted? For the first and perhaps the only time in her life she strongly questioned the judgment of the intelligence that had led her this far. True, she was at first charmed by him. There was not only his unquestioned good looks, there were his virtues and that seemingly incorruptible nobility that she had enjoyed stripping away. He had been gutted like a fish in the market. Slash—slash—and the complaisant carcass was all that remained of what had been that paragon of goodness. The question that now concerned her was, had it been overdone? Was he up to what lay ahead?

The tunnel, so low it required him to stoop at times, opened into a wider place. He had followed the beam of light in Olivia's hand as it moved ahead of him. The footing was raw earth tamped down. Nothing had been said between them for several minutes. The light then stopped; angling downward, it fixed upon some dull white objects in a heap at one side. He came up to her and peered down.

He resisted what he somehow knew. There stirred in him vague memories of sun-bleached animal bones on a New Mexico desert.

"They're not early Christians, if that's what you're thinking," she said. "Look here," she added, shifting the beam of light upon a darker mound that he recognized as a heap of rusted, begrimed rifles, as well as other bits of military equipment to which clung shreds of coarse fabric of an indecipherable color.

"German," he muttered, recognizing the shapes of a pair of helmets.

"There are more interesting souvenirs," she said, moving off. Carefully skirting the grisly accumulation, he followed. He had to stoop low in order to enter still another chamber.

A propane lantern that Olivia had lit blinded him for a moment. The harsh light revealed a puzzling litter. Close by was a crude wooden bench. An array of tools and wiring suggested whoever had worked there had been interrupted.

"David, here—" she called from across the chamber.

He saw what appeared a heavily reinforced rack of wooden beams. Cradled upon it were two rows of bulky metal objects of a dull gray color. His first impression was they were immense kegs of wine.

Approaching closer, he moved his hand over the smooth metal surfaces. Thoughts of wine kegs fled. In the shadows at the rear were the symmetrical fins, in front the nose cones with their sensitive fuses.

"Aerial bombs," he said incredulously.

"Eight in all," she replied. "One would set off the others, am I right, David?"

"I—I don't know."

"You *do* know," she scolded.

He examined them closer. Wires led to a plate that had been removed from the side of a missile in the rack's center. "These are old," he said without looking up.

"Forty years, more or less."

He faced her. He explained the explosive charge inside—either liquid or solid—could be unstable.

"They'll work, be assured of that," she said.

"I mean they could go off when you don't want them to." He shook his head in disbelief. "You've been living above this... you knew they were there."

"I knew, David. Only I knew. And now you know."

"All these years," he said in wonder, recalling the skeletons outside.

"Relics of the German occupation of Rome." She went on to explain that the German S.S. intelligence had somehow learned that the palazzo was to become the headquarters of General Mark Clark and his Fifth American Army command after they had evacuated. Despite the fact that Rome had been declared an open city, someone had consid-

253

ered it too good an opportunity to be missed to strike a telling blow at the Allied leadership. Von Kesselring in Berlin had been informed of the plan, and more because he felt his authority had been challenged than for any affection for the Americans, he struck against the plot with his own Abwehr. The plan along with those who had prepared it, died; and the secret, since it served no one to recall it, was forgotten. "These have just been waiting, David. Waiting for us. For this occasion."

"I don't understand," he said. "Why? What can you possibly—"

Olivia let him get no further. She spoke of the summit meeting soon to happen. This was to be followed by the affair at the palazzo at which she was to play hostess. She spoke of the distinguished guests. Feeling like he was in some sort of trance, he listened as her plan unfolded. How at the proper moment, at the height of the festivities, the toasts to peace and good will, the congratulations—how it would all be shattered in one fiery blast. "Can you see it, David? *Can you?*"

"Yes," he said quietly, eyes staring.

He could only wonder how it could be that he was feeling no shock. Only a confusion. A puzzlement.

"Why?"

As though lecturing a schoolboy, she patiently explained how each side—the Russians and the Americans—would at once accuse the other. "The meeting itself was arranged out of necessity. You can be sure distrust and suspicion was there from the start. Then this. It's a terrorist act to be sure, but as in all terrorist acts the consequences are what count." She put her hand on the aerial bomb meant to be the detonator. "As this one will set off the others, so what we do will set the world on fire."

She spoke of silos opening like blossoming flowers. Oceans spitting out missiles. "No sooner will it begin, David, than it will be over. You've seen tropic twilights. One moment the sun is there, the next it's darkness."

Again he had the terrible sense that he was empty of feelings. Emotions. He visualized the events as she told of them, and yet he was feeling nothing. Olivia and he were one of a kind now.

CHAPTER TWENTY

The news of the summit conference in Rome sent a chill through Shula.

The trident and the woman who wore it were somehow involved, were her first thoughts. The purpose of the summit was to avert the latest world crisis—a last desperate hope. Olivia's purpose, she reasoned, was to create crisis. Having her in the vicinity of an infinitely delicate peace conference could only be an invitation to disaster.

Flying over the Mediterranean from Israel, she peered down to the rippled blue of the sea, wishing her thoughts were as serene. Trouble lay ahead, she was certain. What would come of an encounter with the Principessa Olivia was enough to concern her. She now had the added problem of the extra security she was certain blanketed the city in preparation for the conference. Her identity was surely known by the authorities and she would be quickly picked up.

She was caught between a rock and a hard place. She had defied Zev Cohen's orders; she was, in fact, deserting. But she had to take that risk, distasteful as it was to her. Later would come the excuses—the explanations; hopefully they would be accepted—if her mission was successful. If not, nothing mattered. Her first priority was to find Dave. After that—together—they might have a chance against the woman. The threat represented by the terrorists looking for her would be lessened, she knew, by the fact they would be driven underground by the heavy security, except possibly those willing to accept the higher risks of doing some mischief in order to wreck the conference. All in all, the journey to Rome represented many fearful possibilities.

The El Al 727 had hardly touched down at the Leonardo da Vinci Airport when her fears were confirmed. Police and military vehicles were out in force. In the terminal building she recognized the plainclothes agents outnumbering uniformed guards carrying automatic weapons at ready. She could readily pick out the former, even identifying their service: the S.I.D., the Ministry of Interior's secret service, as well as several members of DIGOS, the carabinieri's special bureau dealing with political crimes and intelligence operations which she considered as effective as any of their counterparts on the Continent. Once or twice she suspected several sharp-eyed loungers as American and Soviet agents.

I'm a real smart-ass, she speculated at one point,

if I think I'm to get through this.

She had taken the usual precautions of a change in appearance and a new passport, but these precautions seemed childishly transparent as she stood in the long line at passport control where the usual sharp-eyed agent was now backed up by an S.I.D. man who peered over his shoulder, checking each photo with the face of its owner. His bleak, suspicious eyes sought known extremists, or others he suspected as members of that international brotherhood. Only when the S.I.D. gave the word did the control officer bring his rubber stamp down upon a passport page.

It was almost her turn.

The long line grew impatient with the slow, deliberate processing. Just ahead of her was an obviously German couple complaining loudly in their own language about Italian inefficiency. She left the place in line and moved in ahead of the couple.

"Fräulein! Sie können sich nicht vordrängen!" the man objected.

"In your hat," Shula said quietly. *"Ich bin eine Americanerin,* and I'm in a hurry."

The woman joined with her husband, and in a few moments a furor broke out along the entire line, which was precisely what Shula hoped for. The police came from various parts of the terminal, and characteristically fueled the fracas. By now the passport control officer and the S.I.D. man were screaming at everyone from behind their glass partition. They made the mistake of closing the window, but this was only for a moment.

Another official joined the two and ordered the window reopened. Processing was now hurried, and in a few minutes Shula was climbing into a taxi.

With the summit still a week off, Rome was in a fever heat of preparation. As Shula had expected, security was a major preoccupation. It was as her cabdriver from the airport had said in his own Sicilian dialect that she couldn't understand: the city's tight as a nun's asshole. Not only was every police and intelligence agency of the host country dashing about "touching all bases" but the advance teams of the Americans and Soviets, with contempt for the Italians, went about following their own procedures. Motorcade routes were made secure. Rooftops and other vantage points for potential trouble were posted and watched. Even manhole covers along planned routes were welded shut. Teams fanned out over the city, sweeping up known extremists as well as others considered a risk. Every building where a social event or a meeting was to be held, or where the principals and their staffs were to be housed, was meticulously swept for "bugs," their staffs put through a clearance process.

She recognized Dave's battered, light suitcase with the broken zipper. It was in a small storeroom of the Hotel Caprice, and the assistant manager had agreed, after she had signed a waiver, to allow her to check. Although the desk clerk had given her a difficult time, the assistant manager recalled she had been a guest. Her story was a tale of unrequited love and abandonment. Her pregnancy was only delicately hinted at. She stooped to open the bag.

"No! Signorina!" the man warned, fearful of his responsibility. She had wanted to see if the weapon she had given Dave was there.

"He had my picture. My letters."

The man was adamant. Anyhow, she had learned what she came for. Dave had simply disappeared.

The Vatican was her next stop. At the admission office at the St. Anna Gate, she came up against the arrogant authority of a minor clerk. Scanning an indexed file, he looked up at her bleakly.

"No," he said. "No Padre Martenius."

In her inadequate Italian, she tried to make clear he worked in the College of Cardinals. "I'm certain of it," she said.

Making no secret of his resentment of the trouble she was causing him, he reached for a phone. After some unintelligible conversation, he replaced it and glowering at her for wasting his time, said, *"Nièntе! Non conosciuto!"* He then turned to another visitor.

"He works here! He does!" she shouted in exasperation.

Curious glances were turned toward her. She went to a window overlooking the inner square. Outside a pair of Swiss Guards stood at attention, their absurd uniforms belying their effectiveness. She knew very well that their halberds were purely ceremonial, maintaining a tradition. Modern automatic weapons were somewhere within easy reach. Despite this, she was tempted to risk dashing through. As if reading her thoughts, the clerk behind the counter called across the room, *"Vietato l'ingresso!"*

An angry retort was on her lips, but a soft voice beside her said, "Don't say it."

Father Michaels was a black. His smile was warm and friendly and she was grateful he had prevented her from doing the foolish.

"Addis Ababa used to be my parish before we became unfashionable," he said. "Before that, believe it or not, it was Bed-Stuy' in Brooklyn. In fact I was born there."

She found herself smiling. "Me too," she said.

"Of course," he said, not having to explain the chemistry of recognition.

"Borough Park," she said.

"I once worked in a car wash on Coney Island Avenue," he said, adding, "I learned more about human nature there than I did at St. John's. Now, what's your problem?"

She explained Father Jan Martenius was a friend. "I must see him. That idiot there says he doesn't work here. He does."

Father Michaels spoke for a while on the telephone then returned to her. What she saw in his face as he came toward her, alarmed her. She felt a familiar chill that had often served her. A premonition of disaster.

"What is it?" she said, as he came up to her.

"You said you knew Father Martenius."

Knew. The tense. "I know him," she said.

"The man is dead."

She stood staring, hardly listening as the sparse facts were given her.

"Was he alone in the car?" she asked.

"Apparently."

"Did anyone know where he was going?"

"A village in the Abruzzi was mentioned. It was on his request at the motor pool. La Rocca, yes."

La Rocca. She recalled it as the ancestral home of the Amontaldi di Donati family. Olivia's home. Where she was born. And Jan was going there.

"I'm sorry," the black priest was saying.

"Sorry?" she said blankly.

"Your friend. Father Martenius."

"Oh, yes. Thank you. Thank you very much, father."

Sitting in the taxi, she sought some logic in what was happening. Accident, the priest had said. Was anything accident, she wondered? She had the sense of everything moving at a faster pace. Gaining momentum. A pattern was shaping.

She directed the driver to drive slowly about the Palazzo Amontaldi di Donati. Twice the high walls were circuited, and she had a fair idea how impregnable they were even if there hadn't been a security net of police and military. Guards were posted on each corner and a brace of soldiers carrying automatic weapons were at the gate. She paid off the driver before the hotel across the street from the gate, and pretending she was a tourist, sauntered across to the gate.

"Is this a government building?" she asked innocently in her poor Italian.

"No," was the curt reply.

"Then why are you here? You and the others?"

His reply was an eloquent shrug. "Eh!"

"I don't understand," she said, flashing her prettiest smile.

At this point a sergeant came up and told her to move off. Another smile would be wasted, she knew.

The number Shula dialed was known only to Mossad members, and the cryptic message she left was to be delivered to someone called Walrus. An hour later, seated in a café opposite the Termini, she saw a denim-clad young man pull up in a Lambretta. As he padlocked the machine, he scrutinized the neighborhood with an expert eye. Entering the café he spotted Shula almost at once and made his way to her table with its view of the front door and all who entered through it. Before sitting he glanced to the rear to make sure there was a rear exit. A safe place, he decided, he knew Shula would select.

Ari Dubov, code-named Walrus by reason of his heavy mustache, was an Israeli sabra. He had been through two wars, the last as a tank commander. During the blockade of the Egyptian Third Army he had been badly burned. A long convalescence had turned his life around. He had been trained as a musician, a cellist; but the angers he had nurtured for what he considered a political betrayal by the United States and Great Britain in calling off the blockade, had burned out from him any further interest in Bach and Prokofiev. He subsequently had found purpose for his life in the

Mossad, where his courage and other qualities, sharpened by his anger toward the enemies ringing Israel, made him an invaluable operative.

The eyes in the ravaged face met her own with caution and unfriendliness, which held back the lie she was about to tell. She had prepared a tale to do with gaining entrance to the palazzo in order to pilfer documents having to do with P.L.O. arms suppliers. She meant to suggest it wasn't an assignment since Zev Cohen wanted her "on ice" for a while longer. She would have liked to offer it to Zev as a fait accompli—if Ari would help her get inside, that is. Nothing more.

Sitting opposite him, picking up on his hostile vibes, she held back. She was in trouble enough, with even a courtmartial somewhere in her future. To drag her friend Ari into her problems would be unfair. But why was he uptight, she wondered? Could it be he was still miffed because of the Via Veneto incident? It was true, she had involved the organization into her personal affairs.

Almost as if reading her thoughts, the man called Walrus said, "So? The same American?"

She nodded grimly. Her eyes returned to the Formica tabletop on which she had been describing circles with the bottom of her damp glass of amaretto.

"You want some kind of help," he continued. "You wouldn't call me otherwise."

She looked up, meeting his bleak stare. "I must get into the Palazzo Amontaldi di Donati," she said. "For some reason it's guarded. Heavily."

"For some reason!" His tone was frosty. Mocking.

"Yes."

"You don't know the reason."

"There's security everywhere."

"As heavy as at the palazzo?"

"What is it, Ari? What's going on?"

He could see nothing in her expression to suggest she was dissembling. "What if I told you an affair's to be held at the palazzo? Among the guests will be the president of the United States and the premier of the Soviet Union. If the pope himself shows up, I wouldn't be surprised. Despite what happened to him, he'll want to be there since much of it was his doing."

Her stare was incredulous. Somehow she had known it was something of this magnitude, and yet the confirmation left her stunned. It was so unreal to her, almost as it had been from the very start—a marriage of reality and mysticism. They had been kept separate—compartmentalized—in her mind. Now here they were come together— joining to tear the world asunder. Reality was now beating at her head as if it were a tightened drum. The leaders of the world's two greatest powers, increasingly paranoid in their feelings toward each other—fingers poised over their respective nuclear buttons—and they were to be under the same roof with that woman. The pieces of the puzzle had come together for her, and still it was almost too grotesque to accept. Both heads of state killed at what was supposed to be a peace conference. It had all been programmed . . . She recalled a saying of her father: "The history of man is written in riddles."

"Shula, what is it?" Ari was saying. She blinked. Her thoughts returned to him. "What is it?" he repeated.

"I—I didn't know of the affair," she said. He saw she was speaking the truth.

"What's it to do with the American you're chasing?"

Chasing! The word was a blow. Her fight against Olivia—the trident search—some might call it a noble cause, but she had never thought of it that way. It was just something that once she had committed herself to it, the importance was as natural as self-preservation, which, by extrapolation, it was.

How she would have liked to have shared the secret with Ari, but he was the ultimate realist, born and raised on a kibbutz. Being a tough pragmatist meant survival. Could he possibly deal with the almost fantasy notion of the trident? She knew his feelings toward her father and the old men like him. Pain-in-the-ass obstructionists with their unbending, uncompromising orthodoxy. Guardians of the Written Word! Arguing whether you have the right to defend yourself if an Arab wants to cut your throat on shabbat. What would he think, she wondered, if he knew of the *aruv* she carried in her pocket.

"So he's a goy," he went on. "He prefers a real princess to a Jewish one."

She started to rise to leave.

"Sit down," he said. Somehow she did. "Zev wants you back in Jerusalem," he said. So that's it, she thought. He knew. He knew all along. "It was an order," he went on.

She now understood his anger. He had a duty to obey Zev's order, and he had his feelings toward her. Involuntarily she reached her hand out and touched his. "Ari—"

"You wouldn't do this for your friend. For anyone," he said, almost gently.

"No."

"So it's something else."

She no longer hesitated. Adroitly she put the situation into an entirely different context. There was no mention of the trident or anything suggesting the supernatural . . . Dave Turrell, a newsman, had stumbled on a conspiracy—a plot to disturb the delicate nuclear stalemate through an act of terrorism. The trail led directly to the Principessa Olivia Amontaldi di Donati. "If I can check this out," she said, "I can expose the plot before the summit—"

"He's inside the palazzo."

"I believe so. It's what I want to find out."

"Let him come out."

"He would if he could," she said.

There was a pause. She could sense his sharp, well-trained mind sorting out these bizarre facts. Searching for the lie. She could follow how he was thinking. He knew what a woman in love was capable of, but she had deserted, disobeyed Zev, something Shula Gorin would never do. Not for any man.

"You love him?"

"Yes, Ari," she said. "But it has nothing to do with it. I just know if anything happens during the summit—anything to stop the process, the consequences could be too terrible . . ." She hesitated a moment . . . "I know what you're thinking."

"What am I thinking?"

"If it isn't Israel's problem, it's not your problem."

"So?"

"You're wrong. It's ours—it's everyone's problem."

CHAPTER TWENTY-ONE

Not once—even as a child—could Olivia ever recall questioning her fate, her mission. To ask, even if she knew there would be no answer, why she had been singled out for this role would have been, literally, out of the question. There was no protest . . . who would she protest to . . . ? In her unique case she was as deficient in will as she was in normal scruples. She was the perfect one for her task; letting herself be carried onward by an irresistible force she neither doubted nor questioned. A plan—a purpose—was at times vaguely defined; she sensed this, and it became increasingly easy for her to comply since it brought her incalculable rewards. Inexorably she had risen from a peasant family's sorry condition to her present place. It was Faustian in every respect except a choice had never been offered her. No bargain had been struck. She was a chosen one, just as Hillel Gorin had once called Dave chosen.

Shame, guilt, even compassion were nonexistent for her. She was an instrument. Her course was inexorable, its logic increasingly clear. She was unique—and this alone was a heady compensation.

Hostessing dinners, receptions, functions of any kind held no terrors for her. Her grace, flair and competence made them appear effortless. The forthcoming reception and dinner, however, was of another magnitude, requiring consultations with many ministries as well as foreign embassies. The logistics and the protocol were of incalculable complexity, requiring hours of her supervision, if only to accommodate the tastes and idiosyncrasies of the principals.

To the vexation of caterers, chefs and the countless other participants who believed sincerely that their contributions were of prime importance, one element intruded. Security had priority over all activities, and the men whose responsibility this was seemed to have their hands into everything. They were everywhere, under everyone's feet, in everyone's business. Nothing escaped their attention and probing, and they seemed impervious to complaints, flare-ups of temperament and the general dismay they caused.

This was the frenetic state at the Palazzo Amontaldi di Donati two days before the affair. The principals were already in Rome. They had been to the Vatican. They were now in the Quirinal, sitting opposite each other with the fate of the world balanced precariously among the cool, obfuscating words of high diplomacy.

The passionless gentlemen at the Quirinal exchanged views on troop movements—on embargoes—on the deployment of warships, yet not once was it mentioned how long a child five miles from a ground zero nuclear blast would take to die from radiation sickness. The experts of their backup staffs might have had this somewhere among their books and charts, but somehow it had been omitted from consideration—even in the quantum leap of calculated number of actual casualties. Sanctuary from responsibility and guilt—absolution even—was found among the dry husks of statistics peculiarly devoid of pain and suffering. The Pentagon and Kremlin computers had no software for human misery. Mass incineration was too mind-boggling, but let's talk anyway, the gentlemen had said, and talk they did, since it remained their only hope.

Dave, when he wasn't with Olivia or alone at his task in the catacomb replacing the frayed wires of the trigger-bomb, or preparing a shortwave radio relay hidden in the desk of her sitting room that would activate the delay fuse within the bomb, had time for his thoughts . . . Why was he doing this? What was the sense of it? He knew he had this unnatural need for Olivia—a mortal illness, and he couldn't understand it even as he paid homage to it. Something was amiss in his own mental circuitry, he suspected. It was almost as if some vestigial shreds of his former self refused to allow him to surrender himself entirely; and the fear he was doing something terribly wrong haunted him.

Moving his hands gently over the smooth round surfaces of the missiles he had polished clean, he experienced a warm, tactile sensuality. He recalled vaguely that some of the men in his company had felt that way about their weapons. Even after the war he knew such men, presumably hunters, sportsmen. His beclouded mind cast up other, more recent seminal recollections. The bombs—Olivia's body—they were at times interchangeable. The symmetry of both, their smooth, curving firmness. Touching one was not unlike touching the other. Why did those old war memories he had thought forgotten keep haunting him, he wondered. The fire and acrid smoke mixed with the stink of jungle muck—how come, he once thought, the smell of ginger came through to him as unmistakably clear and strong as if he were on Mott Street, Chinatown. Screams of dying torn from faces with eyes being introduced to Death crossdissolved with Olivia's face. She had no business among those horrors, yet the image persisted. The war—those bombs—her. He sought to disassociate her from death and violence and brutality, but it was futile. She was an obverse side to the coin.

Olivia sensed these thoughts and became concerned. She felt hesitation in him. Resistance. Some final thread of reason hadn't been severed completely. Her apprehension grew. She had come to this crucial point in her life and now felt threatened.

These fears were compounded by the advance teams of intelligence and secret service operatives working over the palazzo, leaving not a single square inch unexplored and checked out except for the upper floors, which had been made off limits. As part of the host country, DIGOS was the Italian anti-terrorist bureau which had final say in all security matters. However the Americans and the Soviets deferred to Anatole Castelli, chief of DIGOS, only so far as protocol dictated. Suspicion and distrust were inherent in their roles, essential as their sharp eyes and hair-triggered UZIs. They had their own manuals and procedures for what was called executive protection, and they had no intention of entrusting their leaders to a nation they secretly held in disdain.

Olivia had made a sudden appearance in the cellars where a DIGOS team was poking among the rubble. Her objections brought bureau chief Castelli down from a conference he had been holding with his Soviet and American counterparts on the first floor.

"Your Grace..." the wiry little man said, hurrying toward her, concern written over his ferretlike face. His black, shoe-button eyes betrayed him, though. The cunning and suspicion there canceled out his obsequious show that she was somehow inconvenienced by his men. "Everything will be replaced. You won't know they have been here."

"You're...?"

"Anatole Castelli, Your Grace. Bureau chief of DIGOS."

Olivia never once glanced at the thin, yellow wire running along the conjunction of wall and low ceiling which she knew ran from the catacomb to her sitting room, rigged by Dave in the early morning hours when he worked without fear of discovery. Her manner quietly imperious, she belabored the unhappy official for disturbing her life. "There are priceless heirlooms here, Signor Castelli. Destined for the National Museum. Your men push them about as if it were so much trash." She turned to an unhappy worker standing back. "What are you looking for? What do you hope to find?"

"Your Grace, Your Grace," Anatole Castelli said, coming to the rescue, taking the brunt of the principessa's anger, "please address yourself to me. These men do what I tell them. If they have been careless—"

Olivia had her eyes on one of the men standing dangerously near the wire at the end of which, a hundred yards away, was the bomb. If he reached up, his hand would touch it. If he did, or was about to, it was of course possible something unfortunate might have happened, as happened to so many who put Olivia's purposes in jeopardy. As it was he indolently reached into his pocket for a cigarette, which he now lighted.

Olivia chose to jump on this. "*There*. He now lights one of his filthy cigarettes. Fool," she now said to the startled agent, "it is forbidden to smoke in the cellars."

The woman's attack intimidated even Castelli, who enjoyed a special position in a city so often victimized by terrorism. "Your Grace, Your Grace—"

"Out, out of here," she said, pointing. "All of you. I will call off the entire reception."

Anatole Castelli knew Olivia's reputation, and the high places to which her influence reached. He snapped a few words, and Olivia watched sternly as the cellar emptied.

But Olivia's troubles had only begun.

From her upper-floor window one late afternoon, she watched as Dave paced the garden. It was clear to her he was a man wrestling with a problem. Was it possible the hold she had over him was slipping, becoming more tenuous? Would it last the short while longer she needed? She sought in vain to gauge the extent of his disaffection, and it disturbed her. She whose gaze could penetrate the earth itself, she who understood most men's hearts and motives was now confounded by this dilemma in one whom she had considered totally captive.

Earlier at lunch that day, amidst the white-and-gold opulence, she had commented upon his mood. "Aren't things going well, David?"

"What's that?" he had said, looking up from a hardly touched plate.

"You seem unusually quiet. Preoccupied."

"No."

"Is that equipment you ordered right? Was it what you wanted?"

"It's okay. Fine."

"Is it all"—she hesitated at this crucial word—"ready?"

He nodded. "It's in your desk drawer. The red button only needs to be pushed. I thought of using a shortwave transmitter but it's too dangerous with all the walkie-talkies around."

"David, you're very clever," she said. "I'm proud of you . . ."

He nodded vaguely.

"How much time will there be for us to leave before it happens?"

"Twenty minutes. I thought that would be enough . . ."

That had been earlier that day. Now, gazing down at him in the garden, she saw a disturbed, worried man. What was going through his mind? Was there a miscalculation—an overreach in putting him into this position? Was the magnitude of the act too much for him to deal with? She rejected these thoughts. They were doubts and considerations for a mind in control of itself. His wasn't . . . at least it wasn't supposed to be. Everything hinged on him. She had come to regard him with contempt. Now he'd become a real concern. A threat?

He sat on a marble bench in the garden observing the activity about him. Crews were at work preparing the grounds. Strong lights were being rigged on high scaffolding to light the entrance and parking area. Looking across to the roofs of the buildings adjacent to the palazzo, he could see the teams of men taking positions, making them secure. Army soldiers were posted at other strategic spots within the park. Maps, diagrams and walkie-talkies were in evidence everywhere.

He got up and walked toward a group of men

poring over a blueprint spread out on a small table. "Excuse me," he said, "who's in charge of American security?"

A mix of technicians from the various involved security forces paused in their work. They looked at Dave with blank stares. He was no stranger about the premises and was usually disregarded as a harmless fixture. He repeated the request, adding, "It's important."

"Inside, sir," an American said politely, but with no great warmth. "In the communications room, I believe."

"Thank you," Dave said. As he went off the others looked after him. The American shrugged and the conference resumed.

Agent-in-charge Lester Fallon could have been a Mormon. Clean-cut, well-tailored, everything about him suggesting a take-charge competency. He succeeded in pretending not to be annoyed at Dave's interruption. The small room near the kitchens had once been a pantry. Now it was a complex of electronic equipment connected up with satellites in the sky as well as with Air Force One, even now at the Leonardo da Vinci Airport.

"What can I do for you, sir?" he said to Dave.

Dave hesitated. He knew what he was about to say would sound insane—outrageous. It would be dismissed by its very extravagance. If he himself wasn't sure of his own sanity, what would anyone else think? "There's a plot to assassinate the president," he said simply. Simply! It was sufficient to stun the room. Work stopped. Everyone turned their heads toward him.

"Is that so, Mr. Turrell?" Agent-in-charge Fallon said evenly. "Tell me about it, sir," the Secret Service man said, stressing the "sir."

"There are eight aerial bombs beneath the palazzo."

"Aerial bombs—"

"Yes."

"Except for the princess's private quarters, the palazzo—top to bottom—has been given a thorough search."

"Not thorough enough," Dave said.

"Meaning?"

"Are you aware there's an old catacomb just beyond the cellar?"

The room was silent now. It was a room crowded with the latest in electronic technology. The security experts of three sophisticated nations had scoured the premises, and now this character, probably paid for his services in bed by the lady of the house, was telling them they had goofed. Overlooked a mere eight aerial bombs.

"Tell us about this catacomb and the bombs, Mr. Turrell," Fallon said.

Dave looked about. He knew where he stood with these men. Turning again to Fallon he described the catacomb beyond the cellar and how the bombs came to be there.

"What do you know about the bombs themselves?"

"They're German, World War Two type. I can't tell whether the charge is liquid or solid, or in what condition they're in. They're in the five-hundred-kilo class." Dave noticed his credibility mounting as he spoke. The nomenclature was impressive.

"I was an engineer in demolitions in Nam."

"Are the bombs armed?"

"One is," Dave said. "Armed and ready to go. It'll blow the others."

"You have any idea who armed the bomb?"

Dave hesitated before saying, "Yes."

"Tell us please."

"I did."

"You—"

"Yes."

"Why are you coming out with this now?"

Dave shook his head. He'd thought about the question, and had found no answer. How could he know that some vestigial part of himself had refused to die—to become part of *her* and her cabal. Much of him was still benumbed, confused . . . Fallon repeated the question. Dave could only answer . . . "Because it's wrong . . ."

"Yes," the agent said, struggling to hold on to his poise. "Where's the detonator now?"

"Would you like to see it?"

"I would."

Dave led the way to Olivia's sitting room. Beside him was the Secret Service agent-in-charge. Two clones of the agent followed behind. Tension was high, and no one could think of anything to say. Coming to the sitting room door, Dave was about to open it when Fallon reached out to stop him. Dave turned in surprise.

"Upstairs is off limits to us," Fallon explained. "The princess could be upset by this." He turned to one of his men and said a few curt words. The latter spoke into his walkie-talkie and for several awkward moments they stood about, waiting.

The message came in several minutes. The principessa wasn't to be found, nor had she left the grounds. Agent-in-charge Fallon, with a nod of his head, gave permission for Dave to open the study door. He went directly to the regency desk. The men were close behind him. He carefully opened a drawer. Nothing. He burrowed among papers and small leather-bound books. Still nothing.

"A little trouble, sir?" Agent Fallon, directly behind him, said even more politely.

Dave stared at the drawer and its contents. Bewildered. He was a man coming out of a drugged sleep—orientation was difficult.

"I wouldn't worry about it, sir," Agent Fallon said, clearly more relaxed. He even smiled.

"The bombs..." Dave said, looking up. "The bombs in the catacombs."

Fallon was now openly annoyed, he had other things to do. Still, he had been too well trained to leave anything that could come back to haunt him.

"Okay, Mr. Turrell," he said. "Let's be quick about it."

Leading a procession down into the cellars Dave felt a sense of panic. He was aware he was having problems with orientation. With other things. But was he becoming entirely unglued? At one point he reached up to the shadows of the cellar ceiling, searching for the thin wire he had run upstairs from the catacomb. It wasn't there...?

"What's there?" Agent Fallon asked. "You're looking for something."

"No, no," Dave hastily said. It was a dream he was walking through. None of this was happening. Olivia herself was an illusion.

They had come to the heavy Biedermeier chest.

"Help him," Agent Fallon ordered several of his men as Dave struggled to move it. With the aid of the other men, the commode was moved aside.

Nothing.

"What is it, Mr. Turrell?" Fallon asked.

"There should be a boarded-up opening here," Dave said, staring incredulously at the rough surface of the cellar wall. He rubbed his hand over it. It came away begrimed. The wall was as it had been for years. That was obvious. He looked about to find the three operatives regarding him distastefully.

"Something wrong, sir?" Agent Fallon said, his voice now edged.

"I . . . I don't understand," Dave said, shaking his head.

Fallon sent his men back upstairs to their tasks. Six foot two of bone, hard muscle and restrained accusation. He forced himself to keep his mouth shut as he listened to the selective roll call of his later years. There was a nastiness about it—and he felt a growing anger—hearing it all relived in this stranger's words. His military record was succinctly told. Later the agency job. "You did well, as usual, Mr. Turrell. Employment rating fine. No personal problems. Moderate drinking habits, preference for scotch with a twist. No known barbiturates or narcotic involvement. No known homosexual alliances, although you did recommend for employment one Geoffrey Osman, who resided at Sixteen West Eleventh Street with a Robert Wiley." The eyes searched Dave's.

"So?"

Fallon shook his head. "Comes the sixty-four thousand dollar question, Mr. Turrell."

"Yes."

"You gave it all up. Good job. Everything. To buy the Pojoaque *Double-Dealer*, a broken-down newspaper headed for the toilet. You bought it and right away changed its editorial policy. Big-deal defender of the Indian cause. Followed by more strikes and violence at the borax plant than they'd ever had before. You were friendly with a Dr. Dan Crespi, a known Indian activist, arrested on three separate occasions. Illegal entry once, causing a public disturbance twice. Shall I go on, Mr. Turrell?"

"No," Dave said. He felt sickened.

Nevertheless Fallon persisted. "I just want you to know, sir. You've been of special interest to us. You haven't been ignored. Your relationship with the princess could be more than it seems, if I make myself clear. And now this farce—this waste of time. I don't believe it's a diversionary tactic. My personal belief, *sir*, is that you're just screwed up. If I were you, I'd get it attended to."

He sat in the darkening room, once the prince's upstairs study adjacent to the bedroom. He sat stiffly erect in an old slipcovered chair facing the curtained window with its partly closed wooden shutters. The evening sounds from the city beyond only partly filtered in.

Reality, it occurred to him, was also only partly reaching him. Olivia's hold over him clung like a stubborn, unwanted smell. He was grateful for even his partial escape. His effort, nonetheless, had failed in spite of his belief that he was his own man again—well . . . almost. The bombs were still there, weren't they? Primed, triggered.

The darkness of the room grew, relieved only by the hotel lights beyond the palazzo wall, diffused by the curtains. More or less, light didn't matter. Agent Fallon had seen to it that he be brought to his room, and he was certain he was under surveillance. The irony of it struck him. Here he was, wanting more than anything to give the alarm, and the very people entrusted with the president's safety were keeping him from doing that. Aside from them, who was there to believe him . . . ?

She came into the room, as though materializing from the dark. No door had been opened. Had it? Had she stepped out from the glass of the mirror on the wardrobe? She stood there—radiantly beautiful, smiling. Dave turned his head about slowly, aware she was there even before he saw her. She touched a light switch.

He stood up, and at once noted a sadness in her expression. Nothing else, nothing sinister or menacing, just a touch of sadness. Disappointment.

"Ah, David," she said, "what have you been up to?"

He looked away from that relentless stare. "I couldn't let it happen," he said. "It has to be stopped."

"But you know—as I know—it won't be stopped. It can't be. It will happen the way it was meant to happen, one way or another. And it was presumptuous of you—and dangerous—to interfere."

"I'll still try," he said, meeting her eyes once again.

"Yes," she said. "I see that. I even know what you're thinking at this moment. The weapon on the wall behind me. One of Antonio's ridiculous toys. You're thinking how you would like to put it in my heart. True?"

It was indeed true. He'd barely glanced at it and she knew.

"Say it, David," she said. "Witch. Witch. The word I grew up with was *'iettatrice,'* which means the same thing. It doesn't matter."

It was, of course, a move of desperation. He knew it even as he made it. He just couldn't think of any alternative—in fact, he knew there was none. He had no credibility, and she was the Principessa Amontaldi di Donati with all that meant. No alternative. God damn her—this abomination had to be smashed.

"Go ahead, David," she said, stepping aside.

And he tried. He took the few steps to the ceremonial sword on the wall. He reached up. It was nearly in his grasp.

And then he froze. Grew rigid. Still facing the wall, his arms upraised, he sank to the floor. A skilled hypnotist might have managed it. Not to mention a witch—though of course that was preposterous. Of course.

For several moments Olivia gazed down at him. There was that familiar detached look in her eyes, as always in such circumstances. Then her eyes blinked. A curtain came away from behind them. She remembered the chef was waiting for her below. A decision for dessert had to be made. Was it to be cherries jubilee at the dinner or something rather less flamboyant?

CHAPTER TWENTY-TWO

It was two hours past midnight, and the streets of Rome were enjoying a respite. The Fiat Cinquecento circled the palazzo enclave with Shula at the wheel, Ari beside her.

"Slow down here," he said. They were about to pass the gate with its sentries. "Don't turn your head."

They were now passing the unbroken line of vehicles usually parked at right angles to the wall along its perimeter.

"Slower," he directed. "There—that white Mercedes fifty meters away."

"Yes."

"That's where there's an opening. A small gate. Locked. I found it yesterday. I don't know where it leads, but if you want to get inside it's all I can suggest."

They were almost abreast of it. In the darkness

she could barely make out a break in the wall made by a heavy grille of some kind.

"Yes," she said. "I see it."

They were already past. Ari told her to circle the entire block once again. She listened as he told her the precise nature of the security around the place. The military jeep would cruise the same route at twelve minute intervals. They would have their light on the wall. Each corner had its posted sentry by which he could see the entire length of wall.

"That small gate," he said, "has a heavy padlock. I don't know the last time it's been opened. If it's rusted, forget it. I don't have a cutter."

"You'll manage it, Ari." She reached over to touch his hand. She knew at what personal cost he was helping her, and her heart went out to him.

"You know what you're to do."

"Be back here in eight minutes."

"You'll stop, but don't kill the motor." They were almost abreast of the white Mercedes. "Slow now," he said. She heard the click of the door latch.

She slowed. Ari opened his door and slipped down to the pavement behind the white Mercedes. She glimpsed him in the rearview mirror as he scurried between the parked cars. She came to the corner, turning left instead of following the wall. She glanced at her watch. Ari would open the gate, she felt certain. The threat, she knew, was less in the gate than in the patrol. He would have at least six minutes with the lock before the jeep came into view.

She parked in front of the lighted showcase of an

elegant leather shop catering mostly to tourists. Alligator bags, reptile shoes, wallets of ostrich and other exotic skins. Her thoughts went to the woman she expected to confront shortly. What to expect. With her knowledge of myths, her thoughts went to that mischievous spirit of ancient Egypt, El Naddaha, the Bride of the Nile, whose beauty and eroticism lured men to their deaths. And they did so willingly in the hope of sharing her embrace through all eternity. The sharp clatter of a garbage can cover, dislodged by a cat, brought her out of her grim reflections.

She glanced at her watch. It was time. She started up the motor, and in a short time she was once again circling the old brick wall.

She slowed as she approached the white Mercedes. There. She saw the movement in the shadows between the parked vehicles. She'd hardly brought the car to a stop when the door at her side was flung open.

"Out," Ari urgently said.

Clinging to the wall and its protective shadows, she watched the car go off. No good luck. No shalom. Nothing. But she knew if he hadn't succeeded in opening the lock he wouldn't have left her.

The patrol jeep came about the corner, cruising slowly, scouring the wall with its powerful light. She crouched behind the front of the car until the light swept over her head and passed on. The rough bricks of the wall felt damp as she inched along. Here and there were tufts of grass that had rooted in the mortar itself.

The gate itself was less than an average man's height. This in itself dated the gate for her—people were shorter several centuries ago. She didn't yet dare use the flashlight she'd brought with her, but by touch alone she found the padlock hanging open from a thick chain. Frequent paintings of the old iron gate had frozen it to its frame, she realized after several efforts to budge it.

"Oh, God, no," she breathlessly muttered. "This can't be the end . . ."

Bracing both feet against the wall, she gave it her best try. Almost. It was moving. Another try and she could feel the reluctant movement as it gave way with a series of creaks that she was afraid would alarm the whole neighborhood. A minimal opening allowed her to slip into the blackness beyond. She closed the gate.

Now she did bring out her penlight, not really strong enough to penetrate the darkness. She could just make out that she was in a low tunnel with an arched Romanesque roof of paving blocks that seemed to have been hurriedly mortared. Early sixteenth century, she estimated, recalling the turbulent history of the times . . . warring families—the Colonnas against the Borgheses, the Borgias versus the Buoncampagna di Ludovicis or perhaps the Amontaldi di Donatis. Alliances changed daily. White nobility fought against black. Soldier popes worked their intrigues as they preached the gospel of peace. Their palazzi had been built as veritable fortresses. Such a passageway, she speculated, could be either an escape route or lead to underground dungeons.

She continued on, groping her way more by touch than by the weak light. The stones underfoot had been smoothed by usage and wetness from an underground source. Feeling somewhat reassured that the passage seemed upward in a more or less straight direction, she kept on, not daring to think about what could be at the far end.

Abruptly a door confronted her. It was a heavy, crude affair of oak with hand-forged bolts reinforced to withstand any battering. Hinges and a latch were of thick wrought iron. Her heart sank as the narrow beam of light picked out its formidable features. At one point, the light fell on the handcarved coat-of-arms of the Amontaldi di Donatis with the proudly crested *corona chiusa*, the very same she had seen in burnished brass and enamel on the front gate to the palazzo grounds.

With a prayer, she lifted the heavy latch. Surprisingly, it yielded. She took a step forward and stood still, listening. The darkness had a new, indefinable quality. The air was still cool, musty—adding to her sense of isolation. All at once she felt inexplicably chilled. There was that atavistic sense that she was not alone. Another presence was there—with her—about her—*within* her?

"Who's there?" she called out, startled by her own quavering voice.

Nothing. The silence was profound, the darkness stygian. And yet, calling out, she had sensed the slightest echo, suggesting to her a large chamber of some sort. As she cautiously moved forward she was at once aware of the change in footing. Smooth. Firm. Casting her light down, she saw beneath a patina of grime a floor of dark, mottled Carrara marble of a brownish hue.

She twisted about abruptly, once again aware of another presence, now even more powerful. Simultaneously she felt more than heard a thrumming. The closest thing she could associate was the thrum of a dynamo. And yet it was nearby, its presence pervasive. She swung her small light about. It settled on nothing to indicate the boundaries of the chamber.

Out of nothing then . . . from no single source came a faint illumination. A pulsing glow, more an emanation. Its wavering, spectral quality reminded her of an aurora borealis she'd once seen in upper Norway. The light—the ionizing tension in the air—had a natural explanation, she sought to reassure herself without too much success.

Shula Gorin, at that moment, knew pure terror. For the past several years she had faced desperate men, situations which could mean death, weapons of many kinds, but this had its own quality. It wasn't even thinking; it was feeling. A fist had gripped her heart, her pulse raced. She wasn't aware of it but her mouth was agape in an effort to suck in more air. She fought for control. Panic, she knew, fed on itself.

The glowing at least gave her an idea of where she was. She was standing dead center in the nave of a small church, which she took to be the private chapel of the noble family. For some reason it had been closed off, not used, retaining its pristine characteristics. The nave had neither pews nor benches, which was the custom of the Renaissance. Here the servants and commoners attached to the family once attended mass and did their praying. She looked up to the rear. Among dim shadows she could see the balcony, where members of the noble family would sit for the service, avoiding physical contact with their lessers.

In the baroque ornamentation, she could see, were typical curlicues and flourishings of gilded plaster and stucco. The simplicity of a straight line was abhorred. Ceiling and apse were covered with frescoes by a master she couldn't name. Glory to God was expressed everywhere, and the Virgin and Child were attended by twelve ceramic disciples. The railed sanctuary of the chancel above the altar had been given the full treatment. A baldachino supported by four marble columns rose above the tabernacle and its holy sacrament. The antependium glittered with its "sanctus ... sanctus ... sanctus ..." embroidered in heavy threads of silver. The focus was on an immense crucifix dominating the chancel, behind which was a fresco depicting the Resurrection ... she suspected it might be a Pinturicchio. She recognized a kneeling mourner as none other than the pontiff Alexander VI. Within the railed sanctuary, at either side, were three large candelabra with unlit candles. Two small chapels had their own frescoes and altars.

This was a superb example of baroque, Shula knew, built to lift the faithful out of the misery and poverty of the times into the magnificence and glory of a better life in heaven. It was difficult not to feel a peace and serenity amidst such grandeur.

She herself had experienced this on many occasions. The cares of the world fell away before such enthusiastic paeans of joy, and for her it had little to do with religion ... it was a celebration of beauty and the higher aspirations of man.

Yet here it was different, she felt. Terribly different.

Death, not life, seemed to charge the air. It seemed to hover over everything like an obnoxious, palpable cloud. As her eyes grew accustomed to the eerie lighting she could make out details of the ceiling fresco. What should have been angelic putti mischievously cavorting about a cerulean sky were leering imps staring down at her with malevolence. Christ, on his cross above the altar, turned his head to glare down at her. The love, the compassion seemed gone from his countenance. The thrumming she had felt rather than heard grew louder. It rolled over the chamber like distant thunder, and it wasn't caused by an errant breeze through the lower-register organ pipes, though she hoped it might be ...

Another new sound came to her. A distant tinkling. She thought for a moment of wind chimes in a garden. A counterpoint to the ominous, heavy rumbling of the organlike sound.

A concentration of greenish-blue light engulfed her, giving her the sense she was center-stage. She peered about. A tableau of awfulness in which she was the centerpiece. The tinkling grew louder. More urgent. She looked for its source. She could see the long crystals of several large chandeliers overhead trembling. An earthquake? Unlikely, she thought, dismissing it as obvious, and this was no time or place for the obvious. She was in a realm where the laws of nature were derided, where logic and reason were betrayed. She was startled by a chandelier crystal coming loose, falling in a clatter on the stone floor. Glass splinters flew like sparks of myriad colors. She caught a motion on an altar column. This was too much. Impossible. Hallucination . . . a cherub of gilded plaster was drawing back his tiny ridiculous bow, turning like a mechanical figure on a medieval clock tower. The arrow was aimed at her. Even as she thought how absurd . . . the damn thing flew, narrowly missing her.

Her surreal agony was just beginning. Another crystal came loose—this one apparently falling not by its own weight but with a velocity suggesting it had been propelled at her. Another. Still another. Now other things came loose from their places. Candles from the candelabra—all missiles directed at her with a calculated force. A deadly barrage—candles, crystals, bits and pieces of wood, plaster-ceramic torn from the chapel and altar. A protean fury seemed unleashed.

Shula stood as if rooted. There was no escape— escape never even occurred to her. She just stood there helpless and vulnerable. Once—twice— again she was struck.

The *aruv*.

If ever, she felt, a talisman was needed to prove its effectiveness against evil, it was now. Here was the test. "O Mother Rachel," she prayed, "now,

now, help me . . ."

She whipped out of a pocket the skein of red woolen thread. In a single gesture she unspooled it on the marble floor, describing a circle about seven feet in diameter, as best as she could estimate it.

Seven feet. One each for the seven centers of heavenly power she was now calling on. Earlier she had recalled a teaching of the thirteenth-century Spanish Kabbalist, who had said:

> "When God gave down the Holy Law, He opened the seven heavens, and all saw nothing was there in reality but His Glory. He opened the seven abysses before their eyes, and they saw that nothing was there but His Glory."

The vaulted chamber was now an arena for the confrontation. And here was to be the outcome.

The charmed circle about Shula held firm. The Antagonist, everywhere in the chamber, raged, stormed and beat itself against the invisible shield described by the red thread of the *aruv*, the talisman said to have been sanctified by God Himself.

The missiles—that's what they were in effect—now came at her in a storm, shattering against the invisible barrier, building into a barrier of debris, mounting higher and higher, even burying the slender woolen thread.

Her glance was somehow drawn to the upper reaches of the chapel, where a solitary figure could be made out. It was a woman, she knew. The Principessa Olivia, standing tall and proud as she peered down at her triumph.

Olivia relished her victory. The woman's survival was a temporary thing. Irony was everywhere. Here she was, seeing the parts of the chapel bloody and tearing apart that woman whose identity she had known just as she had known Dave's at their first meeting. She savored every drop of blood, the woman's agony and what must be her terror. Olivia's powers at that moment were limitless. She was as close to her source as she had ever been. Only one thing was missing, something inside her said; and here she committed the mortal sin of pride.

Her triumph had to be seen. Witnessed. Not by anyone, but by—Dave. This, she almost instinctively realized, was the reason he had been permitted to survive. As the Enemy's delegate—his representative, as it were, he had to view his own conquest, if only to concede.

He lay as he'd fallen. But now life seemed to return to him. For several moments he lay still, eyes opened, staring up at the ceiling of the darkened room. Then he got to his feet. Standing still for several more moments, he gave the impression of listening to an inaudible voice.

And then he moved, stiffly at first, going to the door, opening it and leaving the room. He traversed the long, deserted corridor. Downstairs, everything was frenetic activity, last-minute preparations for the dinner-reception on the following evening.

He was ignored as he walked past groups of men and women scurrying about, issuing orders, following them. He seemed oblivious to them, as if he were in some private limbo. It wasn't unlike his first visit to the palazzo, when entering the gate unchallenged he walked directly to where Olivia was—apparently waiting for him.

One of the American secret service agents spotted him leaving the palazzo.

"Hey there, Mr. Turrell. Wait up!"

Dave continued walking. The agent, catching up with him, politely told him he was to stay in the palazzo's upper floors. "You're off limits down here, sir."

The movement was as quick as it was unexpected, which was perhaps the only reason it succeeded. Without change in his now detached expression, Dave's hands shot out and grasped the man by the lapels of his jacket to fling him away with a strength that was hardly natural for him.

Moving off into the dense brush and foliage, he plunged straight ahead, as if drawn by some unheard voice, until he came to the furthest part of the small park. There he came to the ivy-overgrown private chapel. Ripping away weeds and foliage from the long-unused door, he succeeded in pushing it open. He entered the darkness. He came into the balcony as Olivia was staring down at the spectacle happening on the nave floor. Shula returned that stare from within her charmed circle. The tumult was dreadful. Debris was let loose, battered itself against a power that wouldn't yield. Shula stood untouched within her sanctuary.

"Bitch!" Olivia called down above the din.

Dave, standing beside her, looked down. And what he saw caught and held him. It was like a blow. There was a moment or two of confusion as recognition was kindled. And as it took hold, his torpor seemed to vanish as if he were returning from a long journey through a dark tunnel. The animation that had been extinguished in his eyes returned. Slowly he turned his head to the woman beside him. Olivia's eyes met his, and what she perceived startled and terrified her.

She knew it was over. She had failed.

Whatever had usurped the chapel had gone, retreated. A kind of grace replaced obscenity. Hatred was banished in the face of joy. The cherubs on the walls had recovered their innocence. The fetid air that had permeated the place was gone. Christ on His cross had returned to His beneficence. Love and compassion were in His features, along with eternal sadness from His understanding of man, who had put Him there.

As Shula and David held each other, Shula's eyes went to the balcony. Her sudden stiffening caused him to look up as well.

Olivia was gone.

She stood rigid, peering down at the spectacle below, seeing in the havoc the ruin of her own life and purpose. Olivia had little doubt that the carefully contrived pattern of her life, often beyond her own comprehension, was now unraveling. The alarm would shortly be given and this time, she sensed, she could expect no mystic interference to block the enemy. Something inside her felt emptied. She suspected—was even certain—she stood alone now for the first time in her recollection. Abandoned. Where was her failure? Where had she failed? Was it perhaps in her impulse to keep Dave alive so that he could see her victory over that woman? Was this then the penalty for her vanity—and her human failing?

She found herself back in the palazzo. The hour was late and the rooms were empty. She was drawn into the *salone da ballo,* now festively decorated for the following evening's event.

She was drawn, unaccountably, to the very spot where Prince Antonio had fallen to the inlaid marble floor. She stood tall, straight, her lovely head slightly cocked in a manner to suggest she was listening to unhearable voices. It was that familiar posture when she had been receptive to it. Him. But this time there were no voices. There was no presence. There was nothing. And the pain of it could be seen in the terrible sadness in her eyes.

Now came a sharp hiss. Her head slowly turned. At the far end of the chamber a huge bouquet of carnations, crysanthemums and sprays of ferns mingled with lilies of the valley and baby's breath, seemingly fresh and newly watered—yet as if it were dried tinder it exploded into flame. Had she ignited it and forgotten? Had He . . . ? The salon quickly became an inferno.

She watched passively, unable, unwilling to move. She watched and understood. Slowly she walked into the darkness of the billowing smoke.

Hurrying through the tunnel toward the street, Shula led the way with her small light. Suddenly she stopped.

"Dave?"

He was not behind her. She retraced her steps and found him looking back.

"Come *on.*"

He continued looking back. "Dave, we must go," she said, and took his hand and pulled at him to go on. Stumbling ahead, they heard the sirens even before they reached the gate. They finally emerged into bedlam. A ruddy glow lit the sky. Men, some in uniform, were running in all directions, others were screaming hoarse commands. The blue lights of the police and military vehicles mixed with the glow of flames reflecting off the buildings opposite the palazzo. Windows became glaring red eyes as smoke clouds billowed up.

David and Shula were quickly caught up by a pair of carabinieri, who hustled them behind a barricade hastily set up in front of the hotel.

Flames engulfed the palazzo, of which only the upper floors were visible from their vantage point. They watched in silence. The fire brigade was now coming into the street, adding to the noise and confusion.

Shula turned to look at Dave. The flame's glow gave him an eerie appearance. But there was something else. His eyes stared, his mouth was slightly open. Her head turned to see what could have such an effect on him.

And then she saw. In an upper window, silhouetted against a background of flame, was a figure, standing straight. It could only be Olivia, she knew; as she also knew some communication was happening between them.

The ground convulsed. A great explosion wracked the old structure, sending debris, smoke and flames upward in a lurid, obscene blossom. The high thick walls protected the cowering spectators from the blast itself. When the smoke eventually cleared, the area was silent for several moments. The low moan of sirens, all else had become still. The centuries-old building within the walls had simply vanished. Fallen into itself. Into its own ancient grave.

"It's over," he said, "at least for a while."

"Yes."

Neither wanted to confront the prospect of the trident appearing on another child. At another place. Once in a lifetime was enough . . .

He took her hand.

"What do you know about Elat?" she asked.

"Elat?"

"It's a place in Israel. At the very southern end. The sand is white, the water clear as anywhere in the world." She spoke about having some unfinished business in Jerusalem. "An explanation of what I've been up to to a man called Zev Cohen, who in a million years will never believe me. But then, who would? After that, my friend—Elat."

"And shalom," Dave said, to her delight and surprise.

"Shalom," she said, and dared to hope that peace might actually come true.

MORE EXCITING READING
IN THE ZEBRA/OMNI SERIES

THE BOOK OF COMPUTERS & ROBOTS (1276, $3.95)
Arthur C. Clarke, G. Harry Stine, Spider Robinson, and others explain one of the most exciting and misunderstood advances of our time—the computer revolution.

THE BOOK OF SPACE (1275, $3.95)
This "map of tomorrow," including contributions by James Michener and Ray Bradbury, is a guide to the research and development that will transform our lives.

THE FIRST BOOK OF SCIENCE FICTION (1319, $3.95)
Fourteen original works from some of the most acclaimed science fiction writers of our time, including: Isaac Asimov, Greg Bear, Dean Ing, and Robert Silverberg.

THE SECOND BOOK OF SCIENCE FICTION (1320, $3.95)
Glimpse the future in sixteen original works by such well-known science fiction writers as Harlan Ellison, Spider Robinson, Ray Bradbury, and Orson Scott Card.

THE BOOK OF THE PARANORMAL & (1365, $3.95)
THE MIND
Sample the mysteries of altered states, psychic phenomena and subliminal persuasion in thirty-five articles on man's most complex puzzle: his own mind.

THE BOOK OF MEDICINE (1364, $3.95)
Will you live to be 200 years old? Is pain on the verge of elimination? In twenty-four illuminating articles discover what is fast becoming reality in the world of medicine.

Available wherever paperbacks are sold, or order direct from the Publisher. Send cover price plus 50¢ per copy for mailing and handling to Zebra Books, 475 Park Avenue South, New York, N.Y. 10016. DO NOT SEND CASH.

THE BEST IN SUSPENSE FROM ZEBRA
by Jon Land

THE DOOMSDAY SPIRAL (1481, $3.50)
Tracing the deadly twists and turns of a plot born in Auschwitz, Alabaster — master assassin and sometime Mossad agent — races against time and operatives from every major service in order to control and kill a genetic nightmare let loose in America!

THE LUCIFER DIRECTIVE (1353, $3.50)
From a dramatic attack on Hollywood's Oscar Ceremony to the hijacking of three fighter bombers armed with nuclear weapons, terrorists are out-gunning agents and events are outracing governments. Minutes are ticking away to a searing blaze of earth-shattering destruction!

VORTEX (1469-4, $3.50)
The President of the US and the Soviet Premier are both helpless. Nuclear missiles are hurtling their way to a first strike and no one can stop the top-secret fiasco — except three men with old scores to settle. But if one of them dies, all humanity will perish in a vortex of annihilation!

MUNICH 10 (1300, $3.95)
by Lewis Orde

They've killed her lover, and they've kidnapped her son. Now the world-famous actress is swept into a maelstrom of international intrigue and bone-chilling suspense — and the only man who can help her pursue her enemies is a complete stranger . . .

DEADFALL (1400, $3.95)
By Lewis Orde and Bill Michaels

The two men Linda cares about most, her father and her lover, entangle her in a plot to hold Manhattan Island hostage for a billion dollars ransom. When the bridges and tunnels to Manhattan are blown, Linda is suddenly a terrorist — except *she's* the one who's terrified!

Available wherever paperbacks are sold, or order direct from the Publisher. Send cover price plus 50¢ per copy for mailing and handling to Zebra Books, 475 Park Avenue South, New York, N.Y. 10016. DO NOT SEND CASH.